THE
WOODS
ARE
WAITING

A NOVEL

KATHERINE GREENE

CROOKED
LANE

NEW YORK

Copyright © 2023 by Abbi Horne and Claire Cathrin Riley

Published in the United States by Crooked Lane Books, an imprint of The Quick Brown Fox & Company LLC.

Crooked Lane Books and its logo are trademarks of The Quick Brown Fox & Company LLC.

Library of Congress Catalog-in-Publication data available upon request.

ISBN (hardcover): 978-1-63910-380-5
ISBN (ebook): 978-1-63910-381-2

Cover design by Meghan Deist

Printed in the United States.

www.crookedlanebooks.com

Crooked Lane Books
34 West 27th St., 10th Floor
New York, NY 10001

First Edition: July 2023

10 9 8 7 6 5 4 3 2 1

Never compromise on what you believe in.

Keep silver in your pockets,
Walk with dirt in your shoes,
Or he'll poke your eyeballs from their sockets,
And boil your bones in stew.

Stay away from the hickories,
Stay away from the trees,
Don't sing, don't shout, don't run about,
Or he'll never let you leave.

Watch out for his rough fingers,
His eyes as red as blood,
Whisper a prayer, you'll need them there,
As he pulls you into the mud.

PROLOGUE

Long ago

THEY WERE BEAUTIFUL in the way children are. Innocent. Carefree. Frozen in the nostalgic reminiscence of forever childhood.

The youngest's hair was flaxen gold. The eyes of the older girl were as blue as the sky. The boy had a smile like the sun.

They were loved. So loved. By their mothers. By their fathers. By their neighbors. By their friends.

Happy and joyful, full of promise.

They held hands, the three of them, and skipped merrily toward the edge of that great, big open field. The world lay at their feet. Nothing but endless possibilities.

"Stay away from the woods," their mothers warned as they left to play. They bit their lips nervously as they watched the children giggle together, already plotting ways to disregard their mothers' anxious directives. Such is the way of children. Always eager to discover for themselves the evil that lay outside their home, no matter the consequences.

Their mothers gave them the silver coins and instructed their children to sprinkle dirt into their shoes. Like the other grown-ups, they knew the importance of protection. They had learned to fear what lay beyond their doorstep.

"Keep silver in your pockets, walk with dirt in your shoes, or he'll poke your eyeballs from their sockets, and boil your bones in stew."

The children sang the silly nursery rhyme and cataloged the basic facts. Filed them away as concrete truths. Yet they thought their innocence would keep them safe. Foolish are the young.

They held onto their superstitions, believing these would save them. Never knowing that it wouldn't be enough—could never be enough.

Because what waited for them among the hickories was more sinister. Something silver and dirt could never keep away.

Flaxen hair, sky-blue eyes, and smiles like the sun were soon lost to the stories, becoming a new, tragic chapter in a tale that had twisted and evolved as the years went by.

Until only blood remained.

Until only the dark existed.

Stay away from the hickories,

Stay away from the trees . . .

CHAPTER

1

The Present

–Cheyenne–

I HESITATED.
The tree line was in front of me, and I thought about turning around and heading back the way I had come.

But I couldn't.

With a world-weary sigh, I pressed on, the forest enveloping me in its constricting grasp. The dense, suffocating mass unfurled in the center of my chest. It was a tactile, physical sensation that was unlike anything I had ever felt in my life and had only ever experienced *here*.

In the woods.

It was as if the very molecules inside my body reacted to this singular space. Like the trees wanted to kill me.

Or embrace me, never letting go.

The sun had only just dipped behind the mountains. Outside the forest, the world would be awash in the hazy light of almost nightfall.

Not here.

Not in the woods.

Here, it was already pitch-black. As if the light never touched the hickories and firs. As if the leaves purposefully kept it out.

In this deep, thick forest.

Go back. Go back. Go back. Now. Now. Now.

I wanted to do as my instincts screamed. But I couldn't. Duty could be extremely self-destructive.

My car continued forward, and my ears were assaulted by the horrific sound of branches scratching against metal like fingernails. I kept my eyes firmly on the narrow gravel road in front of me. I didn't dare look anywhere else. I knew what I'd see. Murky, endless nothing.

I thought about the tiny apartment I had left behind in Roanoke. Of my patchwork sofa I had picked up at Goodwill for ten bucks and carefully reupholstered. My bed with its lumpy yet comfortable mattress covered with quilts and pillows. I had done everything I could to make it feel like home. For a while, I'd even convinced myself it was.

But here I was.

I squinted, barely able to see, but it didn't matter. I would know the curves and dips of this road even if I were traveling it blind. As I crawled through the dark, my heart hammering away, a dark shape moved through the trees in front of me.

As if dictated by muscle memory, I reached into the center console and grabbed the old silver coins that I kept there. I had picked them up at an antique shop and kept them in my car. *In case of emergencies,* I had told myself. But an emergency that required old-time silver coins wasn't one I wanted to think too much about.

I gripped them in my palm and closed my eyes. The words came unbidden, tumbling out of my mouth in a soft, impassioned whisper.

"Protect me from evil. Protect me from those of the evil will."

I had been back in Blue Cliff for less than twenty minutes, and I was already acting like a superstitious idiot. This place had that effect on me. On everyone.

I opened my eyes and quickly deposited the coins back in the tray with an aggrieved huff. The world was quiet once more. Convinced I had been imagining things—my nerves a jangly mess—I started moving again.

I arrived at my destination five minutes later without further incident. The gravel road gave way to a large clearing where a small, rustic-looking house stood shrouded in darkness. In the beam of my headlights, I could see the large hickory tree to the side of the porch, glinting madly with the glass-blown orbs Mom hung from the heavy branches to ward off evil.

I wanted to give myself a moment to get my bearings. I had a script I wanted to follow. I had been practicing it for over a week. Ever since I'd gotten the call that brought me back here.

* * *

"She's not doin' good, Cheyenne. You need to come home." Police Chief Donald Hickman's gravelly voice was thick with concern. When I'd seen his number flash across the screen, I'd almost sent it to voicemail.

But I hadn't.

"What do you mean? If this is about some ritual or—"

"Have you heard about the boy? The one that's gone missin'?"

Of course I had heard about the boy.

Everyone had. My tiny hometown had made national news once again.

"Yeah, I read about it," I told him.

"It's set somethin' off inside her. She's changed. It's like before, but worse. And with the town in an uproar, I can't be out here watchin' her, like normal. No one can. We need your help. You're her daughter. You have to take care of her."

No!

I couldn't go back. Not to Blue Cliff. Not with a child missing. The need to stay away was rooted in absolute survival. It's what had kept me away all these years. It's why the thought of returning filled me with dread.

"I have a job, Chief. I have a life—"

"You have a life here, Cheyenne. In Blue Cliff. And family too. And a mother who needs you. I need you. Your town needs you." His voice went rough. "You're an Ashby. Don't you forget that."

*   *   *

If only I *could* forget.

And here I was, crawling back like the prodigal daughter I was.

It was disturbing how easy it was to leave that new life behind and return to the old one.

I could have sat in my car all night, staring at my old home, but it was the middle of February, and the front door was hanging wide open. I left the keys in the ignition and the headlights blazing so I could see as I got out of my car. The cold air chilled me instantly.

I stepped along paving stones that appeared to have been recently set. I could just make out the property in the darkness, and it looked well maintained. I noticed a new path made of fine gravel that curved around the side of the house to where the root cellar was. I couldn't imagine the freshly painted porch swing was my mother's handiwork, but it was nice to see she hadn't been left to rot in the woods.

As I approached the open door, my shoe skidded, almost sliding out beneath me. In the harsh glow from my phone screen, I could see the line of gritty white salt that had been sprinkled along the doorjamb. I let out a resigned sigh and braced myself as I stepped over the threshold, aware of what would be waiting for me inside.

The smell hit me first. The air was thick with the smell of burning wood. Several bundles of pine branches, used to cleanse a space for protection, lay burning by the open window. It was freezing inside despite the fire that raged in the woodstove.

I quietly closed the door behind me and lowered the window. The place was eerily quiet except for a rhythmic scraping sound coming from the back of the house. I made my way into the large, open room that comprised the main living space, and followed the narrow hallway into the cramped kitchen.

That's where I found my mom.

Her small form was hunched over as she frantically swept the floor, and the back door was open, leading out to the woods beyond. She would stop every few moments to sprinkle something onto the floor while mumbling unintelligible words. I stood watching her, horrified yet not surprised.

Constance Ashby had always been a force to be reckoned with. Even when she was ranting and raving about things that scared the hell out of me, she had an aura of power that was undeniable. It made her impressive and terrifying. She was the strongest presence in my mind. I had felt her even when we were separated by miles.

The woman in front of me appeared shrunken, as if the weight of the world had literally crushed her. Her once-thick, dark brown hair was stringy and streaked with gray. My mother had never been a large woman, but she was no dainty thing either. Now, she looked as if a strong gust of wind would blow her over.

I had only been gone for five years, but my mother looked as though she had aged forty. She obviously hadn't been taking care of herself, and this went further back than a couple of weeks.

My stomach clenched and my chest ached at the sight of her. The guilt became a living, wild thing inside me.

I am a horrible daughter.

Candles flickered on the counter, casting deep shadows across the floor. I went to turn on the kitchen light, but it stayed dark. The electricity must have gone out. It wasn't unusual to lose power for days at a time in our remote location. I knew it had nothing to do with an unpaid power bill. I had never known my mother to pay for utilities in her life, but we'd always had what we needed anyway. One of the few perks of being an Ashby.

The Ashbys took care of the town and in turn, the town took care of the Ashbys.

I zipped up my coat, wrapped my scarf tighter around my neck, and slowly made my way toward the woman sweeping in a state of delirium.

"Mom," I said softly, touching her shoulder. She continued sweeping. Stopping only to sprinkle on the floor what I could see were dried herbs. Now that I was closer, I heard the same chant I had spoken in the car earlier, echoed from her lips.

"Protect me from evil. Protect me from those of the evil will."

A blast of frigid wind blew in from the open doorway. I skirted past my mom, who was still lost in her ritualized behavior, and quickly shut it. This seemed to break through to her. She stopped sweeping and looked up, blinking rapidly as she stared at me. I got the feeling she didn't recognize who I was.

My heart clenched painfully.

I am a horrible daughter.

Her eyes, which had once been vibrant, were sunken into her face. She looked as if she hadn't slept in days. Maybe longer.

"Mom, it's me. Cheyenne," I whispered, afraid to speak any louder.

I tried to wrap my arms around her, but she flung my hands away.

"No. You won't trick me this time." She looked around the kitchen, breathing loudly. "How did you get in here? You shouldn't have been able to cross the salt!" Her voice rose to a screech.

Unfortunately, this I recognized. My entire body braced itself for the escalation. The one I had become intimately familiar with as a child.

I took a step back. "Mom. It's really me. It's Cheyenne. Your daughter—"

She started chanting louder, flinging the dried herbs in a circle around me. This was getting out of control. I had to break through the trance she was in. But I was out of practice. It had been so long since I'd had to do it, and I was worried I had forgotten how. At one time, I had been the only person able to get through to her when she got like this. It had been my most important job.

And the reason I had left.

Steeling myself, I grabbed a hold of her upper arms and held her still. I was a good four inches taller than my mother and easily had thirty pounds on her. I could feel her bones beneath my fingers.

"Enough, Mom. Enough!" I said loudly and firmly, giving her arms a squeeze. "Look at me," I commanded. When she snarled and spat, refusing to meet my eyes, I shook her. "Stop it, Mom. Stop it now. I'm not *him*. I'm Cheyenne. Look at me."

She stopped struggling. Her entire body sagged as the fight left her. She lifted her head and looked at me. Her eyes brightened. "Cheyenne?"

I loosened my grip on her arms but knew better than to let go. "Yes, Mom. It's me. It's your Cheyenne." I suddenly felt smaller. And younger. Like I was a child once more.

My mom grabbed the front of my jacket, wringing the material in her hands. "What are you doing here? You shouldn't be here."

I was used to this sort of reaction from her. It wasn't new. But pairing it with her clear exhaustion, I was definitely more worried than I had been before I arrived. "I came to see you, Mom. I heard you weren't doing so well." I tentatively put my arm around her and began to slowly lead her from the kitchen. I bypassed the chaotic living room and walked straight down the hall to her bedroom at the end. I opened the door, expecting to see more of the mess that dominated the rest of the house, but was surprised at how spartan it was. Aside from the old wooden dresser in the corner, there was nothing else in the way of furniture in the room.

At some point in the past five years, my mother—or someone—had removed the ornate hickory sleigh bed and replaced it with a thin mattress on the floor. The floor was dotted with chalk figures and symbols. Some I knew, others I didn't. Burnt candles ringed the bed, and we had to step over them so I could help my mom onto the mattress.

She lay down easily enough. I covered her with a coarse blanket. I noticed she didn't have a pillow, so I quickly went to the living room and grabbed one from the couch, along with another throw blanket that draped the arm. I brought them back and gently placed the pillow beneath her head. Why was she living this way? What was going on? I knew I wouldn't get answers tonight, but I despaired at the sight of her and the house that had once been filled with life, even if tinged with darker things.

To find my mom like this, her mind so clearly deteriorated, was excruciating. How could I have stayed away for so long without knowing this was going on? Was this only because of the missing kid, or did it go deeper than that?

I tucked the blanket around my mom's shoulders, noting the fine tremors that racked her body. She was probably freezing, but there was little I could do when the electricity was out.

My mother watched me intently.

"Try and sleep, Mom. You look like you need the rest," I told her softly, leaning down beside her again.

My mother grabbed my hand, her fingers icy, her grip painful. "You shouldn't be here, Chey. You need to leave. Before *he* knows you're back." Her voice was like gravel, her words spat out with a venom not meant for me.

I sighed. "Mom, no one knows I'm here—"

"You never listen! Don't go into the woods. Stick to the road, you hear me? There's something coming. I can feel it. It's everywhere. *He's* everywhere. The birds are quiet. The animals are hiding. I've felt *him* coming closer for months. I can't keep him away. Not this time." She tried to sit up, but I gently pushed her back down onto the pillow. "*He'll* find you. You have to leave before he knows . . ." Her words drifted off as her eyes became heavy. It was as if the energy that had been fueling her was slowly fizzling out.

"Sleep, Mom. I won't go into the woods, I promise. I'll stay on the road. He won't know I'm here. I'll be careful." I told her what she needed to hear.

My reassurances seemed to do the trick. She relaxed. But before she closed her eyes, she pressed a hard lump into my hand. "Keep this with you. Don't leave the house without it."

I looked down at the gleaming obsidian and quickly tucked it in my pocket. I hated my mother's superstitions. They had ruined her life, and I had worked damn hard to ensure they didn't ruin mine too.

"Okay," I said, getting to my feet, seeing my mother had already fallen asleep. I quickly left the room, quietly closing the door behind me.

I stood in the silent, dark hallway, not knowing what I should do now. I hadn't expected such a whirlwind upon my arrival. I sagged against the wall and tried to get myself together.

I was already feeling the emotional toll of this place. I hadn't adequately prepared for it. I had made myself forget how hard it was to be here.

Squaring my shoulders, I walked to the front door. I quickly went out to the car and grabbed my duffle bag, purposefully ignoring the creeping sensation that crawled up my spine. The feeling that I wasn't alone.

I was never alone in these woods.

The trees were quiet, the birds silent. It was like a vacuum of noise that felt both oppressive and consuming.

"The birds are quiet. The animals are hiding.

"I can't keep him away. Not this time."

It was easy to dismiss my mother's words as those of a woman barely in her right mind. But standing in the woods—in the skulking night—I felt my thoughts drifting to that awful place reserved for childhood nightmares. Nightmares created by the woman who should have kept them at bay, not invited them in.

Mom had filled my youth with fear and horror, and I felt both scratching at my insides, waiting for me to let them back in.

I took the keys out of the ignition, the headlights turning off, leaving the world in total blackness. I slammed the car door closed and glared toward the dark, dark woods. I refused to hasten my steps as I returned to the house, but I scanned the yard before going inside, in an age-old habit that infuriated me.

The house was now still and cold. Too cold. I went around and closed the windows and then blew out the candles. I found a battery-operated lamp on the coffee table and turned it on. I took in the state of things and felt overwhelmed. My skin itched with wanting to clean and straighten.

Instead, I ignored the debris of my mother's turbulent world and carried my bag to the door across from my mom's. Without giving myself a chance to retreat, I turned the doorknob and walked inside. I went to flip the switch and was pleased when light flooded the room. It seemed the electrical outage had been temporary. Now, with the shadows gone, I took in my old room and was shocked to find that it was the one spot in the house that hadn't changed at all.

The air didn't feel stale like disused spaces should. I sniffed, catching the cloying scent of lavender and rosemary. There wasn't a speck of dust on any surface. The bed was neatly made. My old posters were still hanging on the walls.

The fact that my mother had taken such an effort to maintain my childhood bedroom, in the condition it had been when I left, hurt my heart in a way I hadn't been expecting.

Later as I lay in a bed in a room that hadn't changed, I felt the tears come. I had worked so hard to escape this place, yet here I was, plunged right back into it. I covered my face with my hands and sobbed for all the ways that I was still tied here. To this life. No matter how hard I tried to run from it.

Finally, after what felt like ages, I closed my eyes.

And while I drifted off to sleep, I thought I heard the soft whispers of the forest in my ears, welcoming me home.

Or warning me away.

CHAPTER

2

—Cheyenne—

M OM WAS STILL asleep when I woke up the next morning. I opened her door a crack and found her curled
up beneath her blanket. I hated seeing her sleeping on a
mattress on the floor, and I wondered why she had removed
the bed. I would have to do something about that.

Quietly I closed the door and headed to the living
room. In the harsh light of day, the house was worse than it
had first appeared. Every square inch of surface was covered
in candles and herbs, crystals and carved sticks. Evidence of
my mother's delusions were everywhere I looked. It made
me want to scream.

My mother's house consisted of only five rooms, all on
one level. The living room was filled to the brim. There was
hardly any space to sit down. She had never been a hoarder,
but obviously that had changed over the years.

On one side of the room sat a large oak table covered
in what appeared to be knickknacks and random trash—
decaying plants, burnt wood, piles of rocks. But if you
looked closer, and knew exactly what you were seeing, you'd
know this wasn't clutter. You'd know this was the remnants

of some sort of ceremonial offering. The rotting plants were elderberry and pokeweed. I noticed rosemary falling in drying clumps onto the floor. The wood was etched with symbols, and the rocks—that shone with a dull luster—were all the colors of the rainbow. The crystals were some of my mother's most cherished possessions.

I controlled the urge to sweep it all to the floor and instead walked to the kitchen, which was just as cluttered as the living room. Crystals and candles were everywhere. The air stank of burnt herbs.

The room was small, the large, roughly hand-carved table taking up most of the space. I was ten when Chief Hickman replaced the open fireplace that had been used for the past hundred years with an electric stove. An old-time icebox still stood outside the kitchen door, though we had no need for it in the twenty-first century. Apparently, until Mom, the Ashbys had stubbornly refused to enter the modern era.

For the time being, I ignored the disorder and opened the twenty-year-old refrigerator in the corner. It was empty. There wasn't even the clichéd head of moldy lettuce or curdled milk.

I then moved to the cabinets. Except for the plates and cups, there was no food there either. What had Mom been eating? No wonder she was all skin and bones.

If I was going to be staying here for any period of time, we needed food. And my mom needed to start taking better care of herself.

I quickly showered and dressed. Then I picked up the black obsidian Mom had given me last night, and though I thought about putting it in my pocket, I instead opened a drawer and buried it beneath a pile of old T-shirts.

Town was the last place I wanted to be. But I had come back to Blue Cliff to be with my mother, and I couldn't avoid it forever, though I wished I could.

It had snowed overnight. It was only a couple of inches, enough to look pretty without making it impossible to get out. Driving through the woods during the day was less daunting than after sundown, but no less smothering. The dense trees felt as if they were pressing down on me. The road, a narrow lane cutting through the forest, was in bad shape, which forced me to drive at a snail's pace. Someone had tried to fill in the potholes, with little success.

I attempted to ignore the way the wood's shadows played tricks with my eyesight. It was hard not turning my head every time something moved just out of view.

It's only a deer.

It's only the wind blowing the branches.

There was an otherness about the woods. It opened its cavernous mouth and swallowed me whole. As a child, it had been my constant companion and my eternal captor. It was the whisper in my ear, the chill on the back of my neck, the sounds that were both real and imagined.

Hickory Woods was all encompassing and more than trees and dirt. It was my story's beginning.

And perhaps its end as well.

The drive into the town of Blue Cliff was a short one, no more than fifteen minutes. The forbidding yet beautiful presence of the Appalachian Mountains made them look as if they were only an arm's length away. The grayish-blue slate rock the area was named for dotted the landscape in broken, irregular chunks.

The closer I drove to the heart of the town, the more anxious I became.

I was a mature woman, damn it—*grow a backbone!*

Why did I care what a bunch of hicks thought about me? Their opinions didn't matter. I had left all that shit behind.

As soon as the thought entered my head, I knew I wasn't being fair. These people were a rugged bunch who looked out for each other. Everyone was family in one way or another. My internal antagonism was rooted in my deep-seated guilt that I wasn't ready to deal with.

I didn't want to face what I had left behind.

As the fields and woods turned to houses and streets and shops, I slowed down, taking it all in. Blue Cliff, Virginia, was a town stuck in a time warp. Nothing had changed in the five years since I had left. There was something depressing but also comforting about that. Sure, there were new flower planters outside the town hall and what looked like a new clothing store on the corner of Hickory and North Streets, but that was about it. Blue Cliff had been frozen since the day I left.

Except for the vans. And the obvious outsiders milling about outside the town hall and roaming the square. They didn't move with a familiarity that I would expect in someone born and raised here. These were "outta-towners." They didn't belong.

Strangers didn't happen upon Blue Cliff unless they came for a very specific reason. And these kinds of strangers had taken up residence once before. Five years ago.

I noticed a perky-looking redhead dressed in a pretty pink skirt and a frilly white blouse, looking as if she were freezing in the frigid wind. She faced a man holding a heavy camera, her face assuming an expression of serious concern. And she wasn't alone. Reporters were everywhere. Taking notes, talking to cameras, accosting people on their way to the Breakfast Barn for their morning cup of coffee.

I parked my car outside of Grady's General Store. I didn't lock it when I got out. People in these parts didn't bother with pesky things like security. Though maybe they should have.

I slung my purse over my shoulder and walked with purpose toward the store. I passed the old community message board that was still tacked to the brick wall on the outside of the tiny grocery. Curious, I stopped and had a look. There was a flyer announcing the church raffle next month. The rotary was putting on a pancake breakfast this Thursday—all welcome—with a two-dollar entrance fee. The Kiwanis Club was holding a meeting next Monday. There was a notice for the upcoming Historical Society potluck supper, to be held at 21 Hickory Hill Drive. I knew the address. I knew the overdone ornate columns and sweeping verandas, even if I had never been particularly welcome there.

This was all normal business for a normal town, except Blue Cliff wasn't normal.

A faded smile peeked out from beneath the brightly colored notices. I could see the familiar, innocent face of ten-year-old Olivia Bradshaw looking back at me. Her missing poster was sun bleached and worn with age, still stapled to the corkboard, with a long-lost hope for a happy return.

My stomach churned.

I looked around. On the lamppost, was another fresh-faced youth, Danielle Torrents, forever immortalized by the frantic desperation of the hand that had stuck it there so many years ago.

Growing up, I'd been used to the missing posters dotting walls and park benches. They were the constant reminder of Blue Cliff's dirty, awful truth. The "lost" children. The ones who weren't ever coming home. Olivia Bradshaw was there. So was Michael Caruthers. And of course Danielle. They were the ones from my lifetime. The ones whose grisly deaths had precipitated my escape.

But there were others too.

Some of the flyers and posters were more than fifty years old, stapled one on top of another. Each addition added a new layer of grief to an already traumatized community. I knew that people's refusal to take them down was rooted in shame and guilt. A desire to remember at all costs. But

I wished they would get rid of them. It didn't do anyone any good to be constantly reminded that this was the town that "gobbled up children"—as a national news outlet had dubbed Blue Cliff in a scathing in-depth series five years ago.

Yet, how could they forget when history kept repeating itself?

A newer poster caught my attention. The colors were still vivid, as if only printed yesterday. And most likely it had been. It was the picture of a young boy, with a gap-toothed smile and wearing a blue plaid shirt, who only two weeks ago had been running around with his friends and climbing trees in the woods he should have avoided.

Hadn't anyone warned him that the hickories could steal him away?

Missing. Dakota Mason. Last seen on February 2nd. $1,000 reward for information leading to his return.

A thousand dollars.

A drop in the bucket to some, yet for most of the people around here it was a small fortune. But did the money really matter when it came to the life of a child gone too soon?

Like the ones before him, Dakota had ventured into the woods and never come out. I had read about it in the papers and had seen the news segment on CNN. It was as if he had vanished into thin air.

Like Olivia.

Like Michael.

Like Danielle.

One day he was there, the next he wasn't. And all that was left behind was the raging panic of unanswered questions.

Missing Dakota Mason was one of the main reasons I hadn't wanted to come back. I had been to this dance before, and I was eager to sit it out. If Chief Hickman hadn't insisted I was needed, I would have stayed in Roanoke. But it seemed the chief, the man I had known and loved my entire life, had expertly used my once-buried sense of duty against me.

The aged hickory trees lining the street reached toward the sky with their bare, skeletal arms. I noticed something dangling above my head and curiously reached up to touch it. I rubbed my fingers along the rough contours of the small doll wrapped in twine. My stomach twisted, and I tasted copper as I bit the inside of my cheek.

I walked slowly along the sidewalk, noticing similar dolls—or poppets as my mother called them—hanging by their arms from the low-hanging branches. They were crude things, fashioned from corn husks and string, others of sticks and straw. I knew them well, having helped my mom make them hundreds of times before. But they were hidden things, meant to be kept in pockets and locked away in drawers. Seeing them out in the open, a town's superstition on display, disturbed me.

They created a ghoulish sight as they swung slightly in the breeze.

I glanced at Dakota's sweet smile again, the shadow of the hanging poppet swaying across the wet paper. A growing sense of disquiet rumbled low in my belly, and I quickly walked to Grady's General Store, relieved when the door shut out the image of dolls and innocent, missing faces.

I grabbed a basket and filled it with fruits and vegetables. I picked out some venison, thinking I could have a hand at making Mom's venison stew. I made sure to grab some instant coffee and milk, and a pint of grape-nut ice cream for good measure, before making my way to the checkout.

So far I hadn't run into anyone, partially because the store was pretty much empty. I should have known my good luck wouldn't hold.

Ed Grady, the owner, was working the register. "Cheyenne Ashby, is that you?" His weathered face broke into a tired smile, and he immediately came around the counter to envelop me in a tobacco-scented hug. "My God, girl, it's been too long." He held me at arm's length, giving me a narrow-eyed inspection. "You're too thin. And you look tired. City life doesn't seem to suit you."

I knew Ed meant well. He had grown up with my mother, and the two were old friends. I remembered him and his wife, Linda, visiting often when I was younger. Linda and my mom would chat while Ed chopped enough firewood to last us the entire winter.

The years hadn't been good to him. He had always drunk too much moonshine, which he made in a not-so-secret still he kept a mile off the narrow road that headed up the mountain. As a result, his middle had expanded to nearly twice the size it used to be. His once-red hair had thinned, and the whites of his eyes were now a concerning shade of yellow. Busted capillaries lined his bulbous nose. But his smile was as bright as ever.

"City life is treating me fine," I assured him with more than a little bite.

"Your ma didn't tell me you were comin' home," he said. Was he being accusatory or was I feeling unnecessarily defensive?

"Probably because she didn't know," I muttered, loading the groceries onto the counter. Ed started ringing me up, putting my items in a plastic bag. Clearly, Grady's General Store had yet to get with the more environmentally conscious times.

"It's good you're back. Connie could use the help. With everything goin' on with the Mason boy, she needs someone to look after her properly." Ed pressed his mouth into a firm, judgy line.

"Well, I'm here now," was all I said. I was ready to get out of there, but it seemed good ol' Ed was taking his time ringing up my handful of groceries.

"There've been some changes since you left. Delilah Reynolds got a new hip. The church auxiliary raised funds to replace the bell," Ed informed me. I wanted to roll my eyes but didn't dare.

"That all sounds great," I responded, not meaning a word of it.

Ed's eyes lit up. "Oh and my boy Reggie has moved back home. He's been such a help to Linda. Children should be willing to take care of their parents." Ed's words couldn't be more pointed if he'd sharpened them with a blade.

What he failed to say was that his twenty-something son had recently been released from jail for voyeurism. He had been picked up at least four times that I knew of, though it was probably more. Reggie was a weirdo who liked to look in people's windows. He'd always made me uncomfortable when I was younger. Every town had that one person everyone silently raised their eyebrows about. The fact that Ed and Linda were universally loved and admired made it difficult to hold their questionable son accountable for his behavior. Reggie Grady had more slaps on the wrists than anyone I knew. I was surprised when I read that he was finally sent to jail for a six-month stint. But it seemed you could only look the other way for so long.

Blue Cliff was a town of characters. Some good, some bad.

"I'm happy for you two," I replied, knowing it was the right thing to say.

"I was just out to see your mama last week. Linda didn't come. She broke her back last year in that big snowstorm and still isn't up and around the way she used to be," he went on.

"Sorry to hear that," I replied politely.

"Linda's been growing her herbs in the new greenhouse I built for her in the spring. She made sure to get a bundle of dill together for Connie. Made it up into a pretty wreath for her to hang above the door. Can't be too careful out there in those woods. We like to make sure she's protected. Especially with what happened to the Mason boy."

I could tell he wanted to talk about Dakota Mason. It was the way of people in small towns. They speculated and hypothesized until they were blue in the face. Ed and his friends would talk of nothing else for months—if not years. In Blue Cliff memories were long.

Ed dropped the ice cream into the bag and finally gave me my total. I handed him my debit card, stopping myself from tapping my fingers in impatience.

"That's nice. I'm sure she appreciated it," I murmured.

"Took her the ashes from the pinewood fire we burned at the new year too. Pine acts as a shield, you know." He slowly put my card into the reader and waited. He hadn't taken his eyes off me. "Linda and I worry about her out there all by herself. Things are different now. The darkness is back, Cheyenne. We all feel it."

Oh jeesh, not this.

"It's a shame about Dakota, but I'm sure there's a reasonable explanation," I countered, feeling physically exhausted by the conversation.

Ed's face grew thunderous. "There's nothing reasonable about it. It's like before. More babies will go missing. Especially now that murderer's free."

I didn't have to ask who he was referring to. The whole country knew the story of railroaded Jasper Clinton, wrongfully convicted of killing Blue Cliff's children. He was the poster boy for a miscarriage in justice. Evidence had recently come to light that exonerated him. So Jasper had gone and gotten himself a hotshot appeals attorney and filed a writ of habeas corpus, saying his constitutional rights had been violated. And it seemed they had been. Jasper's attorney claimed evidence had been purposefully withheld during his trial five years before.

The appellate court agreed, and Jasper was released, the three life sentences for the murders of Danielle Torrents, Michael Caruthers, and Olivia Bradshaw overturned.

And now another child in Blue Cliff had gone missing.

I knew Ed Grady wasn't the only one in town thinking the timing was mighty suspicious.

"It seems as if Jasper wasn't the guy though, Ed. The evidence must have been compelling for the judge to release him." I should have known better than to voice an opinion contrary to Ed Grady's. His broad chest puffed up, and he looked ready to spit nails.

"There's no way Chief Hickman and the department got it wrong. I'm sure you remember my brother, Adam— he's been a deputy for the past forty years. He worked that case. He knew from the moment they found little Livvie Bradshaw's body who'd done it."

Ed spoke in absolutes. When it came to the horrific murders of three of the town's children, everyone had an opinion. And most of them aligned.

Jasper Clinton was a murderer. And that murderer was now free.

"Now with Dakota missing, everyone will see we had it right. You know, Marge Evans said she saw Jasper havin' dinner with his parents at the Cracker Barrel off I-81 just two days ago. So don't ya see? He's in the area!" Ed was getting himself worked up.

"I'm sure the police are looking into every possible lead, including Jasper," I told him calmly. I was worried the older man was going to drop dead from a heart attack, with how red his face had become.

"Of course they are. Chief Hickman runs a top-notch operation. They'll find Dakota. They'll get Jasper back in prison soon enough." Ed rubbed his nose with a tissue. "Well, don't be a stranger, Cheyenne. It's good to have you back where you belong."

Where I belong.

It didn't feel like comfort—more like ownership. As if Blue Cliff had a slice of my soul and didn't plan to give it back. I all but grabbed the bag that Ed held out for me. "Thanks. I'll see you around, Ed."

Once outside, I stood on the sidewalk, letting the different emotions wash over me. I watched the unusually busy town move around me and wished I could run again. Fast and far away.

"*Missing.*"

"*Child murders.*"

"*Hickory Woods.*"

The words on everyone's lips punched me in the stomach, like an assault.

Another lost child. Another round of whodunit.

I had survived it once.

But I wasn't sure I would survive it again.

3

—Natalie—

"COME ON, NAT, let me take you to breakfast." Hunter's expression was hard, though he attempted to soften it when he looked at me. "It's been a rough couple of days."

He leaned against the narrow counter, his green eyes watching me with the assuredness of a man who was never refused. Hunter's broad chest and shoulders stretched the clean lines of his expensive suit. His light brown hair was expertly styled. His face was clean-shaven to show off the hard lines of his jaw, and his clothes were perfectly pressed. A Caruthers was nothing if not always well presented. Despite his somber mood, his expression still held a hint of his typical playfulness. It was hard to read him properly, though I knew he had to be hurting.

It was barely nine, and my assistant, and friend, Jamie Fry, wasn't in yet, but that didn't stop Hunter from trying to coerce me away from Bartlett's, as usual. In his eyes, I didn't need to work. I was already well looked after, and a job was unnecessary. I hated that he thought so little of my career—my dream—but I had learned to ignore his digs over the years. My parents were the same, so I had developed a thick skin.

"I understand, but I can't leave the store," I said, carefully pulling out new stock from the large box that had been delivered. "I know how much effort you've been putting into searching for Dakota; I have too, remember, but that means the store has been closed a lot and I can't afford that." He made a noise of condescension, which I chose to ignore, as I carried an armful of dresses over to the rack. "I'm sorry. Maybe we can meet for lunch instead?"

Hunter scowled. "Nat, I'm not asking for you to close your precious store all day—just an hour or so. I was up all night with the search party, and I'm exhausted. Not to mention Mom and Dad have been at each other's throats for days. Her drinking is out of control again. And with all the reporters in town, it's a goddamn nightmare. But you obviously have more important things to do." He turned from me, and I reached for him, out of habit as much as affection.

I bit my lip, sympathy and annoyance vying for supremacy. "I'm sorry," I said again, turning him back to me.

"You know there was a sighting of that murdering bastard, right? At a gas station off the highway. Dad and I drove down there as soon as we heard, but he was already gone." Hunter's features turned frightening, his gaze faraway.

I worried what Hunter and his dad might actually do if they caught up to Jasper. Five years had only compounded their feelings of hatred. Their need for justice was their only drive now that Jasper Clinton had gotten his convictions overturned. Hunter's little brother, Michael, had been brutally slain five years ago, along with Olivia Bradshaw and Danielle Torrents. Neither the families nor the town had ever recovered from the loss. Jasper, the man everyone thought responsible, was now a free man.

Hunter's ma drank to wash away the pain, and his dad, Chase, the mayor of our small town, worked all hours of the day. And my fiancé was the brother that lived in the shadow of a murdered child.

"Hunter . . ." I began, but he cut me off abruptly.

"Please, Nat. This place isn't exactly bustling with customers anyway."

I felt the familiar tug of irritation at the pointed barb.

Hunter reached for my hand. "I really need to get my mind off things for a while." It was impossible to say no to him, especially given the situation. I couldn't imagine how hard things must have been for his family, not only with the five-year anniversary of Michael's murder coming up, but now also Dakota Mason's disappearance. It didn't help that Blue Cliff was teeming with journalists eager to cover the juicy stories that our town kept handing to them on a silver platter.

No one had gone unaffected by the deaths of the three kids. It was one of the hazards of living in such a small town. One person's tragedy was every person's tragedy.

But living in a close-knit community wasn't all bad. There was a comfort in being looked after by your neighbors. It was harder to become the main character in a true-crime podcast when everyone knew your business. It's why I'd stayed. The thought of leaving these familiar streets and losing sight of the mountains brought a sense of panic that I couldn't live with.

But familiarity hadn't saved Hunter's brother. It hadn't saved Olivia or Danielle either. And it hadn't stopped Dakota from going missing. None of them had been kept safe, nor the many children that came before them, all lost to the woods.

It was Blue Cliff's greatest shame. It was the rotten core at the center of an otherwise good heart.

"Please, Nat," Hunter wheedled, taking my hand, his gaze pleading. As if on cue, Jamie Fry pushed open the door, the little bell ringing above it to announce her arrival.

Jamie was a sweet girl, if a bit flaky. Timeliness wasn't one of her better qualities. But her ma and my ma had been in the Rotary Club together for the past fifteen years, so of course I had hired her.

"I'm sorry I'm late. I was up all night making posters with my mom and Mackenzie." She bustled in, a whirlwind of slightly chaotic energy and too much hairspray. She looked exhausted. Dark shadows ringed her eyes, and her skin was pale.

"We're putting the posters up after I finish work this evening," she remarked tiredly, her features pulled taut with worry.

"How is Mackenzie holding up?" I knew that her younger sister and Dakota had been friends most of their lives. Kids in Blue Cliff were a tightly bound group, so his disappearance would be hitting them all hard.

"Not great. It's hard for anyone to understand what's going on, but for kids it's just . . ." she shook her head, her eyes filling with tears. "I needed Mackenzie to see us doing *something*. She's so scared and worried. She can barely sleep. She thinks *he's* comin' to get her, because of course all the kids are saying *he's* come out of the woods to get 'em," she finished in a whisper. "It's hard getting a nine-year-old to believe a person did this and not a monster in the woods. Maybe it's better for her not to see that evil lies in people too."

I placed a hand on her arm. "I'm so sorry. If you need to go home, that's okay. I'd understand."

Jamie wiped tears from her eyes and took a deep breath. "No, I need to be here to take my mind off things. I would've been here sooner, but none of us got much sleep last night."

"Don't even worry about it. It's not a problem," I replied, my voice kind. I could hardly scold her for being late given the circumstances.

Hunter cleared his throat, drawing our attention to him. "So, Jamie, now that you're here, I'm going to take Natalie to get some breakfast. You're okay to look after this place for a little while, right? I'll bring you back something too."

"Oh, yeah, that's fine. I've got it. You two go." Jamie waved us on. "Bring me a muffin. I forgot to eat before I left the house."

I narrowed my eyes at Hunter, annoyed that he'd asked Jamie. I could hardly say no now, though. "We'll be back within the hour. Thanks, Jamie," I said to her.

Heading around the counter, I grabbed my jacket. Hunter held the door open, and we slipped out into the cold morning air.

I took his hand as we walked across the street. Traffic was busy for this time of morning. I guessed it was a collection of things: the snowstorm predicted to blow in over the weekend, as well as the journalists who had been circling like vultures since Jasper's release and then Dakota's disappearance. I'd had to ask Police Chief Hickman to put up a "No Trespass" notice in the shop's window after being inundated with reporters looking for any piece of information they could get.

Blue Cliff was once again in the spotlight for all the wrong reasons.

*   *   *

Normally, our hometown was everything a small town should be. It consisted of a handful of stores and one main road. One way in, one way out. We were surrounded on all sides by thick, dense forest. The official name of the forest was Hickory Woods for the overpopulation of hickory trees in the area. But everyone called them Ashby Woods for the family that had always lived in the heart of them.

We were miles from the highway and tucked into the side of the mountain. If you weren't deliberately going to Blue Cliff, you'd never find it. Not much had changed over the years, which, in my opinion, was part of its charm.

We sometimes got tourists, drawn by our proximity to the Appalachian Trail and the few Airbnbs that were little more than glorified hunting cabins for people wanting to vacation off the grid. We were a town mostly untouched. You wouldn't find a Walmart or a Chili's. We hadn't even had broadband until a year ago. To say we were cut off from the rest of the world would be an understatement. But that was another thing that I liked so much about it.

"Well, hell has gone and frozen over," Hunter muttered, bringing us both to a stop.

I followed his gaze toward Grady's General Store, my features going slack with shock. "Is that Cheyenne Ashby?" I croaked.

She was older and a lot thinner, but despite the differences, she was still the same Cheyenne.

Long, dark hair tied back, skin so pale you wondered if she ever went outside. Even as a kid, when she spent all her days running around in the woods, she'd never tanned. From this distance, I knew her eyes were a piercing blue that could look straight through you. She was striking, with the kind of looks that grew on you the longer you knew her. To those who had loved her, there wasn't a more beautiful girl around.

Her arms were wrapped around a bag of groceries, her expression was fixed in annoyance as she watched a reporter speak to my aunt Margaret—"Marge"—Evans, who seemed to enjoy being in front of a camera. Chey had to have felt the weight of everyone staring at her, as they weren't being subtle about it. People were openly gaping at her. Chey's reappearance, particularly during a time of such disquiet, was definitely a cause for gossip.

I had given up expecting Cheyenne to come back, so I was stunned to see her. Over the years, I had stayed in contact with Constance, Chey's ma. She had been like a second mother to me and had given me a safe haven when things had been hard. Chey may have been happy to walk away from her family, but that didn't mean I had to, and my bond with Constance had only grown. But I couldn't replace her daughter, so for Connie's sake, I was glad to see Chey.

"Do you want to go say something to her?" Hunter asked. I gave him a sharp look. He knew our history and why I never spoke her name. How could he even suggest it?

No, my still bruised heart wanted to shout. But somehow I managed to sound indifferent when I replied, "Sure."

Hunter and I headed through the snow to greet Cheyenne.

Chey had always wanted to escape. Anywhere, so long as it was far away from Blue Cliff. I'd never understood her wish to leave. Blue Cliff felt picture-perfect with the summer farmer's market and the Ole Time Festival in the fall. Blue Cliff was the sort of place that people read about in books. A town seemingly untouched by the outside world.

But Cheyenne had left without a backward glance, a postcard, or even a goodbye hug thrown to the girl she had been friends with her whole life. Yet now she was back. And by the looks of her, she was none too happy about it.

"Hey, Cheyenne, never thought we'd see you back here," Hunter said, oozing cold sarcasm.

"Yeah," she replied shortly. She avoided looking at me until it seemed she couldn't help herself. "Hey, Natalie." She said my name as if she really didn't want to.

"Hey, Natalie."

That was all I got? I wasn't a woman who easily lost her temper. I was a "kill 'em with kindness" kind of gal. Ma had raised me to be a polite, respectable woman who knew how to keep her cool. To be endlessly civil, no matter the situation. I was brought up in the tradition of "bless your heart." But right now I was close to losing it.

Bless her goddamn heart.

"Hey yourself," I replied with my best "aw shucks" smile. "You're looking well."

Cheyenne shuffled the groceries in her arms. "Thanks, you too." She seemed as if she wanted to be anywhere else.

We stared at each other, the years apart flooding between us. There was so much I wanted to say to her, but I couldn't get the words out.

"Did you hear Natalie and I are getting married?" Hunter lifted my left hand to show off the noticeable rock. "It cost an arm and a leg, but she's worth it."

There was more awkwardness. I wished Hunter would shut up. I felt unfairly annoyed at him.

"Pretty," Cheyenne murmured, only giving a passing glance to the ring I was so proud of. I felt a pinch of hurt in my chest, and I forced myself to breathe around it.

"I'm surprised to see you," I said. The words came out relatively calm, which was the opposite of how I felt. "What brings you back? I thought you'd sworn off Blue Cliff." Chey's face hardened, her eyes flashing in something that looked like irritation.

"Just figured it was time to come for a visit. Thought Mom might need me."

Hunter squeezed my hand. "Well, we all look after Ms. Ashby when we can. A single lady out there in the woods all by herself needs the help. I haven't been able to head out there to check on her myself—I'm pretty busy now that I'm the town planner. Lots to do, you know. But others have been looking after things, especially the chief. This town takes care of its own. Even when their own family isn't up for the job."

Hunter could be a real jerk at times. And he never minced words. He didn't particularly like Constance, but that wasn't the point. His comment was about hurting Cheyenne.

"Hunter," I hissed. Looking back at Chey, I softened. "I visit with her from time to time. I know she's capable of looking after herself, but it's easy to get isolated out there." I made myself unclench my hands, which had somehow balled into fists since we had started talking.

Cheyenne forced a smile, and the ice between us cracked fractionally. "That's nice of you, Nat. I'm sure she appreciates seeing you."

A car honked its horn, and we all watched as Chris Miners pulled his beat-up Chevy to the curb. Winding down the window, he leaned out and waved Hunter over. Chris gave Cheyenne a cursory glance, his eyes widening slightly in recognition.

"I'll be right back," Hunter said before heading over to him.

He and Chris weren't exactly friends, but Chris ran the local paper, the *Blue Cliff Bulletin*, so he was always a good source of information. Like his father, Hunter wanted to know everything that was going on. They weren't men who liked to be blindsided.

*   *   *

I was left feeling uncomfortable now that it was just Chey and me. We used to be best friends and went everywhere together. At one time, we were made up of childish secrets and shared experiences. Now the only thing that existed between us were unspoken words and resentment.

Snow had started to fall, and I buried my chin in my scarf to keep warm.

"I'd better get going," Cheyenne stated, her arms tightening around her bag of groceries.

I shuffled restlessly on my feet. "I hope Constance is doing alright. She's had a rough time, particularly after you left. She was cut up for a good, long while." Chey opened her mouth to say something, but I shook my head. "That wasn't a dig, Chey. It's only the truth. She missed you. I tried to fill in as best I could. And she's been okay. Up until . . ." I looked around, nodding toward the reporters hovering nearby. "I'm sure you've heard about Dakota Mason. He's Fred Mason's son. Remember Fred? He was a year ahead of us in school."

"Yeah, I remember Fred," she answered. "Is there any news about the kid?"

I shook my head again. "Not yet, but we have to remain hopeful, right?"

Chey smiled slightly. "You haven't changed, have you? Always looking for the bright side."

I shrugged. "I guess not." I cleared my throat. "Listen, this thing with Dakota has really upset your ma. She's been agitated. Speaking about things I haven't heard her talk about in a long time. Last week, I found her out at the old cemetery digging up dirt from the graves. She wouldn't let me take her home, so I stayed with her until she was ready to leave. I think we were there for almost two hours." I blew out a breath. "It reminds me of the last time. I know she was bad back then, and she's the same this time. Swearing *he* took Dakota. I just thought I should let you know."

"I appreciate the warning, but I think I can handle her. I'm used to this, unfortunately."

"I know," I replied rigidly, "but she's not good. Hunter heard that she left a gutted rabbit on the Mason's front step. She told them to leave it there. That maybe *he'd* accept the offering and bring Dakota back. They were understandably upset."

"Jesus Christ," Chey muttered tiredly. "I'll have to drop by and apologize."

"It's okay—I've spoken to them already. They understand, and in a way they appreciate what she's tryin' to do. But, just . . . just watch her. She's troubled. It's stirred up a lot of stuff . . ." I let my words trail off.

"Thank you. It means a lot knowing you were looking out for her, but I've got it covered now." She checked her phone. "Crap, I didn't realize it was so late. I need to get back. It was good seeing you again."

"Oh, okay, sure. Well, I guess I'll be seeing you around." I stepped to one side to allow her to pass. But despite my own defensive pain, I knew how hard it must have been for her to come back. Especially given what she was coming home to.

I reached out and placed my hand on her arm. "I think things will get a lot better for Constance now you're here," I assured her. Some of the tension left Cheyenne's shoulders, and she drooped slightly. Her eyes moved to the town hall where my aunt Margaret had finished up her interview and was walking with a determined purpose toward us. I knew Chey should leave before she made it across the street.

"You'd better get going before my aunt Marge crosses that road. You may have been gone for five years, but even you can't have forgotten what an interrogation from her feels like." I couldn't help but chuckle as Cheyenne groaned.

"Five years isn't long enough to forget something like that." She smirked. She looked at me. Really looked at me. In that way of hers that both saw everything and nothing. "See ya around, Nat." Then, before I could respond, she turned on her heel and left quickly.

I stared after her for several moments, feeling awash with emotions I had forced myself to put aside.

* * *

I forked eggs into my mouth, barely tasting them. The Breakfast Barn was busy with the usual crowd. The hustle and bustle of the waitstaff hurrying back and forth to tables, filling coffee cups and putting steaming plates of food in front of diners was normally soothing. But not today.

Hunter was tapping away on his phone while we ate, something I found rude but was used to. As if sensing my scrutiny, he looked up and smiled at me. My heart fluttered a little in an echo of the puppy love I'd felt once upon a time. God, he was handsome.

"Work," he said with a dismissive wave of his hand. "You know how it is."

"Anything important?"

"Something's always going on." He leaned back in his chair. "So, Cheyenne's back after all this time." Hunter picked up his coffee and took a long sip. "I wondered if we'd ever see her again. No one has heard from her in years. She's got some nerve, strollin' back after ghosting the entire town."

"Don't be mean," I warned him, acutely aware that despite his good looks, a cruelness dwelled within him.

He lifted his hands in surrender. "All I'm saying is if Cheyenne thinks things are going to be easy, then she's got another think comin'."

"Cheyenne's life was never easy. You have no idea what it was like for her. With the way her ma is and her family's reputation." I frowned.

"I'm sure living with Constance was tough, but some of us had worse things to deal with than a kooky, superstitious mom and weird horror stories. *Our* horror stories were real, and yet we stuck around—we stuck it out. Some of us understand the importance of community and family and honoring our commitments," he snapped, his entire demeanor changing.

I wanted to tell him that there was more to those woods than made-up horror stories. That I had seen things out there that couldn't be explained. That most everyone in town knew there was an element of truth to those tales. Hunter's family were the outliers. Their pragmatism made them stand out. The Caruthers had never bought Constance's herbs or had her draw a ring of protection around their house. They may be from Blue Cliff, their family going back generations, but they made a point to turn away from the beliefs that sustained everyone else.

Knowing he wouldn't understand, because he'd *never* understood, I instead reached across the table and placed my hand on top of his. "I know it must be hard for you and your family right now." It was the only thing I could say when he got like this. When memories of his brother came to the surface and threatened to crack through.

He shrugged again, his eyes on the tablecloth, his features stony. "Every year is hard. You'd think it would get easier, but it never does. And now with Dakota . . ."

The urge to go around the table and put my arms around him was strong, but I was cut off by one of my best friends, Jackson Campbell, approaching our table. His smile was warm and genuine. He hadn't changed much since we were kids. He had the same floppy brown hair and kind brown eyes. Most of the girls in our school had had a crush on him at one time or another. I had never looked at him that way, though, mostly because he was the closest thing I had to a brother.

And because I knew, even as kids, that he and Chey were meant for each other.

"Hey, Jack. How are you?" I smiled fondly.

Jack, Chey, and I had grown up together here in Blue Cliff, just as our parents had done before us. We had been the three musketeers. Where one was, so were the other two. Eventually, Jack and Cheyenne started dating. For a lot of people that would have destroyed the friend dynamic. The old saying "three's a crowd" could have applied, but our relationship was different. Ours was a bond that went deeper than boyfriends and girlfriends. So when they got together, our roles simply shifted to accommodate the change. And when Chey left, Jack and I remained as close as ever.

"I'm good." He inclined his head toward Hunter. "Hey, man."

There was no love lost between Hunter and Jack. Jack had always tried to get along with my fiancé, but Hunter didn't believe that men and women could be friends. He had always been wary of our friendship, which was ridiculous.

Hunter gave Jack a sly smile, and I already knew what he was going to say before the words left his mouth. "So, you'll never guess who we ran into." He paused for dramatic effect before dropping the bomb. "Cheyenne Ashby."

I cringed at his bluntness. Jackson had loved Cheyenne. Deeply. And I suspected he had never stopped. He had dated on and off since she had left, but nothing serious or long term.

Jack's eyes shot to mine, his tired expression morphing into something else entirely. "She's back?"

I nodded. "Yeah. We saw her a few minutes ago."

I watched as Jack digested the news. A myriad of emotions crossed his face. Jack had never been one to hide his feelings. He'd make a horrible poker player.

A large hand clapped down on Jack's shoulder, startling us all. The Blue Cliff police chief, Donald Hickman, stood behind him, a wide smile on his handsome face that was at odds with the somber mood of the rest of the town. The chief was a tall man with thick muscles. When I was a kid, he'd wrap those big, burly arms around Chey and me and squeeze us. We all loved the chief. He never had a bad word to say about anyone, and that kindness ran right through to his core, shining out of his soft gray eyes. And even though we felt an affectionate closeness with him, he'd only ever been "Chief" to us. It felt wrong—disrespectful—to call him anything else.

"Well if it isn't two of my favorite people." He spoke with a fondness that was both endearing and natural. Jack and I shared a special relationship with the chief of police. We always felt looked after.

"I'm not sure if I should be offended by not being included, Chief," Hunter chuckled.

Chief Hickman grinned. "I always have time for a Caruthers—you know that. You and your brother are important to this town and to me." At the mention of Michael, Hunter's smile faded slightly.

"You look tired, Chief," I observed with concern. "And you need to sew a button on your uniform," I teased, pointing to his brown shirt.

He glanced down at his chest. "Good thing I can work a needle and thread." He gave me a wide smile. "And I'm fine, Natalie. It's been a long couple of weeks, is all."

"Still no news on Dakota?" Jack asked, and the chief shook his head.

"I'm hopin' no news is good news," Chief Hickman replied. He turned to Hunter, his face full of concern. "How's your mother holdin' up?"

"She's okay. But this stuff with Dakota is bringing it all back for her. And with Clinton out of jail, she's terrified he's taken Dakota." Hunter grit his teeth. "Have you found the bastard? I've heard people have seen him. We all know he's the one who has Dakota. He needs to be stopped."

Chief Hickman moved closer to Hunter, his reassuring presence calming him somewhat. "You have my word, Hunter, we're lookin' for Jasper. If he has Dakota, we'll make sure he pays and goes back to prison where he belongs." We all felt a little better with the chief at the helm of the ship. "Mind if I swing by some time to see your mother? Maybe I can put her mind at ease," he offered.

"I'm sure she'd like that. But don't be taking on too much. You have enough on your plate with Constance Ashby." The irritation in Hunter's tone was evident.

"Oh, nonsense. I don't mind one bit. We take care of our own in this town."

"Well, maybe you can pass off some of those duties to Cheyenne now that she's back." Hunter didn't even try to hide his distaste.

"Chey's in town? I didn't realize she would be comin' back so soon. She was supposed to call when she was on her way." The chief's expression darkened briefly. "I tried to warn her how bad Connie had gotten with all the ugliness goin' on, but seein' it for herself . . . well, it won't be easy."

I wasn't surprised Chief Hickman was the one to tell Chey about her ma. I had gleaned over the years that he was the only one in Blue Cliff she had maintained any sort of contact with. Did it hurt that she chose to talk to the chief and not to me? Sure. But I understood it. He had taken on an almost paternal role in her life, especially after her dad took off when she was young. He was the only functional parental figure she had ever had.

The chief looked at me expectantly. "Maybe you and Jack can check in on her." He glanced between us. "There was a time when no one could tear you three apart." His smile was indulgent before his mood became serious. "We need to stand by each other. And the three of you should be helpin' one another. It's how it should be." He pulled on his gloves. "I better be getting back to the station."

"I'll tell Mom that you'll be coming by. And I'll be sure to have Darla bake one of her famous cobblers for you," Hunter said as Chief Hickman turned to leave.

"That sounds perfect, son." He held out his hand and Hunter shook it.

"I'd better get going too." Jack gave us a brief wave before following the chief out of the restaurant.

Hunter's people-pleasing smile melted away as soon as we were left alone once more. "Looks like Jack's still a pathetic, lovesick puppy, even after all these years. What an idiot," he muttered in disgust.

"Hunter, stop it," I warned. Jack was, and always would be, off-limits. Hunter could criticize just about anyone, but not one of my oldest and dearest friends.

After that we drifted into shallow small talk, neither of us in the mood to discuss the sadness that seemed to have a hold on our town. There were too many grieving parents for such a tiny place, and everyone knew it. Though we would never, ever say it out loud. Giving voice to the fear was as good as inviting it in. And we worked hard to keep it out of our homes and away from our children. Though it seemed to always find us anyway.

Hunter's parents knew this. As did Olivia's and Danielle's.

And now Dakota's too.

We all knew what it meant when a child went missing in Blue Cliff. Eventually they would be found, but not in the way we all hoped for.

Because the woods had claimed another one, forever lost among the trees.

4

—Cheyenne—

I STARTLED AWAKE, THE recurring dream still spinning in my head. I was drenched in sweat, and I felt an uncomfortable tightness in the center of my chest. I blinked in the semidarkness. The air felt heavy. As if I had just missed something—or someone. The aftermath of their presence was everywhere.

Squinting in the direction of my door, I noticed it was slightly ajar, yet I distinctly remembered closing it when I went to bed.

Had my mom been in my room while I was asleep? Something about that was both comforting and unsettling.

I checked the time on my phone. It was a little after eight in the morning. I hadn't been able to go to sleep until well after midnight, so it felt too early to be up. I had only been back for two days, but like when I was a kid, I was having trouble sleeping.

It was because of the dreams. They had always been vivid. And they were always the same.

I was in the woods. It wasn't dark, but it wasn't light out either. It was that misty in-between time when the world was quiet and the air was full. I didn't have a clear idea of how long I'd been there, only that it'd been awhile. I was cold, and my hair was damp, which made me think I'd been standing outside for a significant period of time.

I knew I was scared. The kind of scared that makes your knees buckle and your heart race.

Because I'd been left alone to wait.

For *him*.

I knew he was coming.

I didn't know exactly what I was meant to do when he came—only that I couldn't run. I had to stay exactly where I was. Because it was my duty.

In my dream state I knew these things with absolute certainty that left no room for doubt.

I waited for him.

For him to find me.

There was movement in my peripheral vision, and I couldn't breathe. It felt like I was drowning. My face was wet. My feet were cemented to the ground.

He was coming closer.

I could practically feel his hunger.

Finally I could open my mouth, and when I did, I screamed.

That's when I woke up. Every single time.

I was left with the shaky sensation that I had narrowly escaped death.

It was a messed-up dream that I'd had a thousand times before. It could almost be real.

This town, this house, these woods were bringing back things I hadn't thought about for a long, long time. These dreams were simply a manifestation of all the bullshit I had been force-fed my entire life.

Finally, I gave up trying to go back to sleep and slipped out of bed. I dressed casually, putting on a heavy cardigan to ward off the chill. I opened my curtains, to see that it had snowed. Again. By the looks of it, a lot too. The trees were heavy with the white stuff, and it was still falling. I had almost forgotten how oppressive winters could be in the mountains. I realized had I waited another day or two to travel, I wouldn't have been able to get to Mom.

Perhaps the reason I was having the dream again had to do with how strange it was to be back. It felt like slipping on a pair of shoes that still fit, even though I should have outgrown them a long time ago.

I wondered if Mom was awake. I hadn't really seen her since that first night. Yesterday, after I got back from town with the groceries, I found the house empty. I noticed her heavy winter coat was gone, as well as her thick walking boots that she kept inside the kitchen door. I knew she was out in the woods somewhere and most likely wouldn't be back until well after sundown. I'd heard her come home a little after ten last night, her steps heavy as she made her way to her bedroom. She had stopped outside my door, and I wondered if she'd come in.

But she continued to her room, the decisive click of the door shutting behind her.

Growing up, it wasn't unusual for Mom to go into the woods for an entire day. Sometimes it was to collect herbs and flowers that only grew closer to the mountain. Sometimes she came back empty-handed, with a shattered expression, refusing to say a word to me. I didn't know what she did on those days when she'd go straight to her bedroom and light candles, wafting burning pine needles, and murmuring unintelligible words in a constant, panicked drone.

I didn't know where she went, but I knew it was a place I didn't want to follow.

I had learned at an early age how to take care of myself. One of my first memories was of being left at the house by myself for hours while my mom went on one of her "woods walks."

"Don't disturb the salt. And don't let the candle go out. Keep the windows closed and the door shut. Don't let him in if he comes. He can't cross the salt. Remember that, Chey."

Don't let him in.

Him.

The man—if that's what he was—who had dominated my entire life until I left, desperate to wrangle it back from his grasping, bloody hands.

The Hickory Man.

Keep silver in your pockets,
Walk with dirt in your shoes,
Or he'll poke your eyeballs from their sockets,
And boil your bones in stew.

The children in Blue Cliff had grown up on the legends of the Hickory Man. He was our local boogeyman. The omnipresent evil that haunted Hickory Woods, where Mom and I lived. The stories of him went back hundreds of years. Back to the very first settlers in the foothills.

When the crops wouldn't grow, it was because of the Hickory Man.

When the milk went sour, it was because of the Hickory Man.

And when the children went missing . . . everyone knew it was because of the Hickory Man.

Many of the parents of Blue Cliff, the ones who were deeply tied to the old ways, still sent their children out of the house with silver coins and a sprinkle of dirt in their shoes. The origins of the superstitions were lost to most, but they were adhered to all the same. It wasn't something anyone talked about. Why would they? Did you talk about why you brushed your teeth in the morning or why you said your prayers before bed? The coins and the dirt were simply a part of everyday life in our tiny corner of the world. The ritualized traditions remained like some sort of ingrained compulsion. Hard-held belief was an impossible thing to shake. Even if it was crap.

And now it seemed I had decided to come back at the worst possible time. There was another missing child. A new, yet familiar grief had blanketed the town once more. A boy was gone, and the flesh-and-blood man most believed to be a killer had been set free.

It had the feeling of cyclical tragedy that never seemed far away.

It always came back to the children.

And the woods.

And the sense of doom that was impossible to move away from.

I finally made myself leave my room. The smell of burning cedar was strong as I headed to the kitchen. Mom was there, waving a smoking stick into the corners. Seeing me, she put the smoldering wood down on the windowsill and poured two cups of coffee, giving me a wan smile.

I looked at her closely, but warily. She still seemed tired, but the circles beneath her eyes weren't as pronounced today. It appeared as if she had had a good night's sleep. She was still much too thin, but there was color to her cheeks that hadn't been there that first night. After hearing from the chief, I had expected the worst. In part, I had gotten it. But now, in the soft light of this new morning, she seemed something like the old Constance Ashby. Eccentric, but with a sharp mind.

"I'm sorry I wasn't around to see you yesterday. It was a new moon last night," she said. To anyone else, this wouldn't make any sense. But I knew exactly what she was talking about.

"You're not going to ask what I'm doing here?" I demanded, accepting the cup of coffee.

Mom leaned against the counter and looked at me over the rim of her mug as she took a long sip. "I know Donald called you. He told me after he had done it. The man could never keep anything from me."

"Did you tell him to call me?" I accused.

Mom put her mug down and crossed her arms across her chest. "If you must know, I gave the ol' chief a good piece of my mind. He thinks I need your help out here. He's forgotten I've survived just fine on my own for years."

Mom reached across the empty space between us and put her hand on my arm. "You're my child of the trees, Chey. This is always your home. But that doesn't mean it's safe for you to be here. It's happening again. All of it. I see it so clearly."

There it was. My mother's trademark bleakness. It was exhausting.

"Not this again, Mom. It's horrible to hear about Dakota Mason, but it's just that—a terrible, *tragic* situation. It doesn't mean something *more*," I argued. I leveled her with a firm look. "But that's why I'm here." I took a breath. "I know you've been acting out again, like five years ago after the murders. You have to let me help you this time."

"I'm not *acting out*, Cheyenne. Stop treating me like a two-year-old. I'm trying to warn everyone. It's what I'm supposed to do," she exclaimed, her neck flushed.

"Maybe this time, we can leave things to the police. It's not up to you to look after everyone—maybe just yourself for once."

"That's not how things work, Chey, and you know it. I *have* to keep everyone safe. I'm the only one who can." She shook her head again. "I can't let my focus wander, not even for a second. I can't let myself be distracted. Otherwise, more bad things will happen. *He* already has one child, but that won't be enough. One is never enough."

"Did you know that Jasper got out of prison?"

"We can't talk about that," Mom shushed me.

Ignoring her, I went on. "He's out, Mom. He didn't do it."

"I saw him, Chey. In the woods. He was out there with *him*. We were all together in *his* darkness. He got what *he* wanted. What he's always wanted. And now he's back, and the boy paid the price." My mom looked out the window with a worried expression, as if searching for something. I didn't know if she was talking about the Hickory Man or Jasper Clinton.

Five years ago, my mom had been one of the loudest voices against Jasper. When she claimed to have seen him in the woods around the time of the murders, that had been enough to confirm for people that Jasper was guilty. Because the Ashbys were special to this town, and when Mom talked, many listened. People still spoke about my grandad, Charlie, in reverential tones. And his father, Jonah, before him.

* * *

"Drink your coffee, and then I want you to help me sort the herbs I collected yesterday." Mom gave me a firm look. "If you're going to be staying here, we need to take some precautions. The trees know you're back. That means *he* does too." Of all the things I knew I would have to contend with when I'd decided to come back home, this was the worst.

Her blind, illogical faith in things that weren't real.

Mom had her beliefs, and they most definitely weren't mine. But I knew when to pick my battles. I was there to help her. I didn't want to alienate her as soon as I showed up.

"Let me make you something to eat first—" I started to say, but Mom waved away my suggestion.

"I can eat later. No time for that now." Before I could argue, she left the room.

I downed my coffee and joined my mom in the living room. She was sitting on the floor in front of the fire, an old sheet spread out in front of her. Piles of plants she had scavenged from the forest lay around her. With deft, experienced fingers, she peeled off the leaves and cut the roots.

Instead of sitting beside her, I went to the narrow bookcase beside the window. I pulled a large purple binder from the middle shelf. I had been surprised to see it there earlier.

"I thought I got rid of this before I left," I mused out loud.

I opened my old scrapbook up to the first page. I smiled at the yellowed photograph of two young girls, no more than seven or eight, arms around each other, grinning at the camera. One with dark hair, one with blond. One with a tear in her overalls, the other wearing a pretty pink dress. Both appeared happy.

Page after page was devoted to the unbreakable friendship that had existed between Natalie Bartlett and me. There were ticket stubs to movies I barely remembered, pressed flowers from long-ago bouquets. The punches kept coming the more I looked.

Because these were photographs of two people who loved each other. Who weren't just friends, but sisters.

I hadn't allowed myself to process what I'd felt at seeing Nat yesterday. She hadn't changed much. At least not outwardly. She was still pretty as a picture, wearing her blond hair cut in layers that brushed her shoulders. Her hazel eyes were still wide and clear, like some kind of animated princess.

The exchange had been cold, yet brief, which hurt, even though it shouldn't. When I'd left Blue Cliff, I had left everything and everyone. That included Natalie. I had cut her out of my life totally and completely. Or so I thought. I should have known that bonds like ours didn't ever really disappear, no matter how much I wanted them to. Seeing her again, I realized how much I had missed her.

Perhaps I should have called her or tried to stay in touch. But I knew that if I heard her voice, I'd never keep to my resolve to stay away. Natalie was as much of a lure as my mother. As much as the woods. It was necessary to make the escape a final one.

Nevertheless, here I was.

My eyes stung as I saw the massive, eight-by-ten-inch professional photo of myself all dressed up in my sweet, blue Homecoming dress, a huge smile on my face, and in the arms of my date. His smile was every bit as adorable as I'd remembered it to be. Soft brown hair falling across his forehead. Dark eyes bright and happy. I barely came to his shoulders. His broad frame dwarfed me. He had the build of a football player, though I knew for a fact he had never thrown a ball in his life.

Jackson Campbell.

My high school boyfriend.

My first love.

My *only* love, if I was being honest with myself.

Jack had grown up on the farm at the edge of Ashby Woods. I had known him for as long as I had known Natalie. He would often join us on our adventures. Up until the day I left, the three of us had been as thick as thieves. The Campbells were our closest neighbors. Mr. Campbell would bring us choice cuts of meat before they were sold to distributors, and Mrs. Campbell would buy herb wreaths from my mother in the summer.

Jack had gotten up every morning and helped his dad with chores on the farm before taking the bus to school. I remembered that magical day after I had turned fifteen, when Jack joined me at the bus stop. He had obviously just showered and was dressed in a green button-up shirt that hugged muscles I had never noticed before.

Had Jack always been that cute?

I had never looked at him in that way until then. He was my friend. My playmate. He and Natalie knew my secrets, and I knew theirs.

But I hadn't been looking at my friend. I was looking at a boy I wanted to kiss. A lot.

My stomach had been in knots, and it was then that I realized I liked him. That I really, really liked him. And from the shy smile he gave me, I was sure he liked me too.

Things happened naturally between us. We started dating quietly and without the drama of a typical high school couple.

Our relationship never felt all-consuming. It fit into my life in an unobtrusive way. My feelings, which gradually evolved into love, never came at the expense of my relationship with Natalie or my other friends.

He understood my life. He understood what mattered to me. And he never tried to erase who I was before we were together.

And I had left him too. Just as I had left my mom and Natalie.

I was starting to realize what a fool I had been.

I quickly flipped through the rest of the pages, barely allowing myself to look at the pictures and mementos I had collected over a short lifetime.

I was relieved when I turned the final page I had made, which signaled the end of my childhood and the memories I had held onto.

That should have been it. The rest of the pages should have been blank.

But they weren't.

I found a cutout from the local newspaper, the *Blue Cliff Bulletin*. The date was from five years ago.

"Still Missing."

The headline was all caps and in a large font, and underneath were three school pictures of smiling, happy children.

Danielle Torrents.

Michael Caruthers.

Olivia Bradshaw.

I knew their faces almost as well as I knew my own.

I didn't have to read the article to know what it said.

These three beautiful children, all born and raised in Blue Cliff, had disappeared. First Olivia. Two weeks later Danielle didn't come home. Finally, Michael went out to meet his friends by the woods and never came back.

Gone.

*　　*　　*

I remember them playing together, like they always did. Michael Caruthers was kicking a soccer ball while Danielle Torrents and Olivia Bradshaw played tag. Other children were there, but those three were the ones I remembered focusing on. As if, even back then, I knew I should pay attention. Or maybe it was only the haze of memory honing in on the ones that mattered.

I knew each of them. And they knew me. Here in our small corner of Virginia, everyone knew everyone else.

Livvie called out a hello as I cut through the park on my way home after school. Her mom was one of my mother's regular visitors. Livvie would sometimes come along, and I would be told to watch her. I usually took her into the woods, where we looked for squirrels and deer. Livvie, like all kids in Blue Creek, was both terrified and fascinated by the hickory trees. Danielle was her best friend. You didn't see one without the other. Just like Nat, Jack, and me.

And Michael was a lot like his older brother. Full of swagger and confidence, which were slightly less obnoxious only because he was a kid. You could forgive a lot of faults in an adorable ten-year-old with a thousand-watt smile.

They were good kids. Kind kids with innocent hearts. They were loved and cared for by an entire town.

* * *

I turned the page. Another article. This one from the bigger, county newspaper. The headline was more dire this time. More horrific.

"Bodies Found in Search for Missing Children."

Weeks after disappearing, their bodies had been found in the woods.

My woods.

I had unfortunately discovered one of the bodies myself. It made my connection to the murders uncomfortably real.

"Mystery Deepens in the Deaths of Local Children."

All were found wearing the clothes they'd disappeared in. Nothing different except for two things: Each child had silver coins in their possession. They were old coins. Dimes from the days when they were made of silver and not an alloy of nickel and copper.

And their shoes were filled with dirt. When the soil had been sent away for analysis, it was determined to be the rich composite found in Hickory Woods. If you grew up in Blue Cliff, this wouldn't have been a surprise. But it was deeply unsettling.

Because most people believed the ancient protections worked. That when our grandparents told us to carry silver and dirt, it was for a very important reason. Yet, no one understood why, on those particular occasions, with those particular children, the coins and the soil didn't keep them safe. Their failure should have shaken the rigid belief systems to the core. But the opposite became true. People were too afraid *not* to follow the old ways.

It was a foolish superstition, but one that was deeply ingrained and rooted in the desire to save the children from an evil worse than anything they could imagine. Even if it failed a time or two, the fear of what would happen should they *not* listen outweighed any doubts.

Perhaps even more mysterious was the way the children had died. Each of them had drowned, but with no indication that their clothes had ever been submerged. Where could they have drowned? There wasn't a stream or a river for miles. And there hadn't been a body of water in Hickory Woods since Bobcat Creek dried up in the 1920s. When the water from their lungs was tested, it was shown to contain a mixture of heavy metals and a specific type of fungus that could only be found in areas high up in the mountains and in the deepest hollers. Investigators couldn't find anywhere within miles with a contaminated water source, and it was strongly believed that the killer wouldn't have taken the kids far away to murder them, only to bring them back to the very place they were taken from. It made no sense.

So, where were they killed?

It was one of the many aspects of the cases that bewildered the police. The FBI had no answers. The people of Blue Cliff had no closure.

I kept flipping the pages of what had once been my scrapbook, disturbed that it was now filled with the stories of the most awful time in our town's history.

Then there was another face. A pale, sullen man with shaggy blond hair and a mouth etched in a permanent scowl.

"Man Arrested in Connection to the Blue Cliff Murders."
Jasper Clinton.

The killer whose conviction had been overturned. The murderer who had produced evidence proving he was innocent.

Jasper had been different. He and his family had moved to Blue Cliff only the year before the deaths, when he was twenty years old. He had done very little to integrate himself into the community. He was a known drunk who liked to make a scene when he got wasted. I remembered Chief Hickman joking that they were thinking of naming one of the jail cells after Jasper, considering how much time he spent in it.

Natalie and I would often see him passed out on a bench in the park in the middle of the day, clearly trashed. No one liked him. He had no friends. So it made sense that the town pariah, especially a man who was an outta-towner, was guilty of the crimes. But honestly, I'd never pictured him as a child murderer.

Despite my doubts, no one else wondered how he could have done it when he had no basic knowledge of local topography. How he could have navigated Hickory Woods like a local. Quiet grumblings claimed he was helped by the evil that lived in the woods. My mother swore he was in league with the Hickory Man. Others believed the Blue Cliff newbie simply had a really good sense of direction.

It didn't matter that Jasper denied, denied, denied. He had been tried and convicted in the court of public opinion long before he ever went to trial.

I turned the page to yet another newspaper clipping, but the date of this one was from only three days ago.

"Another Missing Child. More Unanswered Questions."

This one was about Dakota. The words were different, but the circumstances were uncomfortably familiar.

He was gone. Except for some small, child-sized footprints in the snow leading into the woods, there was no sign of the missing boy.

Why were these articles in my scrapbook?

I had been home for only a few days, and already it felt like too much. Blue Cliff was a small town—a sad town. Olivia, Danielle, Michael—and now Dakota—hadn't been the first to go missing. They were only the most recent in our long, gut-wrenching history.

The scrapbook held the others as well.

An old article from the fifties showed a picture of a pretty young girl with pigtails. I knew her name. We all did.

Clara Whitmer.

She had been eleven when she went missing after cutting through the woods on her way to town. She was found dead a week later, in the forest, water was in her lungs, with no explanation as to how it got there. It had been the hottest summer on record and in the middle of a record-breaking drought. Not long after, Billy Walker and Janice Brown also disappeared. Their bodies were discovered in the woods, within days of each other, in the exact same condition.

And there were more.

Bradley Moses. He died in 1923. He was only eight when his body was found in the forest after he was missing for more than two weeks. Dirt in his shoes. Silver coins in his pockets. Dead from an apparent drowning. At the time it was believed, as implausible as it was, that he had fallen into the old swimming hole and pulled himself out, then walked three miles before finally dying in a low-lying gully in Hickory Woods, with water in his lungs. A modern perspective would have attributed it to dry drowning perhaps. It had been a horrible accident—nothing more. However, soon after that, the town was mourning Lydia Struthers and Sally Burbank as well.

The last page of the scrapbook contained another, more recent article from a national publication:

"Five Years Later in the Town That Gobbles up Children: What this grisly anniversary means for the people still living in Blue Cliff, Virginia."

The town that gobbles up children.

What a terrible indictment.

I skimmed the article. It recounted all the facts I already knew. It talked of the murders. And it talked about Jasper's

recent release. It outlined the evidence that had been sub-
mitted to the appellate court. I was shocked to hear that
the prosecution, led by Nat's father, Stewart Bartlett, had
failed to hand over key evidence during discovery. Evidence
that included DNA on Michael Caruthers's body that didn't
match Jasper Clinton's. Mr. Bartlett wasn't the only one
whose ethics were being called into question. It seemed the
Blue Cliff Police Department had "misplaced" items found
at the crime scene—an old Altoid tin and a scrap of brown
fabric. It was only this year, when an anonymous source
notified the state attorney general's office about their exis-
tence, that it all came to light.

But this article wasn't only about the most recent child
deaths. It also mentioned Clara Whitmer, Billy Walker, and
Janice Brown. And Bradley Moses, Lydia Struthers, and
Sally Burbank. It mentioned older names too. Other children whose names I had forgotten.

Seeing them written out like that, I thought maybe Blue
Cliff really *was* the town that gobbled up children. Because
that was a lot of kids going missing and later turning up
dead. They couldn't have all been accidents.

What had happened to Clara and Bradley and the others? So many children, so many years apart.

"Why are you looking at that?" My mom's voice was
shrill in my ear. She grabbed the scrapbook, slamming it
shut.

"What was all that, Mom? Why did you put this
stuff in my scrapbook?" I asked, startled by her sudden
outburst.

My mom's eyes hardened. "Because we can't forget. It's
when we forget that he'll make us remember. He's done it
before, Chey. He's doing it again."

She shoved the book back on the shelf. She was clearly
agitated. I watched her, my worry growing. "It's okay,
Mom—"

"It's not okay, Chey. It won't ever be okay. You never understood that." Her eyes were now wet with tears.

"Come on, Mom. Let me help you with the herbs." I took her hand and led her back to her spot on the floor.

This time she let me distract her.

But her words rang in my ears.

Maybe she was right.

We couldn't forget the past, no matter how much we wanted to.

5

−Natalie−

I CARRIED MY CASSEROLE dish carefully up the freshly swept steps of my parents' home. I was arriving solo for once. It felt wrong to be attending without Hunter, but he'd promised he'd meet me there later. He had been held up at the office and couldn't get away for another couple of hours.

"Just compliment your mom's clothes and tell her how pretty the house looks and she'll leave you alone," Hunter had joked, predictably making light of the contentious relationship I had with my ma.

It was the annual historical society potluck supper, and normally almost everyone in town would have been at the Bartlett house. However, these times were anything but normal, as noted by the less than usual number of cars parked on the street out front.

The ceramic dish was hot in my hands. I needn't have bothered bringing a casserole, knowing my ma always catered the event, but it felt like a small defiance. At one time everyone would bring something. I remembered that, as a child, I thought it a fun occasion, usually held in the basement of the Presbyterian church. There were no uniformed waiters handing out canapés or tables of fluted champagne. It was a downhome affair with people I had known my whole life enjoying being together and maybe raising some money for renovations of historic properties in Blue Cliff. Things had definitely changed once Ma took over as president three years ago.

My ma lived for these events, and she was famous—or infamous—for throwing over-the-top parties that people would talk about for months afterward—but not always in a flattering way. She tried hard to make everything glitzy and glamorous, when our neighbors and friends would have been more comfortable with a hog roast and a bluegrass band. She really had lost touch with the town she had grown up in.

I was surprised that she had decided to go ahead with the potluck, given how much appearances mattered to her. Because it seemed in bad taste to host a swanky soiree while the police scoured the woods for a missing child. On top of that, with the spotlight on my dad and his mishandling of the Jasper Clinton case, it felt like horrible timing. I tried to reason with my ma, but she wasn't a woman to listen to anyone's opinion but her own. I knew she would be practically spitting nails with the less than full showing, and I'd hear all about people's inconsiderateness later.

I let myself inside, smiling at Blair Cross, the younger sister of Hunter's friend Jess, who was obviously working the event. She held open the door for me, and I let her take my coat.

I had to admit the house looked amazing. It appeared warm and inviting, with large bouquets of orange and yellow mums interspersed with winter jasmine placed around the large hallway.

"Do you want me to take that?" Blair asked, indicating the covered dish in my hands.

"Sure. Thanks." I handed it to her, knowing its contents would end up in the trash, and then made my way to the large, open-floor-plan living and dining room that usually served as the location for my parents' parties.

Despite the less than heaving crowd, I had to hand it to my ma; she really did know how to throw a party. Even if everyone there was likely present more out of obligation than any actual desire.

People had come decked out in their best clothes that most likely hadn't seen the light of day since last Easter. I picked up a flute of champagne and made my way through the crowd, calling out hellos as I headed toward my mother. I noticed my dad on the far side of the room, by the bar, looking miserable.

Once upon a time, my dad had been the life of every party. He'd been the one to make everyone smile, the ultimate charmer. It was his charisma that had swayed juries and influenced judges. But he hadn't been that man in a very long time.

Everyone's greetings were genuine, and I knew that while my parents weren't particularly liked, I had worked hard since I was a child to overcome that hostility, so that aversion didn't extend to me.

I found my ma holding court, surrounded by some of her historical society friends, glass in hand, hair blown and curled, lips painted a perfect red. I recognized her figure-hugging gold dress as one she had purchased from my shop several weeks ago. As irritating as she could be, that act of support made me feel good.

Especially since Ma had been dead set against me opening my own store.

"You don't need to work, Natalie. People will think you're not being taken care of! It's up to Hunter to provide for you now."

She had made her disapproval well known, and yet despite it, I had forged ahead.

"Hi, Ma," I greeted as I drew close.

She stopped talking and turned to me, air-kissing my cheek. Her heavy perfume almost suffocated me. She stepped back to look me over, her hazel eyes, the same color as mine, appraising me before she gave me a chilly smile.

"Where's Hunter?" she asked without saying hello.

"He got tied up at work—he'll be by later," I assured her.

"That Hunter's a goodun'. We need someone from the Caruthers family 'round here since his father claimed he couldn't make it." My ma sniffed, clearly annoyed. Her twang always grew stronger when she'd had a drink, and right now she spoke like a girl right off the mountain. She hated that accent. But hearing it now proved that you couldn't hide from your roots, no matter how hard you tried.

"Chase isn't here?" I asked in surprise. As the mayor, he made it a point to attend all town events.

"He's not the only one," a woman with frizzy brown hair interjected. I knew Jackie Lytton from church.

"I can't believe so many people didn't RSVP, Daphne. That's a lot of food you'll have left over." Her passive aggressiveness wasn't surprising. Ma's circle of cohorts generally held a barely hidden level of disdain for each other.

"Natalie, Jackie's taken over as treasurer for Delilah Reynolds while she recovers from her hip operation. Though, between us ladies"—my ma dropped her voice in a tone for hushed confidences that the others seemed to eat up; gossip was like catnip to these women—"she had been mismanagin' funds for years. It's downright criminal." She laughed and her friends joined in. Daphne Bartlett poking fun at something criminal felt uncomfortably wrong given my dad's current situation.

"Your potluck is a far cry from the ones in the church basement Janette used to put on, even if people couldn't be bothered to show up tonight," Nancy Pearson, Ma's best frenemy from elementary school commented, looking around my parents' lavish home.

"Thank you, Nancy," Ma cooed. "Do you remember them godawful plastic flowers? And pimento cheese sandwiches, for cryin' out loud." She laughed hatefully, taking another long drink of champagne. "That woman wouldn't know a good time if it bit her." The women snickered together.

Daphne Bartlett liked to play queen of the manor in her ostentatious antebellum-style home that my dad had built for her. But everyone knew that she had grown up in a tiny, one-bedroom house on Cherry Street. I had only ever seen one single picture of the place where she and my aunt Margaret had lived as children. It had been practically falling down even then, which is why it had been demolished years back. Ma's family came from nothing, a fact she worked hard to make everyone forget. She purposefully shunned her past. It was something that irked the other folk in town. Most believed in owning who you were. There was pride in the mountains we called home. There was a loyalty to the trees and dirt that birthed us. Ma's disgust for our town was unfathomable to her neighbors and even her friends—though comments were said behind her back and not to her face. The Bartletts were one of their own, whether either side liked it or not.

"I'm going to find Dad and say hello," I said, needing to escape.

Relieved to be off my ma's hook, I went in search of my father.

"Natalie, hello!" I turned to find Linda Grady standing behind me. I could see Ed at the food table, making his way through the stuffed mushrooms.

"Hi, Linda. It's good to see you. How's your back?"

Linda gave me a pained smile. "I'm still kickin', but I don't know how long I'll be able to stay on my feet tonight.

I reckon I've got another hour in me, though." She squeezed my hand. "Thank you again for the pies and cookies you brought over after my surgery. Even if I barely got a taste in, with Ed in the house. And now that Reggie's home, he's just as bad."

"I forgot Reggie was back. How is he?" I asked politely, though I couldn't care less. Reggie was several years older than me and a total creep. He used to follow me around, to the point where the chief had to have a word with him. Ed and Linda were lovely people; it was a shame their son was such a weirdo. They had lost their daughter to meningitis when she was only three years old. Everyone felt sorry for Ed and Linda, knowing how hard it must be for them to have lost one child and the other being like Reggie.

"Ed's got him stocking shelves at the store. He's been such a help. And like everyone else, he's cut up about Dakota." Linda wiped her eyes with a tissue.

"Does Reggie know Dakota, then?" I asked.

"Of course not," Linda retorted, a note of something like defensiveness in her voice. "He just hates seein' another sweet child lost like those others. He was so upset then too. I'm sure it reminded him of losing his sister. He helped search day and night, ya know. He looked in the papers constantly to see if they found 'em. I had never seen him so worked up."

"It was a tough time for all of us." I didn't know what else to say. Things suddenly felt awkward. Thankfully my aunt Margaret waved me down. "I'd better go say hi to Marge. Take care of yourself, Linda." I gave her a quick hug and hurried across the room.

Margaret Evans, or Marge to those who knew her best, was my ma's younger sister. She hated these things and only came because Ma made her feel guilty. Because of that, she had taken up a spot in the farthest away corner she could find.

"There you are. Your ma has been fit to be tied, waiting for you to show up. I'm sure she had somethin' to say about Hunter not comin' with you," Marge said knowingly.

"He's coming later," I told her.

"You're looking too thin. Your clothes are practically hangin' off you. Come by and I'll make you some of my fried chicken. You always loved that when you were a little 'un." Her comment was a mixture of censure and genuine kindness. Margaret had never married, and so I spent a lot of time with her growing up. While she wasn't as obsessed with appearances as my mother, she was still a hard woman, not someone easy to love. And she was as nosy and judgmental as her sister.

"Sounds good," I replied.

She took a sip of her glass of water and cast a disdainful look at the crowd gathered in my parents' home. "I can't believe your ma went ahead with this thing. What was she thinking?"

"Maybe she thought it would be good to have some sense of normalcy—"

"That's nonsense and you know it." She turned her hazel eyes to me. "My sister simply loves a party, and not even something like the inconvenient disappearance of a child will stop her." My aunt wasn't wrong. "Everyone's talkin' about it, sayin' with what's goin' on with your pa, it woulda been best to postpone it." I knew Margaret loved my mother, but they didn't exactly get along. Aunt Marge, like everyone else, didn't approve of Ma's airs and graces. "It says somethin' when the mayor doesn't even show up."

She was right. Chase's absence was noticeable and would ruffle my ma's feathers more than anything.

Marge made a noise of disapproval. "What is that man doin'?"

I followed her gaze to where Otis Wheeler was standing with Jamie's parents, Abel and Candy Fry. I knew my assistant wasn't with them, as this wasn't her kind of party. Otis was a local jack of all trades. He had his fingers in many pies and seemed to know everything going on with everyone. He was a bit of an oddball, living in a run-down house at the end of Hickory Lane. Like Aunt Margaret, he had never married. He seemed to prefer the company of the kids at the elementary school, where he worked as the janitor, rather than that of the adults. I noticed he had a full glass of what I guessed was homemade whiskey, his drink of choice. His brown shirt was rumpled like he had slept in it, the hem torn. His face was a mottled red as he spoke with animation. My ma must have been furious when she saw him like that. I was surprised she'd let him in the house.

"He's been goin' on and on about Dakota all night. Tryin' to get people to go look for Jasper or some such silliness. He sure is makin' a fool of 'imself. He's a little too involved, if you ask me."

"We're all worried about Dakota. Otis knows him from working at the school, so of course he's upset," I reminded her.

"Sure," she murmured, watching the older man closely.

"I see Dad—I'm going to go talk to him," I told her, watching as he snuck out the door and into the hallway.

I hurried after him and headed toward my dad's office, where I knew I'd find him. However, before I could knock, I heard voices coming from inside, Chief Hickman's low, familiar timbre being the most prominent.

I wasn't sure what was being said, but neither my dad nor the chief sounded happy. Particularly when I realized they were talking about Jasper.

Now I was more than just interested—I was fully invested.

The voices on the other side of the door were no more than mumbles, so I found myself pressing my ear to the door to hear better.

"Any word on Clinton?"

"Not yet. The bastard seems to have disappeared into thin air," Chief Hickman's deep, frustrated voice replied.

"You're an idiot if you think he'd ever come back here. Why would he? He'd be strung up from a tree as soon as he crossed town lines." I wasn't really shocked by the cold bitterness in my dad's voice; he'd been angry and cold for a long time now, but I *was* surprised it was directed at Chief Hickman. "What do you intend to do about him? Something's got to be done, Don," my father continued.

"We'll find him and put him back where he belongs. A man like that will trip up sooner or later. We just need to bide our time."

"Of course, just leave it to superhero Donald Hickman." Dad's sarcasm was plain. "And leave it to me to come along behind you and shovel up all the horseshit. It's how it's always been. But too bad for you—it seems my days of shoveling shit are over, Don. My neck's on the chopping block. Someone's got to be the bad guy, right?" My dad sounded angry, but also resigned. For some reason, that bothered me most. Like the fight had left him. "Just tell me that Dakota . . ." A feeling of unease washed over me as he paused and didn't continue.

"Watch your mouth!" the chief snapped. "I'm doing what I can for Dakota and this town, and that's all you need to know."

I wished that I hadn't listened to their conversation in the first place. Other people's secrets should remain just that: secret.

"You expect me to trust you? After everything?" my dad retorted, his voice now shaky.

"What option do you have?" The chief sighed with impatience.

I'd known Dad was in trouble, but I hadn't really allowed myself to think about how much until now. It seemed he expected to get the brunt of the fallout from Jasper's release.

Footsteps came closer to the door, and I quickly returned to the party.

My phone vibrated in my purse. I pulled it out to see a message from Hunter saying he wouldn't make it. He ended it with a half-baked apology that I was expected to accept.

"Natalie." A raspy voice snapped me out of my bitter thoughts. I jumped at the feel of a hand on my arm.

"Constance. What are you doing here?" I was startled to see her. She didn't usually attend formal town events. That wasn't Constance Ashby's style.

It was no secret that my ma had never liked Constance. I knew it was the bond that Constance and I shared that irked my mother the most.

I took Constance by the arm and led her to a chair next to the wall. She looked tired, her eyes lined with heavy wrinkles. "Linda and Ed thought it would be good for me. Seems they're worried I'm not getting out enough. I suppose my trips into the trees don't count." Her eyes moved around the room. I noticed how some people inclined their head in a respectful greeting while others quickly looked away, as if afraid to make eye contact. There would always be those who were in awe of Constance and those who feared the Ashbys. For me, it was a little bit of both.

"Where's Cheyenne?" I asked, looking around for my former best friend.

"Do you really think she'd come to somethin' like this?" she scoffed.

"She used to come to the potluck when we were kids," I remarked.

"Well, a lot has changed since then, hasn't it," Constance said, pointedly looking at the tray of salmon puffs and champagne glasses on the table beside her. She picked up a tiny quiche and examined it. "What in the Sam Hill is this?" She sniffed it.

"It's pretty good. You should try it," I chuckled, amused by her reaction.

I watched her pop the hors d'oeuvre into her mouth. "Not bad," she admitted, licking her fingers before grabbing another one. My ma would have a conniption if she saw her doing that. "I'll give it to your ma—she sure can throw a party. But she was always coordinating somethin' or another when we were younger." Given how my mother felt about Constance, it was easy to forget that, like everyone else in town, the two had grown up together. Constance watched the crowd with concern. "This was a bad idea to do right now, though."

She reached into her pocket and pulled something out, handing it to me. My stomach twisted as I looked down at the tiny corn husk doll wrapped in string, the exact replica of the ones dotted around town.

She placed her hand on top of mine, curling my fingers around the doll. "I only came to give you this. Because we can't ignore what's going on. Dakota's gone. You must protect yourself."

Even though I felt dread at her words, I was also touched with how, even after all this time, she still looked out for me.

"Thanks, Constance."

Her hand squeezed mine. "I'm worried about you, Natalie. You, Chey, and Jack. You three have always been vulnerable to the goings-on in the woods. Be alert. Don't forget for a moment what happens there. Especially to those who think they can forget."

"This isn't the place to be talkin' about that." My ma appeared at my side, consternation on her pretty face, her champagne glass now empty. "I won't have that nastiness spoken in my home, ya hear me?"

"Even if she's right? Dakota's gone and we're sippin' drinks and eatin' food like it's not happening," Ed Grady said, coming to stand beside Constance, his wife behind him.

My ma looked livid. "We can't let this one awful thing take over our lives—"

"A boy is missing, Ma," I chastised gently, earning me a look that could kill. "Who knows what's happened to him?"

"*He's* back! That's what happened to Dakota." Constance got to her feet. "Natalie, we can't ignore him." She turned to the rest of the room. Everyone had stopped talking and was watching in morbid interest. Their stares seemed to ignite her fury. "He's here, and he'll be coming for the children!" she cried out.

"You need to shut her up," Ma seethed under her breath.

"Constance, let's go talk about this." I tried taking her arm to lead her from the room, but she remained rigid and unmoving. I wasn't Cheyenne, and I didn't have the ability to calm her down like she did.

"Gather the dirt and collect your coins. The Hickory Man is hungry after five years, and he has come to collect. He's already taken Dakota, but the boy won't be the last!" She was yelling now, her arms waving wildly. "Don't you see? If he's kept waiting when he's hungry, he will come and take them himself. He's not the patient kind. I feared this was comin'. I've been tryin' to protect you all! You need to listen to me!" Ed and Linda, two of her oldest friends, did nothing to stop her. They simply stood there, nodding their heads, encouraging her.

Constance produced a handful of herbs from her pocket and started sprinkling them on the floor. *"Protect the innocent. Shield them from his eyes."*

"Stop it!" my mother shrieked. She was visibly shaking. I wasn't sure if it was from anger or humiliation. "Constance Ashby, it's time for you to go."

Feeling protective of Constance, I reached out to take her hand. "Come on, let's get you home."

"You will sit right here, Natalie Bartlett! You are *my* daughter and you're stayin' put. Let someone else handle her."

I realized that she was drawing a firm line in the sand. I had to choose: Constance or her.

"I've got her," Chief Hickman said as he came into the room. He was wearing a smart suit instead of his usual brown uniform, and if the circumstances had been different, I would have told him how handsome he looked.

"Are you sure?" I asked as he gently took Constance's hand.

Chief Hickman put his arm around the smaller woman's shoulders. "It's no problem—I've got this from here. I'm used to walkin' Connie to her doorstep. Ain't that right?" He looked down at Constance, who seemed to change in his presence. She visibly relaxed and became less agitated. It was as if Chief Hickman were a sedative that she desperately needed.

"But, Don, I have to help them," she said weakly.

The chief rubbed her arm as they slowly walked from the room. "I know you do, but you can't go into people's homes and start causin' a fuss. This is meant to be a fun night."

"I was just warning them. I didn't mean to upset anyone." She sounded sad. But whatever else she said was out of earshot as they left the room. I turned back to face my mother's wrath.

"Did you invite her here?" she accused.

"No, Ma, I didn't. But isn't she welcome like everyone else in town?" I countered. Ma and I stared at each other, a battle of wills.

My dad reappeared, drink in hand. He took note of the silent room and the notable tension between Ma and me. "What did I miss?" he asked lamely, sipping his Tom Collins.

Ma glared at him. "Where've you been, Stewart? I've been makin' excuses for you all damn night," she snapped, her voice slurring.

"Thought it would be easier to stay out of the way. Wouldn't want my presence to take the spotlight off you and your party," he said with bite. The cracks had been forming in my parents' seemingly idyllic marriage for years, but they'd never shown it so publicly before.

"You not bein' here makes people talk even more! I've been out here pissin' in the wind all by myself. I looked like a fool," she hissed, trying to keep a smile on her face for her guests.

Dad drank the rest of his cocktail and put the glass down. "I guess there's only room for one of us to look like a fool, right?" He kissed my cheek. "You look lovely, Nat." And with that he walked back out of the room, leaving ma fuming.

I felt all eyes on us. I knew people were silently judging us. Constance's appearance had been jarring, and the gathering fizzled out not long after she left.

Ma's party would be the talk of the town for sure.

But not in the way she would have liked.

6

—*Cheyenne*—

THE SEARCH FOR Dakota had entered its third week. I often heard the sound of police and volunteers combing the woods, their voices loud in the normally silent forest. The search parties, while important, still felt like an intrusion. These people didn't belong here, and it seemed that even Mother Nature was trying to force them out. Because soon the snow hit hard, causing the search to come to a standstill.

I had heard from Linda Grady about Mom's appearance at the annual historical society potluck supper when she came to visit Mom two days later.

"You should have been there for your mother, Cheyenne. She needed you," Linda had stated with judgment.

It had been on the tip of my tongue to hit back with a snarky comment about her own less than perfect child, but I stopped myself.

Mom was still sleeping on the mattress on the floor. When I asked where her old bed frame had gone, she became upset. "It was made of hickory. I couldn't have that in the house anymore. *His* trees should be kept out *there*." When I suggested getting a new bed, one not made of hickory, she had become irrationally mad. "There are more important things to worry about than where I lay my head down at night, Cheyenne."

I was still sleeping badly. Worse than ever before. I was getting, at most, a couple of hours of sleep a night. Every time I closed my eyes, I was in the woods. I couldn't breathe. And I was waiting for the Hickory Man. I was exhausted and, truthfully, a little freaked out.

I woke up on Monday morning, after another restless night, to find a small doll resting on the pillow beside my head. It was the same size and proportions as the ones I had seen hanging from the trees in town, though this one was made with sticks and twine. My insides turned icy.

I scooped it up and all but stomped to the living room. I held it out in front of me with two fingers, as if afraid it would bite me. "Did you leave this in my room?" I demanded.

My mom was sitting in her chair by the fire, bent over something in her lap. She didn't bother to look up before replying. "Keep it in the shadows. It works best in the dark."

"Please don't leave things in my room while I'm sleeping. It's weird," I seethed.

Mom finally put aside what she was working on—more poppets—and gave me a look that had me almost recoiling. "I will protect you in any way that I can. I won't apologize for it. I won't stop it either. So if you're going to stay here, Cheyenne, you will accept my ways and you will live by them. Is that clear?"

I thought about dropping the doll into the potbelly stove but didn't want to antagonize my mother any further. Starting a fight with her first thing in the morning was never a good idea. Instead, I tucked the poppet in my pocket, planning to get rid of it later.

There was a time when I would help my mom make the poppets. I had even enjoyed it. We would fashion the dolls, sometimes of straw and stick, other times of old corn husks. They were made to represent a person who needed help. It could be used for protection. Or to cure an illness. Or to help with fertility. A poppet was simply a conduit for my mom's spell work. The target of her protection, who would then keep it in a safe, dark place.

I knew this doll was meant to be me. It was a personalized protection, but it was one I didn't want. The days of me blindly going along with her nonsense were long over.

Deciding it was best to change the subject, I glanced out the window and noticed that the path was now clear.

"You should have waited for me to do that, Mom," I said, pointing to the freshly shoveled snow.

Mom had resumed her crafting, her fingers moving deftly as she wrapped rough corn husks with twine. "Jack was by earlier. He cleared the walkway and chopped some fresh firewood. Left it by the front door."

My heart flipped. "Jack? Jackson Campbell was here?"

"Normally he comes out this way at least once a week. Or he did before you came back. He usually does odds and ends around the house for me. He's a good boy, raised by good people. Louise and Paul always ask after you. Though I haven't had much to relay over the years." I ignored the gibe.

"And Jack?" The words slipped out before I could stop them.

Mom stood up and came closer, placing her hand on my arm. "Some broken hearts take longer to mend."

Her simple words served a painful truth.

"I need to go into town to pick up some supplies I ordered from the hardware store. Usually Chester Jessop comes out here, but with the snow, he can't make it. I keep telling him to trade in that Buick for a Jeep, but he doesn't listen. Insists he can get around fine. But a foot of snow and he's stuck." Mom tutted with disapproval. "I can walk if you can't—"

"Of course I can take you. Though I'm not sure my car can get through all this snow," I said uncertainly.

Mom waved away my worries. "Jack took care of the road. He bought one of those fancy plows about two years ago. It's been a godsend."

I should have known Jack would continue to look out for my mom. That was the kind of guy he was. But it made me feel incredibly guilty on way too many levels to count.

We both headed to the kitchen, where I put on a pot of coffee. "You seem good this morning," I observed.

"I'm fine, Chey. Stop fussing over me. I've looked after myself with no problem all this time. I don't need you hovering, waiting for me to do something you don't approve of."

I swallowed thickly, trying not to get upset or angry. "Fine." I got a mug from the cabinet and filled it with coffee. "When do you want to leave?"

"After lunch."

"Okay, I'll be ready," I told her.

"First, I need to collect some things from the woods." I watched as she gathered the items she'd need for a trip into the forest. Her cloth tote bag, herb scissors, a small trowel, and salt. Always salt. For "just in case." I wondered what happened to the basket that she used to have. I remembered it had been a family heirloom, passed down from her mother.

"Where's your basket, Mom?" I asked her.

She glanced down at the bag on her arm and frowned. "I'm not sure. One day it was here, the next it wasn't. I've looked everywhere."

She was clearly bothered by the basket's disappearance. "I'll have a look around for you," I offered.

Mom smiled. "Thanks, Chey. I'd appreciate that." She paused on her way out of the room. "Would you like to come? It's been a long time since you've been in the woods. They've missed you."

"I thought you wanted me to stay out of the woods," I challenged.

Mom frowned and seemed to thoughtfully consider my words. "I don't want you straying, Chey. I still mean that. But you'll be with me, and I stick to the paths. I know the trails to follow. You know them too. It's important to stay in the safe places. But I feel like you need to recharge. Your spirit is depleted, sweetheart. You need the woods and they need you."

It was on the tip of my tongue to say no. Yet I found myself nodding. "Sure, why not. I don't have anything else on my schedule." I quickly finished my coffee, then pulled on my winter coat. When I started to put on my tennis shoes Mom gave me a look. "What?" I asked.

"Your feet will be soaked in minutes. Go find the snow boots you left in your closet." My chest constricted at the fact that my snow boots were still there. Where I had left them.

Once I was ready, I followed Mom out the back door. I noticed she moved more stiffly than she had when I was younger. She had always suffered from arthritis in her knees and it seemed they were getting worse. The cold was particularly hard on her joints.

We walked straight into the woods. It was like dipping your head under water—the silence deafening. I noticed almost instantly that there wasn't a sound. No winter birds chirping in the trees. No animals rustling in the brush. I wasn't startled by it. I was used to the absence of noise. There were times the birds and animals seemed to disappear. As if they knew to stay away even when the humans didn't.

It was actually nice after the continuous drone of people traipsing through the hickories in their efforts to find Dakota.

We moved with practiced familiarity, staying close to the places we knew, turning left at the fork, heading toward the meadow and away from the old holler that lay abandoned closer to the mountain.

Hickory Holler, or Ashby Holler as the locals knew it, was the old Blue Cliff settlement from back when the first people came over from Scotland and Ireland and chose this area as their home. Located in the forest close to the foothills, it was protected *and* isolated.

At some point in the last hundred years, the good folk of Blue Cliff had decided to move away from the shadow of omnipresent rock and closer to newer civilization. It probably had to do with the fact that after the advent of electricity, it was too difficult to wire the buildings in the manner becoming popular in the rest of the country. The people had simply picked up and moved. The houses, the gardens, the small school had all been left as it was.

I knew the holler well, having at one time used the now derelict properties as my own personal playground. Natalie, Jackson, and I had spent hours there, away from everyone and everything.

My feet itched to take me in that direction. To trek the miles it would take to reach the forgotten buildings of a long ago past. But I didn't. I followed my mother and stuck to the paths.

On most days the woods were dark. The foliage was so thick the sun couldn't penetrate the leaves. But today, with the snow white and blinding, the world around me was bright and not at all the threatening place of my worst nightmares.

I felt such conflicting things about the forest. It was where I had grown up. I had spent almost all of my childhood thick in it.

But dead children had been found here. I had seen one of them firsthand.

It was in Hickory Woods, not far from my house, that I'd stumbled across the body of Michael Caruthers. I had been walking to Jack's house, not paying much attention to where I was going. I had practically tripped over his tiny form. It hadn't been there that morning when I had gone out to collect kindling for the fire. I was sure of it. But there he was, lying on top of the leaves as if he were asleep. Hands placed by his side, eyes open and staring up at the canopy above him, irises clouded over and unseeing. One small hand was clenched into a fist, and I could see the glint of silver. He had been laid out as if whoever put him there wanted him to be found.

Wanted *me* to find him.

When you saw a dead body, you knew it instantly. It was the preternatural stillness that surrounded it. The almost eerie quiet. There was no question that Michael was dead. I had known without checking for a pulse. And he had been dead for some time too. I could smell the decay.

*   *   *

I had run back to my house, falling to my knees several times in my haste. I had started crying at some point, and at that moment I had desperately wanted my mother. But she hadn't been there. In fact, I'd had no idea where she was. I hadn't seen her since the night before. The police arrived within minutes, and the woods were no longer mine, but instead a crime scene.

So, for me, there was something foreboding about the trees, knowing they had witnessed atrocious evil.

*   *   *

Twigs snapped somewhere to my left. Mom and I both stopped and looked in the direction the noise had come from. I could see someone moving between the trees. The man slunk along, keeping to the shadows as if not wanting to be noticed.

"Is that Reggie Grady?" I asked softly, watching as the blond man, wearing a brown shirt and no jacket, moved just out of view. It was always a surprise to see other people in the forest, though it shouldn't be. But at times it felt Mom and I were alone in the endless trees. As if the wildness belonged solely to us.

Mom watched Reggie, her face stony. "He's always where he shouldn't be. Someone like him isn't welcome out here."

I was more than a little bewildered at the sight of Ed and Linda Grady's son, recently released from jail, wandering around Ashby Woods. What reason would he have to be so close to our house?

"That's odd, don't you think?" I murmured, not taking my eyes off his retreating form. He moved like a man intimately acquainted with his surroundings. As if he spent a lot of time out here.

"Hmm," was all Mom said as Reggie's footsteps faded away.

We carried on with our task. Mom stopped periodically to pick bright red berries from the scraggly looking trees. She handed me the trowel, directing me to find the dormant bloodroot plants and carefully dig them up. "Not all of them. We have to leave some behind to grow in the spring."

She handed me an orange and brown stone. "Bury that in the ground after you take the root. The soil will be frozen, so you'll need some elbow grease." I looked at the tiger's eye, trying to remember what purpose it would serve. It had been a long time since I had been well versed in crystal usage. Mom made a noise of impatience. "It helps strengthen growth. We have to respect the plant, and in turn it respects us." Not wanting to get into a debate about the consciousness of plants, I did as she asked.

Mom was singularly focused on her task. Collecting, rooting through the brush. She was more alive than I'd seen her since I'd gotten back. Completely in her element in the place that she loved.

Getting a little bored, I wiped off my hands and carefully and quietly walked through the trees toward a small clearing I remembered lay beyond the ancient, gnarled hickory tree. I put my hand on the trunk as I passed, smiling slightly. Nat used to call it the "grumpy old man" because of the way the knots had grown into its base in the shape of eyes and a downturned mouth. The bark was peeling in large sections, giving even more of an impression of an elderly gentleman.

While before I had been thankful for the lack of noise, now I realized I missed the birdsong. Knowing they were overhead made me feel almost protected. I looked back and realized I had gone farther than I thought. I couldn't see Mom. A wind started to blow, snow drifting down from the branches above me. I shivered. I was completely and totally alone.

"Cheyenne."

Was that Mom calling me?

Could it be Reggie? The thought made my skin crawl.

It hadn't been a shout or a call from the distance.

It had sounded close.

Right next to my ear.

"Cheyenne . . ."

The woods were doing things to my brain. I was on hyper alert, my ears straining in the silence for any sound. Rubbing my hands together in an attempt to warm them, I stomped through the forest. The trees closest to the clearing were twisted, as if an invisible hand had molded them by force.

A memory came to me of a time when I was no more than six or seven years old. I had followed my mother and Ed and Linda Grady to this very clearing. I carried a bundle of sticks that had scratched my bare arms.

I recalled being excited. And scared. It was the first time I had been allowed on this special trip.

*   *   *

"Don't drop the hickory," Ed warned me *"We'll need every stick."*

It felt like a huge responsibility.

Once we were in the clearing, I carefully put the bundle down and watched as the adults, my mom included, built a strange structure. It looked like a scarecrow, but made of hickory branches. When they were finished, my mother picked it up with reverent hands and placed it in the center of the clearing.

One by one, the other adults placed items at the base of the figure. Ed left the skin of a rabbit. I felt ill and had to look away. It seemed fresh, and I was pretty sure there was blood on the fur. Ed's wife, Linda, left bowls filled with what appeared to be livers. I only knew because Mom made them for dinner sometimes.

Finally, Mom took my hand and led me toward the stick figure. *"We have to kneel before him, Cheyenne,"* she said softly. *"We have to show our deference. Do you have the feathers?"*

I pulled the bright red cardinal feathers from my pocket. Mom had brought the dead bird to the house yesterday and asked me to pluck the feathers. I hadn't wanted to and had started to cry. She ignored my tears and stood over me while I performed the gruesome task.

"Leave them at his feet," she instructed. I obediently did as I was told.

We were joined by the others, and we all bowed our heads like people did in church. But we weren't praying.

"Take our offerings. We give them to you freely and with an obedient heart."

*   *   *

I snapped out of the memory as I walked into the open space. It was only a ring of hickory trees with a clear area in the middle, no more than ten feet wide. I saw a lump of sticks covered with snow and knew exactly what it was. And next to it, lying on top of the snow was a small bundle of twigs and twine. One of my mother's poppets. Had she brought it out here? I leaned down and picked it up, feeling oddly unsettled by finding it there. I didn't like leaving it alone in this place, so I put it in my pocket.

I knew that it was here that we had erected the effigy of the Hickory Man.

*　*　*

Mom could never quite tell me who the Hickory Man was. Probably because even *she* didn't know. She could only say that he was as old as time, named for the trees where he dwelled. Our family's one purpose was to placate him.

"What will happen if we don't?" I had dared to ask once when I was a mouthy preteen, already losing patience with what I considered to be outdated practices.

Mom had gripped my arms hard enough to leave bruises. "Don't talk like that *ever*!" She seemed slightly unhinged. "We protect this town by giving *him* what he wants."

I had wished I could swallow my stupid question, but now I had to know. "And what does he want, Mom?"

Mom had leaned close, her nose almost touching mine. "Blood, Cheyenne. *He wants blood!*"

I had stared at her in disbelief that quickly turned to horror.

"One day this task will fall to you."

That was my first real clue that something was wrong with my mother. And with the rest of the town too. Because she wasn't the only one who believed some malignant force lived in the woods, threatening to destroy us all if he didn't get a steady diet of flesh and bone. Many of the adults I trusted would join my mom in the woods. They'd listen to her stories of the evil that resided deep within it.

The town turned a blind eye to the grisly goings-on, wanting protection from the Hickory Man and all that it entailed. No matter the cost.

He was in every part of our lives in Blue Cliff. He was felt in the herb-infused wreaths people hung from their doors to keep evil spirits from their homes. In the horseshoes hung above entryways.

He was found in the playground song we all grew up singing. And in the deep seated fear that went back for generations.

At first, he was also seen in the murders of three innocent children. Many believed it was the work of the very spirit my mother was meant to mollify.

The silver in their pockets. The soil in their shoes.

A hideous reminder of our connection to the old ways and how they would always affect our lives:

Watch out for his rough fingers,
His eyes as red as blood,
Whisper a prayer, you'll need them there,
As he pulls you into the mud.

And perhaps he was felt in the recent disappearance of another little boy who had strayed into the woods, never to come out.

"*Cheyenne.*"

I wondered if someone was messing with me. But who would be out here in the snow and cold?

I knew the effect these woods had on my psyche. It warped things, making you believe fantastical nonsense. I slipped dangerously into my mother's mindset, worrying that the Hickory Man was out here, biding his time until I came back.

That he was waiting for me.

"Enough!" I said out loud. I looked around at the surrounding trees, my tone accusatory.

"Cheyenne? Where are you?" This time the voice I heard was my mother's. As if on cue, an explosion of bird chatter erupted above me. Not a pleasant trilling, but violent cawing. It sounded like a warning.

I left the clearing, turning my back on the sticks and the memories, and met my mom. She grabbed my wrist and yanked me close. "What did I tell you about straying?" She reached into her pocket, withdrawing the bottle of salt and uncapped it, sprinkling it over my head.

I swatted her hand away. "Stop it, Mom. You're getting that stuff all over me!"

"I can't believe you were so foolish! I told you to stick to the paths and stay close. I turn my back for one minute and you're gone. I expected this when you were a child. But you're a grown woman now. Can't you follow directions?" She was pissed. Before I could argue with her, she was tugging on my arm, forcing me to stumble after her through the woods.

"We need to get home. Now."

"Mom, hold on. Slow down," I called out, but she ignored me. She had become frenzied again, like she'd been that first night I arrived.

"We have to hurry. We can't be out here any longer," she said in a frantic whisper.

I gave up resisting and let her pull me along. A branch snapped somewhere in the woods followed by the rustle of leaves. Mom's grip tightened on my wrist.

"It's okay, Mom. It's probably just a deer. Or maybe Reggie."

There was another snap, exploding like a gunshot in the quiet. It was closer this time. As if whatever moved out there, among the trees, was closing in.

"That's not Reggie," she breathed.

I was starting to think Mom's delusions were contagious, because I picked up my pace, all but running back to the house.

CHAPTER

7

–Cheyenne–

AFTER WE GOT home, Mom shoved me inside and locked the door behind us.

"Stay inside until we go into town," she ordered.

"But—"

"Please, Chey. For once, don't argue with me." She was at the end of her rope, and I instinctively knew to back down.

"Okay, I'll stay inside."

Mom visibly relaxed and quickly lit several candles. She pulled a small leather bag from a drawer, opened it, and sprinkled dried herbs along the windowsill and doorjamb. Then she left the kitchen.

Mom came out of her bedroom a little before one. She seemed more even-keeled. The crazed woman of a few hours ago was gone. "You ready to go to town?" she asked.

"I'm ready." I grabbed my purse and keys, and after putting on our thick coats, we headed to my car. Mom had been right: the road was surprisingly clear. Jack had done a great job plowing, and the gravel made it easier to gain traction.

The main roads were mostly free of snow, but I still took it slow. Twenty minutes later, I pulled into the parking lot outside Jessop's Hardware Store. I started to go in with my mom, but she stopped me. "You don't need to come. Go have a look around. We can meet back here in thirty minutes."

"Sure," I said with a shrug. Mom patted my cheek and walked into the store. Now, with a half an hour left to kill, I wandered down the main street.

I was surprised to see kids clumped together, walking away from the elementary school, climbing into the waiting cars of their parents. Maybe it was a half day or early release because of the predicted inclement weather.

I noticed none of the carefree joy that was typical in kids. These children huddled together as if warding off an attack. Their eyes darted around in hypervigilance. They hurried to their families. There was no dawdling, no delighted laughter as they squeezed out another few moments together.

These were children who felt fear. Who were terrified to walk down their familiar streets. I felt the horror too. I wanted to call out to them, "Hurry!"

"Watch out for his rough fingers, His eyes as red as blood." They were still singing the song. But it had lost its playful tone from when I was young. Now it was a warning—as it had probably been intended. They were hushed as they sang, racing down the sidewalks.

"Whisper a prayer, you'll need them there, As he pulls you into the mud." I found myself singing along. My older and more bitter voice melding with their lost innocence.

Feeling slightly shaky, I turned my attention to the stores as I passed. There was one new addition to the town. It was a small boutique called Bartlett's with an appealing upmarket window. I stepped closer, scanning the front of the store before deciding to go inside.

I pushed through the door, the bell ringing above me, and I recognized the smell instantly. Vanilla. It was Natalie's signature scent. She had been obsessed with the Warm Vanilla Sugar lotion from Bath & Body Works when we were in high school. I would always associate that smell with her.

I slowly made my way through the racks of brightly colored dresses and shirts. There was even a stack of designer jeans. These were high-end items. Clothes more fit for a metropolitan area than a one-horse town like Blue Cliff.

I picked up a flowered peasant top and held it against my front, looking in the full-length mirror.

"That would look great on you. The flowy style suits your frame."

I turned to find Natalie beside me. She put two dresses on the rack before looking at me. She gave me a wan smile. "I wasn't sure I was actually going to see you. Thought maybe you'd disappear into the night again."

Okay, I deserved that.

"This shop is great. Is it yours?" I asked lamely.

Natalie raised an eyebrow. "Thought the name out front was a dead giveaway," she said, rolling her eyes, and I couldn't help but snort. She ran a lint brush down the sleeves of some blazers. "I opened it last year. When Cindy Newbury closed the yarn shop, I thought, why not? I'd always dreamed of having my own store." I could hear the pride in her voice.

"I thought you'd call it Dresses and Unicorns," I joked.

Natalie smiled. "Maybe . . . if I was ten."

I grinned. "You could always do anything you set your mind to."

"Thanks," Natalie said sincerely, clearly pleased with my approval.

Then I had to go and put my foot in my mouth.

"Do you get much business, though? I can't imagine this town being a hub of couture."

Natalie's eyes cooled. "The store gets more than enough business. Even people in this hick town know good clothes when they see them."

"I didn't mean—"

"Sure you did, Chey."

Then icy silence.

"Is it going to be like this every time we see each other?" I sighed.

Natalie raised an eyebrow. "*Are* we going to be seeing each other?"

We were going round and round in circles. It was painful.

"You're angry with me. I get that—"

"I got over being angry a long time ago, Chey. I don't feel much of anything about you anymore." She crossed her arms over her chest.

"Really? Because you seem pretty mad for someone who doesn't feel anything." I crossed my arms, imitating her.

The door opened, the small bell ringing, and a well-dressed woman wearing an expensive-looking peacoat walked in, breaking our silent standoff.

Her cheeks were flushed from the cold, and she clapped her gloved hands together to warm them up. "Getting mighty cold out there."

I noticed the way Natalie instantly plastered on her "butter wouldn't melt" smile.

"It sure is."

"Feels like more snow is on the way," the woman said.

"So the forecasters say." Natalie walked toward her, the picture of hospitality. "Is there anything I can help you with?"

"I'm looking for a dress. Something eye-catching." I noticed that the woman barely looked at the clothes, her disinterest obvious. I was instantly on guard.

"Well, we just got in some new stock all the way from New York. We haven't put them out on the floor yet. Let me have Jamie go get them for you." Natalie turned to the young girl behind the counter. "Could you bring out a few of the dresses that came in with the shipment yesterday?"

While they waited for Jamie to come back, the woman turned her attention to the window facing the street. There was a hawkishness about her as I watched her take in everything. I wondered if Natalie noticed something off about her customer.

"It's busy out there," the woman observed as Jamie came out of the back with an armful of dresses. "Do you think it has to do with the missing boy?" The woman took the dress Jamie offered, without looking at it, her eyes still on Natalie. "What do *you* think happened to him?"

Alarm bells were going off in my head. I saw Natalie frown. "It's not really my place to speculate—"

"Isn't it? You *are* Natalie Bartlett, right? Hunter Caruthers's fiancée? You're intimately acquainted with the tragedy in this town. And your father was the assistant commonwealth attorney that successfully tried the Jasper Clinton case, correct?" The woman gave up any pretense of being a paying customer. Hanging the dress up beside her, she pulled a notebook from her bag. "You must have something to say about the fact that your father is being accused of judicial misconduct. There's talk of him being disbarred—"

"No journalists are allowed in here. Did you miss the giant 'No Trespassing' notice on the window as you came in?" Jamie interrupted, her eyes flinty.

I saw Natalie pull out her phone. "You have thirty seconds to get out of my shop before I call the police. As you said, I'm Hunter Caruthers's fiancée, and his dad is the mayor. So, deputies will be here to carry you out in two seconds flat."

The woman held up her hands. "I'm not writing a trash piece on your town, Miss Bartlett. I want to tell the true story of the people here and how this latest disappearance is affecting them."

"How it's affecting us?" Natalie was getting angry. Her face was red and her breathing shallow. "We can't get a moment's peace because of all you bloodsucking news types bleeding us dry for information. We're grieving. We're sad and we're tired. This town has been through enough. Why can't you leave us alone?"

I watched as the woman furiously made notes as she backed up toward the door. "I only want to tell your side," she insisted.

"You want to hear my side?" Natalie barked. "A little boy is missing. No one knows where he is. Instead of trying to dig up dirt, why don't you put your energy into helping his family find out what happened to him?"

"But what about the three children that were murdered five years ago? Who killed them if Jasper is innocent?" The woman wouldn't shut up, and she was seconds away from getting a fist to the face. From me.

I joined Natalie in pushing the woman out of her store. "I think you'd better get out of here. Because I'm not as nice as Miss Bartlett, and I won't wait for the police to physically remove you," I warned. "I'll do it myself."

The woman had the good sense to look worried but wasn't smart enough to shut up and leave. She clearly wanted her story. "Who do you think killed Olivia, Danielle, and Michael? And are their deaths connected to Dakota's disappearance? It must be someone local, don't you agree? Someone who knows the area? Knows the woods?"

At the sound of the kids' names, I felt sick inside. In this town, it would always come back to the children.

"What I think is an innocent man spent five years behind bars. And a kid is missing. I have no idea if those things are connected. But I don't think anyone who lives in Blue Cliff would hurt a child. That's not how we are. We're all family. We love each other. " Natalie glared at the woman still taking notes. "Now, get the hell out of my shop."

"So you believe Jasper is innocent and deserves to be free? That your father and the police department purposefully withheld evidence that could have exonerated him?" The woman was really testing her luck.

"Look, lady, you're ten seconds from getting my shoe up your ass," I threatened, taking a step toward her.

The woman shoved the notebook back in her bag and scurried out before I could kick her through the door. Natalie turned to Jamie. "Can you go after her? Make sure she's not hanging around out there. Then maybe pop over to the station and let the chief know what happened. Our trespass notice doesn't seem to have enough teeth for some people." She sighed.

"Absolutely. I'll be back in a jiffy." Jamie grabbed her coat and headed outside.

When we were alone again, Natalie seemed to deflate, a note of despair washing over her face.

"Are you okay?" I asked.

"It never ends." Her shoulders sagged.

"I didn't see her anywhere," Jamie said, slightly out of breath as she came back in a few minutes later. "And Deputy Chief Cross said they'd look into what else you can do to keep news people out of here."

Natalie ran a hand through her blond hair, looking frazzled. "Thanks, Jamie."

"I'd better get going," I said, realizing how late it was.

Natalie gave me a distracted wave as I left.

Once outside, I walked over to the missing poster of Dakota tacked to the telephone poll, wishing I could block out the sight of his cute, smiling face.

I noticed a familiar man with dirty blond hair, wearing the same brown button-up shirt I had seen him in only hours before. Out of the corner of my eye, he could almost be Jasper Clinton. I hadn't realized how similar they looked until now.

Reggie Grady was staring at Dakota's missing poster tacked to the community bulletin board. His hands were shoved in his pockets, his eyes intent. He noticed me watching him. His face was a mixture of strange things. I remembered as a kid how I never liked him looking at me.

"I saw you earlier. Out in Hickory Woods," I said, looking for a reaction.

Reggie's eyes were unflinching. If he was bothered with my seeing him, he didn't show it.

"What were you doing out there?" I pressed.

"Why? Do you own the woods or somethin'?" I wanted to look away from him but wouldn't give him the satisfaction.

"No, but my mom says you're out there a lot—"

"So?" he interrupted with a hint of aggression. "I see Constance out there too." There was something implied, but I didn't know what. "Maybe she should keep to her business and I'll keep to mine."

With that, he turned back to Dakota's missing poster, lingering a while longer, before hunching up his shoulders and walking toward his dad's store.

When he was gone, I forced myself to put aside my unease. Five years ago, the people of Blue Cliff had rallied together in blaming an outsider. Jasper was a natural suspect. Not someone they had any connection to. Who would they sling their accusations at this time in the absence of such an easy target?

It was all the same. Especially the ugly parts.

And it was a familiarity I took no comfort in.

8

–Natalie–

THE SUN HAD set hours ago. The winding path leading to the Caruthers' house was dark. Too dark for the way Hunter drove recklessly around the curves.

I chanced a look at him, noting the firm set of his jaw and the white-knuckle grip on the steering wheel. I could feel the rage emanating off him, and I didn't blame him one bit.

An article had been published yesterday in the second biggest newspaper in the state.

"Mayor's Future Daughter-in-Law Stands by Innocent Clinton."

What followed was a story with very little fact and a whole lot of conjecture, mixed with misconstrued sound-bites and ridiculous exaggeration. The headline made it sound like I knew Jasper and that we had some sort of relationship. I asked my dad if I could sue the paper for printing deliberately false information, but he said no judge would rule in my favor. I had to hope no one would actually believe what was written. Because one thing came across in bold black and white: Natalie Bartlett didn't believe Jasper Clinton murdered those kids or took Dakota Mason.

And my fiancé was now furious with me.

"How could you talk to a reporter about my family? About our town?" Hunter had shouted. He was livid. After his initial shouting, he had taken to ignoring me completely, refusing to stay over at my house for the first time since I got my own place. I felt like a Judas.

I was surprised when he showed up at the shop as I was closing for the day, and asked me to come with him to his parents' place. He said his ma was in a bad way, and he could use the support. He had never been able to handle his mother on his own.

"I mean, if you can put aside cheerleading for a child killer long enough to spend time with my family," Hunter sneered, his cruelty directed at me for the first time. I had never been on the receiving end of his anger before.

"Dad'll no doubt bring up the article," Hunter said, turning up the hill toward the house.

"I'll apologize. I honestly didn't say most of what that woman printed—"

"But you said enough," Hunter snapped.

I let out a sigh. "I'm sorry. I didn't think I said anything that horrible. Cheyenne would have told me if I had."

Hunter let out a cold laugh. "I should have known Cheyenne Ashby would be mixed up in this. That bitch knows how to stir shit better than anyone."

I bristled at Hunter's nastiness. "Hunter, don't talk like that about her."

My fiancé glared at me, his expression frigid. "Why are you defending her? She doesn't give a crap about you or anyone else in this town. Don't go wasting your breath on someone who will leave you again in a heartbeat. You don't matter to her, and you never have."

It felt as if he had plunged a knife into my chest. His words hurt—a lot.

"But I'm here, and always have been. By your side, through everything, and it's me that you stab in the back."

"I'm sorry," I said for the hundredth time. My voice had lost all its strength. Hunter had pummeled any backbone I had right out of me.

Hearing my tone, Hunter softened slightly. He reached over and took my hand. "I know you are. And I know you don't really think that monster is innocent. You're not stupid enough to believe that. And I get that around Chey you do things you wouldn't normally do. She's always been the leader in your little duo. So I'll talk to my dad, okay? I'll smooth things over."

I rankled at how easily Hunter dismissed my thoughts and feelings. How easy it was for him to think I was just some silly girl influenced by my more dominant friend. I wondered, not for the first time, how little he really thought of me.

"Dad said Mom's lashing out again. Seems she saw some news show about Dakota, and it set her off," Hunter explained, and I forced myself to push aside my irritation.

I loved Hunter's ma, as any dutiful future daughter-in-law would, but my patience was starting to wear thin. She was hurting and that made her mean. She wallowed in her misery and made sure that everyone around her wallowed in it too.

I couldn't imagine what it must be like to lose a child, and in such a brutal way, but after Michael's murder, she had pushed away everyone, including her eldest son. She had lost two children that day.

Upon arriving, we drove through the open wrought iron gates and came to a halt next to his dad's car. We got out like two people preparing for battle. Hunter automatically took my hand as we walked up the steps to the front door of their large, colonial-style home.

The front door opened before we'd made it up the final step, and I said a quick "thank you" to Darla Dunlap, the Caruthers' housekeeper, as we headed down the hallway. We could hear raised voices punctuated by intense sobbing. We followed the noise to the living room.

"Martha, you have to calm down. Getting this upset accomplishes nothing." Hunter's father, Chase, was hovering by the window, looking at his distraught wife, his expression fraught, his mouth set in a firm line. He seemed relieved when Hunter came into the room.

Chase Caruthers had always been a strong pillar of the community. After Michael's death he'd locked up his emotions and thrown away the key. Feelings were *hard* in the wake of such a horrific tragedy. It wasn't his fault, though—not entirely. The press had hounded his family. They'd come from all over the country to try and interview the parents of the murdered children. The vultures had circled, and it had been relentless.

Hunter's family had survived it, but barely. Now, with Dakota's disappearance, the wounds that hadn't quite healed were bleeding freely once again.

"That little boy is gone! Just like my Mikey. He'll never be able to rest, Chase—I can still feel him," Martha wailed, her face red and blotchy from tears and too much alcohol.

Hunter hurried across the room. "Mom, it's okay. I'm here—what can I do?"

She was sitting on one of the large sofas, a glass of her favorite drink—a Bloody Mary—clasped in her hand. Hunter knelt by her feet and reached for her hands. After trying unsuccessfully to pry the drink from her grip, he gave up.

"Mom? What can I do?" he repeated. I'd seen this scene play out so many times over the years that I already knew the words by heart.

"It's never going to stop, Hunter. Don't you get it? Another boy is gone. He's just like Mikey. They're the same," she shrieked. "Leave me alone—you're not him. I want my Michael!" The sound of his name, broken and shattered on her lips, was haunting.

Feeling as if I were intruding on a private moment, I knew the polite thing to do was leave. Particularly with Chase Caruthers shooting daggers in my direction. I was clearly not his favorite person at the moment. So I quietly slipped from the room, closing the door behind me.

Unsure what to do with myself, I headed to the kitchen to make a pot of coffee, thinking it might help sober Martha up.

Darla was whispering with Otis Wheeler, whom Chase hired to do odds and ends around the house, when I entered the kitchen. They looked up quickly and stopped talking. I knew a gossip fest when I saw one and gave them a knowing look as they made themselves busy.

"I'm going to make some coffee for Martha," I explained, moving to the cabinet to grab a mug.

"Is Mrs. Caruthers doin' alright? She's been . . . tired lately. All this awfulness with the Mason boy has made things real difficult for her," Darla said delicately. Her round face held only affection, and I knew she cared about the family she had worked for during the past twenty years. I had known Darla most of my life. She had been my Brownie troop leader in the second grade. Her son, Craig, was married to my friend from high school, Sissy Jessop. And her homemade lemon bars were the stuff of legend in these parts.

"She'll be fine," I told them.

"I was over at Tammy Bradshaw's place last week. Paintin' the shed, you know. She and Earl were a mess. Dakota bein' missing reminds them of Livvie. It's awful, and what it's bringin' up for those other families is just as bad. This town can't take much more," Otis said. "And the kids are all so scared. I talk to 'em a lot, you know. They trust me. They tell me things. Dakota was a good boy. Always had a lot to say." Otis nodded to himself.

"You knew Dakota well then, huh?" I remarked, remembering how Otis had worked as a janitor at the elementary school for the past thirty years. I remembered him always being around, tidying up the playground, laughing and teasing with us kids.

"I sure did. I know all of 'em. Just like I knew Livvie, Danielle, and Mikey. We have good kids in Blue Cliff." His smile was sad.

"I hate sayin' it, but we all know what happens when children go into those woods. What's wrong with his parents for not telling Dakota the stories? Not givin' him the coins and the dirt?" Darla tutted in that judgmental way that was typical of small towns.

"It's no mystery who's responsible. I heard Jeannie and Randy Newton sayin' that they saw those Clintons at the Comfort Inn near Blacksburg. They said those people were eatin' in the restaurant like they didn't have a care in the world. That's not far from here. That Jasper boy is back and he took Dakota and done 'im just like he done did the other three," Otis retorted angrily.

Darla's normally warm brown eyes became hard. "They need to find that devil and string him up like the old days."

"We don't know what happened to Dakota. Remember, the Bible says, 'Do not judge.' We'd all do well to remember that." When I looked up, Otis and Darla appeared horrified.

The folk of Blue Cliff were unforgiving. And I should have known better than to express a thought contrary to theirs.

"How can you sympathize with those people?" Darla demanded. "Their awful boy killed those sweet babies. He killed our Mikey. They brought evil with them, Natalie. It's taken root again, and the only way to stop it spreading is to find them and make them pay for their sins."

"I'm not sympathizing. I just think—"

"If your mama heard you talkin' like that, you'd send her to an early grave," Otis chided. He was old enough to be my grandpa, and as such, could scold with the best of them. "Talkin' like that about those wicked people." He made the sign of the cross, even though he wasn't Catholic and hadn't attended a church service since the eighties.

"We all trust in the chief. He handled things the right way. If he says Jasper is the killer, then Jasper's the killer," Darla continued. Of course there was no mention of the evidence that exonerated Jasper or the fact that a judge believed him innocent. Jasper Clinton was guilty and always would be in the minds of Blue Cliff. Evidence be damned.

"Even if some people don't have the right morals"— Otis's rheumy eyes flicked my way, and I knew he was referring to my dad in his less than direct way—"our good boys at the police department got it right."

I blushed furiously. "I'm sorry. I shouldn't have said anything," I backtracked, swallowing my irritation. I had been raised to respect my elders, no matter how much I disagreed with their opinions. Or how wrong they were. "I'd better get back to Martha."

"Look after Hunter, Natalie. He needs some love and care right now," Darla intoned darkly.

I heard a crash coming from the other room. Darla and Otis didn't even jump. They were used to Martha's violent moods that always escalated when she started drinking. Darla would go in later and clean up whatever mess Mrs. Caruthers had made, and there would be no talk of what happened. Sweep it up. Throw it away. Never talk about the giant elephant in the room.

After all, Martha was grieving. A lot can be forgiven when someone has suffered a tragedy. Though, deep down, I wondered how long we were meant to allow grief as an excuse for her increasingly erratic behavior.

We look after our own.

Yes, we did. No matter what it took.

"Don't forget the coffee. She'll be needin' that," Otis interjected as I turned to leave.

"Right. The coffee." I gave them a half-hearted smile and picked up the mug before heading back to the living room.

I returned as Hunter and his father were helping Martha off the sofa, though she was making it difficult, her body limp and uncoordinated.

Chase glanced at the coffee in my hands, his expression hard. "Leave it in the hallway, and I'll ask Darla to bring it up."

"I can bring it—"

"I think that you've done more than enough, Natalie," he cut in before turning away.

The three of them left the room without a backward glance. I had been all but forgotten.

*   *   *

"Is she okay?" I asked Hunter a little while later. We sat outside on the porch swing, bundled up against the cold. It seemed more comfortable to brave the elements than sit inside.

"You know how she gets," Hunter replied, his tone subdued. We both stared ahead of us.

I reached out and took his icy hand in mine. My heart hurt for him. Martha could be nasty, and Hunter typically took the brunt of her cruelty. I knew how much a mother's disgust and disappointment could wound.

"Are *you* okay?" I asked, and saw a flicker of pain before he caught himself.

"I have to be, don't I?" He gave me a sideways glance. "I spoke to dad about you . . . about the article. He's pissed, but I assured him you never said any of the things they printed." Apprehension must have shown on my face because Hunter's eyes narrowed. "They were lies, weren't they, Nat?"

I nodded mutely, barely able to look at him. We both knew that I wasn't being truthful, but neither of us would say it out loud. We sat in silence, my betrayal between us. The entire town believed Jasper was guilty, but I believed the evidence. The convictions had been overturned—that couldn't be for no reason. But I had been careful to keep my opinions to myself, at least until that journalist had gotten me angry and I'd said more than I should have.

The door opened, letting out a rush of warm air as Hunter's father came outside. He lit up a cigar, inhaling deeply.

"Damn press are back and looking for blood. Just had two phone calls from newspapers wanting interviews." Chase took a long drag from the cigar, exhaling in an angry puff. "The Bradshaws had to chase one of those leeches off their property with a shotgun, and the Torrents had to change their phone number. Not to mention what the Masons are having to deal with when all they want is to find their son." He stood at the edge of the porch, gripping the rail and staring out at the acres of land that had been in his family since the early days of the town.

He glanced my way, his expression disgusted. "Maybe if people would keep their mouths shut, they'd have nothing to print, and they'd leave our town alone."

"Dad, I explained about that. She didn't say those things"—Hunter turned to me—"right, Nat?"

Both men stared at me, anger and frustration evident on their faces.

"No, I didn't say anything like that," I lied, my voice quiet.

Hunter looked relieved by my denial, but Chase's expression remained cold.

"Well, either way, it seems he has some sympathizers. Otherwise, that supposed evidence would have been burned long ago."

Hunter's face creased with anxiety. "Dad," he began, with a hint of warning. "Be careful what you say . . ."

Chase turned to Hunter sharply, his expression dark. "Anyone, and I mean *anyone*, who believes that child killer is innocent had better watch their back, and I don't care who hears me." He looked at me once more, and I shriveled beneath his scrutiny.

Thank God, Chase Caruthers couldn't see the memories in my head.

*   *   *

"I hate seeing their faces everywhere," I admitted, ashamed to say my secret thoughts out loud. But I knew Cheyenne would understand.

Cheyenne shoved her hands in her pockets and tucked her chin into her collar to ward off the chill. It had started snowing as we got out of school, so we decided to cut through Hickory Downs Park on our way to the woods.

"It is pretty morbid," Cheyenne agreed as we passed another lamppost with the poster of the three kids who had disappeared. "Makes it even worse because we know them."

Chey was right. I used to babysit for Danielle, and Olivia's ma was friends with Constance. And Michael—he was my boyfriend's little brother. Each of the children were known and loved by all of us, so their disappearance was affecting everyone.

"I wish Chief Hickman would find them. They're probably all hiding somewhere, watching us freak out over them. The three of them are always together," I laughed uncomfortably, not believing a word of what I said.

Chey nudged me with her shoulder. "Kinda like you, Jack, and me."

We noticed a guy lying on the bench beneath the skeletal willow tree. One hand hung limply off the side as he raised the other to his lips, taking a long drag from a cigarette. Jasper Clinton rolled his head to look at us as we walked by, his eyes heavy lidded and bloodshot. I could smell him from the short distance, a putrid combination of sweat and booze. I gripped Chey's hand, giving it a tug, trying to get her to walk faster.

"Hey, ladies, wanna party?" his thick drawl called out.

"Come on—let's go," I whispered urgently.

When we didn't answer, Jasper sat up. He wasn't a big guy. His face was thin, and his long, blond hair was greasy. His nose looked like it had been broken one too many times, and now sat off center on his face. He was wearing an oversized hooded jacket with a hole on the shoulder. He looked homeless. Or at least like someone who didn't care about his appearance.

"What's wrong? Scared to hang out with me?" he taunted, his words hard.

Cheyenne pulled us to a stop, much to my dread. "Why would we be scared to hang out with a loser like you?"

"Chey, don't," I warned under my breath. But Chey didn't listen.

Jasper stood up and walked toward us. I let out a pathetic squeak, gripping Chey's hand even tighter. But my best friend held her ground. Her courage was going to be her downfall one day.

"I don't think Loony Connie's daughter should be calling anyone a loser," Jasper shot back, taking another pull off his cigarette and then dropping it on the ground, which for some reason bothered me most of all. Why couldn't he at least throw it away?

"What do you even know about my mom? You're not from around here. You don't know anything about anyone," Chey countered, sticking her chin out. "Maybe it's you who should be scared."

Jasper laughed, but not with amusement. "You people are all the same. Just because a guy hasn't lived here since he was in diapers, you think there's something wrong with him. That he doesn't see how things are." He leaned in toward us, and I instinctively moved back. "Do you ever think that maybe there's something wrong with all of you? This place is messed up. And what's more messed up is you drones don't even see it."

To my shock and horror, Chey grinned. "You might be onto something there. This place is messed up." She put a hand on her hip. "So, you got any weed?"

"Chey!" I scowled.

Jasper looked taken aback, but then he laughed for real this time. "Sorry, I'm all out. But I'm supposed to head out of town this weekend to refresh my supply. Find me next week and I can hook you up. Maybe we could hang out or something." He seemed to relax, which changed the look of him completely. He didn't appear threatening and scary. He looked lost and lonely, eager for our attention. For friendship. He definitely didn't seem like a guy who had kidnapped three kids.

Because that's what everyone thought. When first Olivia went missing, then Danielle, then Michael, fingers started pointing in Jasper's direction. He was the outsider. No one knew him. And he was strange. Always hanging out at the park, drunk and high. He had no friends and didn't seem to make much of an effort to rectify that. And the rest of his family were just as bad. They kept to themselves. Mrs. Randolph told my ma that Mrs. Clinton didn't even say thank you when she took her a pie after they first moved in. You didn't behave like that and expect people to like you.

"Too bad. I could use a buzz right now," Chey said, looking pointedly at the missing posters dotted around.

Jasper followed her gaze, and this time his expression was sad. "I know what ya'll think, and you've got it completely wrong."

"What do we have wrong?" Chey asked.

"That you kidnapped Olivia, Danielle, and Michael?" I added, my voice embarrassingly high pitched.

Jasper turned his sad eyes on me. "Yeah, that. It wasn't me. But I see stuff. Things they don't realize I see."

There was something about him, about the way he answered me, that made me doubt. That made me think our families and neighbors didn't have it right about this weird guy. Chey said I was too quick to see the good in people. What she didn't understand was that it was out of fear. That I was terrified to believe in an evil that existed in people's hearts. That made them capable of horrible things.

But this time I didn't feel that way out of fear, but out of a deep instinct that was just right.

"I swear, I had nothing to do with those missing kids," he insisted again.

"I believe you," Chey said quietly, and I turned to her quickly, startled by her words. Her expression was serious as she looked at Jasper. "But it won't matter."

The sound of shouting and laughter broke the moment, and I saw a group of guys from our high school walking through the park. Jasper saw them too and quickly hurried off, disappearing into the trees.

"Well, that was odd," Chey said after he was gone.

"Yeah," I agreed, feeling shaken. "Did you mean what you said? About believing him?" I asked.

She shrugged noncommittally, and we never spoke of it again.

Cheyenne would never know how that one brief exchange haunted me for years afterward. And how, as the town became Jasper Clinton's judge and jury, I remained silent, keeping my thoughts to myself. How, when everyone else saw a devil, I remembered sad eyes that pleaded with us to believe him.

* * *

Chase paced back and forth, his cigar burning between his fingers.

"That piece of shit can try and hide all he wants, but I've got the best private investigator on the case."

"I thought people had seen him—"

"It wasn't him! My investigator hasn't been able to find hide nor hair of him since he was released." Chase puffed furiously on his cigar, plumes of smoke encircling his head like a cloud. "He's hiding . . . they're all hiding, that whole damn family. They've left town too. But Jasper and his parents can't hide forever. He's going to pay for what he did. One way or another . . ." His words trailed off. Chase Caruthers was a man to be reckoned with, and I believed him when he said Jasper Clinton would pay. If I were the betting kind, I would put all my money on Chase.

He glanced at me again. "Has your father mentioned anything about this?" I quickly shook my head. His face hardened as he scrutinized me. I felt my cheeks heat up.

"Dad . . ." Hunter began, but Chase's glare silenced him.

"Stewart Bartlett helped put that murderer behind bars the first time, and he needs to make sure he does it again, and this time, for good! He's let this town down, and he needs to make it right." Chase walked toward me, coming so close that I could smell his aftershave. Chase stared at me, his eyes boring into my soul, as if looking for something. "Your father's name is important to him. I'd think he'd want to pull it out of the mud. So, you have him call me right away."

My heart slammed against my ribcage. "Yes, sir," I murmured, my tone solemn. Chase held my eyes for a beat too long, making me want to retreat. Then he turned and walked back inside, slamming the door behind him.

Hunter was quiet once we were alone again, and I found him staring at me. He didn't seem the slightest bit concerned that his dad had just gotten in my face.

"I'll speak to my dad," I said cautiously, feeling like this was what Hunter had been waiting for me to say, "I'll make sure he calls him."

"That would be good," Hunter replied stonily. "Jasper getting out has set things in motion, and I don't know if I can stop them. Honestly, I don't know if I want to. He killed my brother, Nat. He can't get away with that."

Worry gnawed at me.

Worry for Hunter and for whatever his dad intended to do. And worry for Jasper.

He may have been labeled a murderer, but he was free now. He had been proven innocent, yet that still wasn't good enough.

I wrapped my arms around Hunter and held him close. The wind blew through the trees, sounding like whispering ghosts.

"Just don't do anything stupid, Hunter," I murmured into his chest. "Please."

His arms tightened around me, but he remained silent, and my fear for the future grew.

9

—Cheyenne—

THE LAST PLACE I expected to find myself was Salty's Bar, the one and only spot for a night out in Blue Cliff. But I was going stir crazy out in the woods with only my mom for company. Not that she really provided any. Most nights she spent holed up in her room, and her days were spent in the woods. I didn't mind spending time alone, but there was only so much isolation a gal could handle. In a moment of weakness, I made the decision to venture into town.

As soon as I arrived at the bar, I ordered straight bourbon and drank it quickly before ordering another one.

"Glad to see you haven't moved onto some froufrou big-city drink," a familiar deep voice commented dryly behind me.

I didn't want to look at my ex-boyfriend that I had never really made my "ex" because we'd never actually broken up. I knew he was probably the last person, besides Natalie, who would be happy to see me.

I heard the stool beside me scratch across the floor as Jackson Campbell pulled it out, followed by the rush of heat as his body crowded in close to mine. He ordered a bottle of Budweiser, and I chanced a peek at him. My stomach flipped. Jack looked good. He'd always been handsome in that boy-next-door kind of way. But now, the boy was gone, and he had become all man. With chiseled features and two-day-old stubble, Jack had the weathered features of someone who'd spent all his time outside—and it suited him.

I took a long, slow sip of my drink, trying to put off the conversation we were bound to have.

"So, you're back," he said.

"Looks like it."

Awkward silence.

"Thanks for plowing our road," I added.

"No problem. I try to help Constance out when I can."

More awkward silence.

"How long you back for?" he asked, his voice rough.

"I'm not sure. I guess as long as Mom needs me," I answered.

This was ridiculous.

I was getting sick and tired of all this baggage hanging around everywhere I went. I swiveled in my seat to face my former boyfriend. He was staring at the TV hanging on the wall, but I got the impression he wasn't really watching it.

"Jack." He raised an eyebrow, but didn't look at me. He continued to sip on his beer and stare at the television. "Jack, look at me." I probably sounded more pissy than I meant to, but I had long since lost the patience to be easy with people's hurt feelings.

He took his time turning toward me. "So you think you're in a position to make demands? All because you decide to waltz back into town looking as pretty as the day you left?"

I didn't know what to say. Thankfully, I was saved from thinking of a reply by the arrival of Natalie and Hunter. I wasn't sure about the reception I'd receive from my former best friend. So color me shocked when she approached and ordered herself a vodka soda and gave me what seemed like a genuine smile.

I noticed that Jack relaxed as he and Nat greeted each other. It was obvious the two were still as close as they'd been when we were younger. I couldn't help but feel jealous at their natural rapport that had once included me. Now, I was very clearly on the outside looking in, and that was entirely my fault.

Natalie took her drink, and I ordered another straight bourbon. She glanced at Hunter, who was sitting with his high school henchman, Jess Cross. The two had always been full of themselves and completely obnoxious.

"Come on, guys. You two can be my backup. Lord knows I'll need it when Hunter and Jess start talking about football," Nat urged. It was on the tip of my tongue to decline, but Jack nudged my arm.

"Let's go."

I took a long swallow of my drink. "Sure—sounds like a blast."

"Stop looking like you're about to donate a kidney," Nat joked as we walked back to the table.

"Donating a kidney might be more fun than hanging out with Jess Cross." I rolled my eyes.

"Be nice, Chey. It won't kill you." Nat chuckled.

"There's no proof of that," I deadpanned, and I meant it. I couldn't think of anything worse than being around Hunter Caruthers and Jess Cross.

So I was surprised yet again when what followed was more or less a decent evening. The tension melted away the more we talked and reminisced. I was able to relax, even if I had to ignore Hunter's pointed barbs and Jess's smirks.

It was like old times. Only now we were older and could drink legally. No more hiding in Jack's barn, sippin' on moonshine and whiskey.

"Remember that time Chey got wasted on those moonshine peaches from Jack's grandpa's freezer?" Nat laughed.

"Yeah, and she puked in the pigpen, and I had to clean it up before they got to it." Jack grimaced.

"I thought they were regular peaches. I had no idea they were soaked in one-hundred-and-eight-proof grain alcohol," I argued with a groan. I couldn't help but laugh at the memory, though I definitely hadn't been laughing at the time.

"You're telling me you couldn't taste the difference between normal peaches and my grandpa's moonshine peaches? Come on, now," Jack scoffed playfully.

"If I could, you think I would have eaten three of them? I was sick for days! I'm pretty sure I had alcohol poisoning." I bumped his shoulder with mine, instigating physical contact for the first time.

We had all been friends in high school, but unlike me, the rest of them had stayed in our town. There was a sense of belonging that blossomed between people who had grown up together. They understood you in a way no one else could. It was a given that the kids of Blue Cliff eventually became the adults of Blue Cliff. I was the anomaly. And seeing their natural closeness, I felt a little bit of regret that I had left all this behind. No one had ever known me the way these people did. For better or for worse.

*　　*　　*

Later in the night, Nat followed me to the bar, and I could tell something was on her mind. Feeling flushed on nostalgia, my mood was lighter than it had been in years. The desire to mend fences was intense, and the desire to recover that sense of normality was overwhelming.

"Spit it out, Bartlett," I joked.

She chewed on her bottom lip. "Why'd you do it?" she asked. Alcohol loosened her tongue, and she seemed emboldened.

"Why did I do what?" I played dumb.

"Leave. Why didn't you say anything? To me? To Jack? I thought we were family. Family doesn't disappear without so much as a goodbye."

I felt the age-old defensiveness take hold. "What do you want from me, Nat?" I sighed. "You want me to apologize for leaving? I can't. Leaving was the best thing for me. You know what was going on back then. How it's still going on. It was too much. Being here, living with my mom's crazy behavior—finding the body—" I couldn't stop myself from shuddering. "I'd finally had enough. The responsibility of being an Ashby was breaking me. So I left and I went somewhere where my last name didn't come with expectations and baggage."

Nat stared down into her glass. "Five years is a long time to not contact your friends."

There it was. The guilt. The pain. I had to face it; otherwise, I'd always feel this lump where my heart should be.

"I am sorry."

Nat raised an eyebrow. "I thought you weren't going to apologize."

"It's not an apology for leaving. It's an apology for being a jerk. I should have said something. I should have told you how I was feeling. And you're right: I should have called at some point. But honestly, I knew if I had talked to you or Jack, I'd never get out, and that was a fate worse than death to me."

Natalie's lower lip quivered, and then she launched herself at me, hugging me tight. I froze, not sure what to do. But I hugged her back, and then we were both emotional and squeezing one another as if we'd never let go.

"I really have missed you," I whispered.

"I missed you too," she replied, her voice cracking.

We pulled apart, both of us laughing a little self-consciously. I rubbed my eyes as I tried to hold back tears. I looked over my shoulder at the table of people who were trying to seem as if they weren't watching us like hawks—and failing miserably.

"And Jack . . . did you miss him too?"

My stomach flipped over. "Yes, a lot. But don't you dare tell him that." Then we were both laughing again, without the discomfort.

We rejoined the table, and I was in a damn fine mood.

Until Chris Miners, the editor of the *Blue Cliff Bulletin*, showed up, letting Hunter know the Clintons had movers loading up their stuff into a U-Haul.

"Was *he* there?" Hunter asked.

Chris shook his head. "Not from what my source could see. But it looks like the family has officially skipped town."

Hunter slammed his beer down on the table. His expression had turned thunderous.

"Who are you talking about?" Jess questioned, his eyes slightly unfocused from the liquor he had consumed.

"Jasper," Nat answered.

Jess's expression darkened. "Jasper Clinton?"

"Yeah," Hunter choked out. "Jasper fucking Clinton."

There was an instant, overwhelming stillness.

Chris was clearly uncomfortable. "I heard there's movement in the investigation into how the case was handled. From the rumblings, it sounds like heads are gonna start rolling."

"Good," I muttered. "They deserve what's coming to them for railroading the poor guy."

"What did you say?" Hunter snarled. He thought he was being intimidating. I was more intimidated by Linda Grady.

"Come on, Hunter—even you aren't arrogant enough to think you know better than an appellate judge. If the evidence shows he didn't do it, then he didn't do it." I shrugged. Natalie looked horrified.

It was like all the air had been sucked out of the room. Everyone froze, waiting to see Hunter's reaction.

"Then who did it, Miss-I-know-more-than-everyone-else?" Hunter demanded. "Or are you gonna start babbling about the Hickory Man like your crazy mom?"

At the mention of Mom, I saw red. I braced my hands on the table and leaned toward him. "You'd better watch your mouth, Caruthers. Wouldn't want the whole bar to see you get your ass kicked by a woman."

Hunter bared his teeth. "Just calling it like I see it. How we *all* see it. You Ashbys are nuts."

"Hunter, come on. That's not cool," Nat said softly. "Please, guys, calm down."

I forced myself to sit back down, relaxing my clenched fists. "All I'm saying is there was new evidence. Evidence compelling enough to set Jasper free. That's how the justice system works. You didn't do the crime, you shouldn't do the time."

Natalie seemed conflicted. "Hunter, maybe Chey's right. There *was* new evidence—evidence that should have come out five years ago, DNA evidence—and it proved he didn't do it. He shouldn't be in jail."

"Are you kidding me?" Hunter yelled furiously, shoving her away from him.

"Don't you touch her!" I shouted. I felt murderous.

"It's fine. I'm fine!" Nat said hurriedly, trying to placate me.

Hunter got to his feet and once again leaned over the table toward me. "It shouldn't surprise me that you're siding with that sicko. Those bodies were found in *your* woods. It was *you* who found my brother." He was practically spitting in my face. "Maybe you two were even in on it together."

"Hunter, that's enough!" Nat said loudly.

"You don't get it, Natalie!" Hunter turned to shout in her face. "Of course not. Little Miss Goody Two-Shoes is too busy sucking up to her bitch friend to realize what a moron she is about everything. Can't you see, Nat? She doesn't want you. She never did. That's why she upped and left without you. You're dead weight and always will be."

Natalie sucked in a breath and looked like she was either going to cry or slap him. I hoped it was the latter.

Jack got up and stood between Hunter and Natalie and me. He towered over Hunter, and I noticed him take a step back. "I think you've said enough. It's time you went somewhere to cool off before shit happens. You get me?"

Hunter looked like he wanted to argue, but Jack wasn't going to back down. After a few tense moments, Hunter turned and left without another word. The door slammed shut behind him. Jess stood up, downed the last of his beer, and took off after Hunter.

"I really want to get out of here," Natalie said, wiping furiously at her eyes. "Is my mascara dripping? Please don't tell me I've got all these people staring at me while I'm sporting raccoon eyes."

"You look fine," I assured her.

Natalie grabbed her purse, slid out of the booth, but then stopped short. "Crap, Hunter drove me here. I have no way of getting home."

"So, not only did he yell at you in front of everyone, but he left you without a ride too. What a prince," I growled, my blood boiling.

"Don't start, Chey. I'm not in the mood to fend off your attacks on Hunter. He's going through a lot. Jasper getting out of jail and then Dakota going missing has brought all of that old trauma back up for him." Natalie started scanning the crowd. "I really don't want to get into this with you. I just want to find a ride home."

"I have my car . . . well, maybe I should have thought how *I'd* get home before having all those drinks." I mentally smacked my forehead.

Jack held out his hand. "Give me your keys. I'll drive your car home. If I remember anything about the way you drive, your car will be safer with me behind the wheel."

"Are you sure *you're* okay to drive?" I asked, not wanting him driving drunk either, but he nodded.

"Only had a couple. I'm fine," he promised.

I dropped the keys in his palm, got to my feet, and gently pushed Nat toward the door. When we got outside, I started to lead them toward my car. Jack and Natalie trailed after me. The parking lot was dark. Too dark to make out the figure that advanced toward us.

"Wait," a voice rasped close to my ear, the stink of booze and body odor making me want to gag. Fingers wrapped around my wrist, clamping down.

I recoiled at the feel of warm breath on my neck. Otis Wheeler weaved unsteadily on his feet, obviously drunk as a skunk.

"Hey, Otis." I attempted to pull my arm free, but his grip was surprisingly strong.

"Have you seen 'im?" he demanded.

"Otis, what are you doing? Let Cheyenne go." Natalie intervened, helping me pry his hand off my arm.

But Otis was undeterred. "Have you seen 'im, damnit?" he growled, glaring at the two of us.

"Who are you talking about? Who have I seen?" I asked. Most thought Otis to be an affable man who loved the kids of Blue Cliff as if they were his own. But something about him was off.

"Dakota. Is he out there?"

At the mention of the missing boy, I went still.

"Come on, Otis—leave Cheyenne alone," Jack said, stepping in. His formidable presence seemed to have an effect on the older man. Otis backed away.

"I know he's out there," Otis wailed.

"I don't know what you're talking about—"

Otis's eyes widened, and he advanced on us again. "He's there. You'll see."

"Okay, Otis, it's time you headed home. I think you've had too much to drink tonight." Jack forcibly moved Otis away from Natalie and me.

"He doesn't mean any harm, Jack. Be careful with him," Natalie exclaimed.

"I need to be out there with 'im!" Otis pointed off into the distance, in the direction of the woods.

Jackson pulled out his phone and made a quick call. When he was finished, he helped Otis to the bench outside the door and sat him down. "Now you stay here. Deputy Grady will be by in a minute to take you home."

Otis didn't argue. He slumped against the wall, as if collapsing in on himself.

"Maybe we should wait with him," Natalie suggested, seeming anxious. "I've never seen him like this."

"I think the best thing we can do is leave the police to deal with him. Adam Grady said he was two minutes away. You don't need to worry about Otis. He'll be fine," Jack said, rejoining us.

"I only saw him a few hours ago. He wasn't anything like this. What's going on with him?" Natalie looked back at Otis, who hadn't moved.

"And what was all that stuff about Dakota?" I added as we continued to my car. "He was saying some pretty strange things."

Natalie frowned. "He's been really upset about Dakota—"

"Too upset if you ask me," I said under my breath.

None of us seemed to want to talk anymore about Otis Wheeler and his weird behavior. Natalie climbed into the back of my car, and I slid into the passenger seat. "Wait— what about your truck?" I asked Jack as he started up the engine.

"I can pick it up tomorrow. I'll cut through the woods to get home after I drop you off." Jack turned onto the main road, heading through town.

"You shouldn't walk through the woods by yourself at night, Jack. You know better than that." Natalie tsked from the backseat.

"I'll be fine. The Hickory Man doesn't care about adults," Jack joked, but I noticed the way his shoulders stiffened.

"I can't believe people still tell those dumb stories about the Hickory Man," I muttered.

"I don't know, I've felt things in those woods. I've seen things . . ." Natalie's voice trailed off.

"You've been living here too long, Nat. That kind of talk messes with your mind. It's a load of horseshit—we all know that," I huffed in annoyance.

"Do we?" Jack countered.

"Come on, Jack—not you too," I moaned.

"All I'm sayin' is strange things happen when you're so close to the mountains. There are places in the deep parts that no one has ever laid eyes on. It's not so hard to believe that somethin' could live out there that's beyond our understanding."

"Something that steals little kids from their beds and leaves their bodies under the trees?" I mocked.

"He never takes them from their beds. It's only if they go into the woods. That's where he gets them," Natalie interjected in a hushed tone.

"If that were true, why didn't he ever take us? We played in the woods all the time as kids, and no scary boogeyman ever snatched us, because here we are."

"Maybe it's because of the silver and the dirt," Nat suggested. "Ma never let me leave the house without a coin in my pocket and a sprinkle of dirt in my sneakers. And that was from a woman who swore she didn't believe in all that *hogwash* as she called it."

I clenched my hands in my lap. "If the silver and dirt protected kids, then what about Livvie, Mikey and Danielle? They were found with silver and dirt, and it didn't keep them safe, did it?"

"I don't know why it didn't save them. It doesn't make sense. We were brought up to believe it would work." Natalie sounded frustrated. "Maybe there are times when even the old protections can't save you. Maybe he's too strong. Too hungry . . ."

"Stop it, Nat," I said tiredly.

"The silver and dirt must work, Chey, because we're here. He never took us—" Nat started to say.

"Or maybe, just maybe, a flesh-and-blood person is responsible and not a myth!" I hadn't meant to shout, but I couldn't help it. I was losing my patience. "There is no Hickory Man, Natalie."

I noticed Jack's eyes met Nat's in the rearview mirror.

"What?" I demanded.

"There was one time . . ." Jack started.

"Jack and I were walking back from your place. We were what? Nine?" Natalie asked.

"The summer before fourth grade," Jack filled in. "It was the day we spent all those hours picking blackberries, and your mom helped us boil them down to make preserves."

"Oh yeah, I remember that. Nothing happened and we were out in the woods for a really long time," I argued.

"It was when we were walking back to Jack's house. We knew we were supposed to take the road. Mrs. Campbell would have our heads had she known, but it was quicker through the trees."

"Nat and I were only a few minutes from your house when the wind started blowing. Really blowing," Jack added.

"It was like a tornado whipping through. The sky was still blue. But it was dark. And the birds stopped singing. It was like they were all up in the branches too scared to make a sound," Natalie whispered.

"It's always dark in the woods, Nat. You know that as well as I do. And there are a lot of times you don't hear any birds when you're out there. It doesn't mean anything," I interjected.

"We could barely see with all the dust and debris being kicked up and then we saw *him*." Jack sounded strained.

"You know you both sound a little delusional, right?" I told them.

"We saw him, Chey," Natalie said. "The Hickory Man."

I started laughing. Really laughing. "Stop pulling my leg, guys. You're telling me you saw some make-believe creature and you didn't tell me about it? Why is this the first time I've heard about this?"

"I don't know . . . maybe because we knew this would be your reaction. You were always so quick to dismiss the stories," Jack countered, and I immediately stopped laughing, feeling sufficiently chastised. I couldn't tell him that as a kid I dismissed it because it scared the shit out of me. It was easier to not believe than to admit it could all be true.

"We were scared, Chey." Jack's voice deepened. "There was this man-shaped shadow in the middle of the trees. He just appeared there. And I swear I heard him say my name—"

"Me too. It was like a whisper in my ear," Natalie added.

The memory of being in the clearing earlier came to mind. How I heard my name on the wind.

"We took off running, and when we got back to my house, we agreed to never talk about it. We didn't want to risk inviting him back if we did," Jack finished.

"It was probably a trick of the light," I argued. "And if it was super windy like that, you probably imagined hearing all kinds of things."

"And then there are the weird memories," Natalie pressed. Her words gave me pause even as my rational brain fought to disregard them.

Jack swiftly turned his head to look at her. "What weird memories?"

"I was young. Really young. Maybe four or five. But I could have been even younger than that—I'm not sure. I would see *him* outside my window. He'd stand there . . . in the shadows . . . like he was watching me. I couldn't really see him. But he was big. As big as a giant. Or at least he seemed that way to me at the time. It's strange . . . I can remember bits and pieces about him. About seeing him outside my window. My dad coming in and seeming terrified—" She shuddered violently, stopping herself. "I asked my dad about it years later, and he claimed he didn't know what I was talking about, that it must have been a bad dream, but I'm pretty sure it was real. That it actually happened."

"Huh," Jack mused. "I've got memories sort of like that too. I swear someone used to watch me through my bedroom window. Sometimes, I thought I even heard someone saying my name. I remember telling my mom, and she got real spooked. Hung some kind of weird plant on my window and told me not to open the curtains after dark. It stopped after a while, but Mom still hangs herbs on the window in my room from time to time."

Hearing Natalie and Jackson's stories unsettled me. I didn't want to tell them about my dreams; I didn't want to feed their unsubstantiated fear. The last thing I needed was another earful of their superstitions.

"Okay, so you guys imagined something outside your windows when you were little. Not surprising considering how we've been force-fed these nutty stories our entire lives. Of course you thought you saw a boogeyman," I retorted dismissively. "But it's not like anything happened. You're both still here."

Natalie and Jack shared a look again.

"Stay away from the hickories, stay away from the trees," Natalie sang from the backseat.

"Don't sing, don't shout, don't run about," Jack sang back. They both looked at me.

I rolled my eyes heavenward. *"Or he'll never let you leave,"* I finished. "We all know the song, guys. Doesn't make it real."

"You shouldn't make fun of it, Chey. What if it was *him* that Jack and I saw," Natalie whispered.

"How could it have been? I thought you said he never took kids from their houses?" I derided, half scared, half disbelieving.

Natalie's brow furrowed as she thought. "Maybe he wanted *me* to go find *him*. To go to the woods . . ." Her voice drifted off, her frown deepening.

"Okay, enough. There's only so much nonsense I can handle for one evening," I intoned dryly. Jack snorted, but Natalie was oddly serious. She wasn't normally the kind of person to talk about sinister stuff. She was the girl who dressed as a princess for Halloween because witches and vampires were too scary. Blue Cliff had changed my old friend.

"Do you guys believe Jasper's innocent?" Natalie suddenly asked, changing the subject. She looked like she was holding her breath. Like it had taken everything in her to ask the question, and I knew why.

I saw Jack's grip on the steering wheel tighten. "Well, he was just released from prison. The justice system obviously thinks so."

Natalie looked thoughtful. "His arrest and conviction *were* pretty convenient," she finally said. "Is that bad of me to think? This case made my dad's career. But honestly, I think they went after the wrong guy."

We lapsed into momentary silence, the thrum of the engine filling the void until Jack spoke again.

"We were all so damn sure he was the guy. Chief Hickman is a good man. I can't imagine him getting it wrong, Or your dad, Nat, but . . ." Jack hesitated.

"But a judge believed this new evidence. Believed it enough to overturn the conviction. That's not done lightly and rarely happens. DNA is pretty irrefutable," I finished for him. Jasper had been a drunk and a bit of a loser. He was an outsider, easily mistrusted, but I didn't think he was a killer.

"Oh God," Natalie breathed.

I turned to look at her, and she had gone horribly pale. "Are you going to be sick? Tell me so Jack can pull over. I really don't want you throwing up in my car."

She shook her head. "I keep thinking about what you said, that if Jasper didn't do it and you're so certain that it wasn't the Hickory Man, then whoever did it is still out there. Those poor kids. And Dakota . . ." Natalie was visibly shaking. So much so that I reached back and took her hand.

Her chin trembled as she fought to control her emotions. Eventually, she dragged her hands down her face and took a deep breath.

"I never thought he did it. No matter what anyone said," she agonized.

"I should be saying you're being ridiculous. But I can't," Jack said, his voice tight.

Natalie chewed on her bottom lip. "It didn't make sense, did it? Why would this young guy randomly murder three kids? Especially in the way he did it? How would he even know about the silver and the dirt? Because the Caruthers would never have given Mikey those things. They've never believed. So how did Jasper know?" Natalie said to him.

"Kids talk, Nat. Michael could have gotten them from Livvie or Danielle—"

"Okay, fine, but he left them in the woods, Jack. Out near Chey's place. Unless you know the paths, you'd never be able to get in and back out without getting lost. He hadn't lived here long enough to know his way through the trees. And they were drowned. Just like those kids from the fifties and the ones before that too. How would he know about the old ones? There are some stories you only hear because you've been raised on them." Natalie looked out the window. "Because whoever killed those kids knows about the other lost children. They know about the Hickory Man. And I am pretty sure that whoever killed Livvie, Mikey, and Danielle also took Dakota. And that means . . ."

We all went quiet.

"He's dead," I rasped.

Natalie nodded. "It's only a matter of time until they find him out there. In Ashby Woods . . . like the others."

"He could be okay. Maybe he ran away, or—" Jack started to say but Natalie cut him off.

"You know as well as I do what happens to kids in the woods. How you're never alone, and then one day, you're at the wrong place at the wrong time, and he reaches out and grabs you." Her voice rose in pitch as she got worked up.

"Stop it, Natalie!" I barked. "Stop talking like that."

"He's out there, Chey. I can feel it," Natalie continued.

"You need to stop listening to my mother. She's rubbed off on you a little too much."

"Then who was it, Chey? Who killed them? Who took Dakota?" Jack sounded freaked out. It was the same tone of voice he'd use when we would watch slasher movies. His knuckles were white on the steering wheel.

"What am I, the police? How should I know?" I sounded angry. I had to get it together. "But stop talking about the Hickory Man like he's real. You sound like my damn mom!"

Jack reached into the center console, lifting the handful of silver I kept there. "For someone who says she doesn't believe, why are these here?" he challenged me.

I didn't say anything right away. I had been called out, my hypocrisy on display for him and Nat to see.

I grabbed the coins and shoved them in the glove compartment. "It's nothing. Just some dumb stuff I picked up at an antique store in Roanoke. It doesn't mean anything," I lied.

I pretended not to notice Natalie and Jack sharing yet another look in the rearview mirror.

There wasn't much conversation after that. We dropped Natalie off first. She lived in a cute one-story ranch house outside of town. Jack left the car idling and walked Natalie to the door, making sure she got inside safely. Then we waited until she turned on all the lights and waved at us before closing the blinds.

Now that it was only the two of us, Jack turned on the radio, clearly avoiding conversation. As soon as we were back at my house, he parked the car, and we both got out.

He hesitated before giving me a quick hug. I wanted to make it last longer. He felt so good.

"Um, do you want to come in for a little bit? Mom's probably asleep, and we could talk . . ." The words faded into the silent dark.

Jack stared off into the trees. A twig snapped. The air seemed full and waiting. A shiver danced over my skin, and I wanted to get inside. I wanted to grab Jack's hand and take him with me.

"Jack," I said his name, soft and unsure.

"I want to, Chey. I really do." He let out a sigh. Another twig cracked, closer this time. "I'm just not there yet. It takes more than a night of beers to undo the last five years."

I wanted to reach out and touch him. I had always been irresistibly drawn to him, even when I was too young to understand what love felt like. My heart clattered and clanged in my chest as if it were trying to break free and launch itself at him.

"I need to apologize—"

Jack finally turned to me, his brown eyes flashing in the gloom. "Don't, Chey. Don't say words you don't mean. You left. You had your reasons. Don't go trying to undo what has already been done."

"I think we should go inside," I said quickly. "Please—"

Jack shook his head. "I can't." His eyes drifted to my mouth, and I felt my body tremble. I forgot about the woods. About the dark, dark night. About the silence and the watchfulness.

I could only see, only think, of Jack Campbell.

"Jack," I whispered his name again, needing to say it. To own it once more.

"Maybe one day I'll come inside, Cheyenne. But not tonight." He curled his hand into a fist as if to stop himself from touching me, and he quickly walked across the driveway, heading home.

I watched him stop at the edge of the forest. He didn't move for a few minutes, and I knew why he hesitated. He had never been one to walk out here alone. His mother had raised him to know better.

Finally, coming to the decision I knew he'd make, he changed directions, heading toward the road rather than cutting through the trees.

I heard the noisy sound of his footsteps fade as he walked away from me. Somewhere, in the opposite direction, another twig snapped, and I could hear movement as something made its way through the woods. I hurried inside and locked the door.

And sprinkled salt across the doorway, to be on the safe side.

CHAPTER

10

—Cheyenne—

"WHAT THE HELL?" I groaned, sitting up in bed. I got up and looked out the window to see an old pickup truck idling in the driveway.

I grabbed my phone to check the time. "Well, shit." It was already after eleven. I had slept the morning away. It hadn't been that late when I got home—only a little after midnight—but I hadn't been able to go to sleep. I blamed Jack and Natalie's spooky stories. Even if they were a load of crap.

I had spent hours scrolling through Reddit pages on the Blue Cliff child murders, and speculation was rife. It seemed our town had attracted an active and vocal community of amateur true-crime enthusiasts who gleefully combed through every tiny detail. And it seemed my opinion—that whoever killed Michael, Livvie, and Danielle had also taken Dakota—was generally believed by those who *didn't* live in our podunk town.

truecrimemaven—6h
The kid is dead. It's only a matter of time until he's found. If I were under the age of twelve, I'd be asking my parents to move out of that town and fast.

blastfromthepast97—6h

What's up with that place? I did a little digging, and kids have been going missing there for like a hundred years. Why isn't the FBI up in that shit? Who knows? Maybe the whole town is killing these kids and covering it up. Everyone is a suspect.

Spending the night deep in the dark recesses of conspiracy theory sub-Reddits led to a very intense nightmare. It seemed all mixed up with the memories Jack and Natalie shared.

I wanted to tell myself they were only nightmares. Nothing to read into. But it was becoming harder and harder to do that. Especially after hearing about Nat and Jack's creepy recollections—they seemed convinced were real. It was difficult to explain away something that was starting to feel inexplicable.

But could childhood memories be considered accurate? They were all mixed up with imaginings and memories of memories. It would be easy to excuse away the things Natalie and Jack shared last night as the hazy remembrance of half-truths and exaggerated reality. But the echoes of my latest nightmare wouldn't let me do that.

Last night, the dream had begun the same way it always did. Me, alone in the woods. Waiting and waiting. My face was wet and I couldn't breathe. Only this time it had ended differently.

This time, *he* came. The Hickory Man. I could only see the outline, but I knew it was him. He was so big. He was all I could see. As he walked closer, I felt myself start to shake in fear. And right before I woke up, he grabbed me. His skin was hot like fire against mine.

With heavy feet, I picked up a change of clothes and headed to the bathroom. I quickly showered in an attempt to feel human again. I got dressed and went to the kitchen in search of my mother. I wasn't surprised she was nowhere to be found.

I put on my coat and went outside to see who was here. The truck had been turned off, and I heard the low murmur of voices coming from around the side of the house. I found my mom and a man kneeling on the ground, digging holes along the foundation of the house.

"Good morning," I called out.

Mom didn't look up—not that I expected her to. When she was in the middle of something, it took an act of God to break her concentration. "Hand me the bones," I heard her say, holding out her hand to the man by her side.

What was she doing now?

The man looked up as I approached, his weathered face breaking into a kind smile. "There's my girl."

I couldn't help but smile back. A real one. "Uncle Donnie!" The giant bear of a man stood up, wiping his hands on his blue jeans and wrapped his tree trunk arms around me in a protective hug.

After a while, he pulled back and looked down into my face. He looked the exact same as I remembered. "You've grown into a fine young woman. You take after your mom." He gave me a chuck under the chin.

"What are you two doing out here in the freezing cold?" I asked.

Chief Hickman handed me a cloth sack. I looked inside to find dozens of small, bleached bones. "What the hell?"

"Your mom's buryin' them at the foundation. Good for protection. She thinks you could use a little extra dose of the stuff, and I agree with her."

I should have known it was something kooky like that. It was on the tip of my tongue to ask what kind of bones they were, but I thought better of it. I really didn't want to know.

"We're almost done here. Just have to go along the rest of this wall. You can help with the binding if you want," Mom offered.

"I'm fine, thanks. I'll watch."

Mom frowned but didn't say anything else. Chief Hickman knelt back down beside her and said something to her, too low for me to hear. She laughed, giving him a playful swat on the arm. Was my mom flirting with the chief? I noticed how close they were. How he'd cup her hand and place the bones in her palm, holding on for a few seconds. Was there something going on between them?

He and my mother had been friends their whole lives, and as such he was a frequent visitor to Ashby Woods. After my dad took off to parts unknown, it was big-hearted Uncle Donnie who had taught me how to ride a bike and shoot a gun. He changed the oil in Mom's car and cleaned the gutters in the spring.

He always made time for me and seemed to like it when I went to him for help with everything from algebra to building a volcano for the science fair.

As I got older, his kindness had never waned. He was like a father to me in a lot of ways, but without the expectation and judgment that came so readily from my mom. That was why when he called me only days after I'd left Blue Cliff, I had taken the call—and had spoken to him on a semi-regular basis ever since. He had an avid interest in my life, though I knew he was simply biding his time until I came home. He, like everyone else, believed my place was here. In the woods.

The talk around town was he'd been in love with my mother since they were kids. That they had dated in high school, and everyone had thought they were going to get married. But then my mom met my dad, who wasn't from Blue Cliff. Tom Jenkins was a stranger, staying in one of the cabins in the mountains on a hunting trip. He'd met Mom at Salty's, back when she worked there as a waitress. I didn't

know much about my dad—and remembered even less—
only that he had hated Blue Cliff. So much that he left in
the middle of the night when I was four years old, and we
never heard from him again.

Chief Hickman had never married, and everyone speculated it was because he carried a torch for Mom. Which
was more than a little sad.

It wasn't the first time I had seen him since being back
in Blue Cliff. He had come by only a few days after I arrived.
A quick visit while Mom was out in the woods.

* * *

*"I wanted to stop by and make sure everything is okay with you
out here," he had said with his wide, contagious smile.*

*I assured him all was fine. I noticed the way he scanned the
house, taking it all in, as if looking for something. As if making
sure it was all the way it should be.*

*His radio had crackled, and I heard someone call him.
"I'll be back out soon to check on my girls," Chief Hickman
assured me with a pat on the cheek before leaving.*

* * *

So I wasn't surprised to see him. And I wasn't surprised to
find him with Mom, helping her with her ghoulish task.

He never openly admitted to believing the superstitions
Mom clung to, but you didn't have to completely buy into
it all to go through the motions. There were people who
might not believe in chanting at the full moon but would
still come out to Ashby Woods for one of Mom's teas to help
cure a cough or increase fertility.

If you lived here long enough, the mountains made
believers of even the most jaded folk.

When they were finished, Chief Hickman helped Mom
to her feet, smoothing a stray hair back from her face. It
warmed my heart to see her smiling like that.

"Would you like some of my winterberry tea? It'll boost your immune system. You're not the spring chicken you used to be—you have to look after yourself," Mom scolded teasingly.

Chief Hickman inclined his head respectfully. "I'd never say no to anything you offer, Connie."

I cleared my throat, and the two of them broke apart.

"Come on, Chey, let's get the chief some tea and cookies. The two of you can catch up. Go sit down by the fire. I'll only be a few minutes." Mom shooed Chief Hickman into the living room once we were inside.

"Do you need any help?" I asked, starting to follow her.

"No, you keep our guest company." She gave Chief Hickman another sweet smile.

I sat down in the armchair opposite the chief. He loosened the laces of his boots, taking them off and putting them next to the log stove to dry out. I watched him pick up a poker and prod the flames to get them going again. He situated himself comfortably in the chair, with the familiarity of a man who had done this a thousand times before.

He pulled a metal Altoid container from his shirt pocket and took out a mint. He offered me one, but I declined. I had always hated the strong mints the chief preferred. The smell made me faintly sick to my stomach. He popped it in his mouth, sucking loudly.

"It's good to have you here, Chey. I've missed you." I felt the usual flash of defensive guilt, but it faded quickly. He was only being nice.

"Thanks, Uncle Donnie. I've missed you too. Though I have to say it's more than a little strange being back."

Chief Hickman leaned forward and put his hand on mine, giving it a squeeze. "You belong here, Cheyenne. You're an Ashby. Sometimes we feel like runnin'. Lord knows I've had the inclination a time or two. But the thing about Blue Cliff is that it stays inside you. You can't run from home for too long. Especially when you're needed." He glanced back toward the kitchen, where Mom could be heard tinkering around. "Your mom's a strong woman, but it's not good for her to be out here in the woods all by herself. Isolation does bad things to a person. And it's been hard for her. I've tried to do what I can, but like I told you when I called, I can't be here as much as I used to, what with everything going on in town."

I stared at the back of his large hand holding mine, noting the faded but still shiny scars in the shape of circles that dotted his skin. They trailed up his arms, disappearing beneath the cuffs of his shirtsleeves.

I didn't know exactly how he'd gotten them, but I remembered my mom telling me a bit about the chief she'd known as a child.

*   *   *

"He was always so much smaller than everyone else. Quiet too. Kept to himself. I hated how the other kids made fun of him because his shoes didn't fit and he never washed his hair," my mom said sadly. I was fifteen at the time and knew all too well how cruel kids could be.

"As if they had any room to talk. Half of our classmates worked on their family farms and came to school in dirty clothes. But there was something about Donnie that made him a target."

"It all worked out though. Look at Uncle Donnie now. There's nothing puny about him anymore. And now he's the chief," I pointed out.

Mom's face was troubled. *"Yes, I suppose it did. I think it shocked a lot of people when he joined the police force. No one expected him to make much of himself. Especially not after his mother died when he was a baby. He only had his father, and Rob Hickman was a mean, no-good drunk."* She winced at the memory before continuing. *"His dad hurt him. A lot. Donnie never told me, but I saw the burns. I saw the bruises . . . we all did. But no one did anything. The older people turned the other way and pretended they didn't see that this boy, one of our own, needed help. 'Round here, you don't go gettin' yourself involved in other people's business."*

She was right, of course. People tended to turn the other way to things that didn't directly involve them. The old term "sweep in front of your own door" came to mind. It still shocked me though. Uncle Donnie had only been a child, and he had needed help, yet no one had done anything.

Mom's expression turned to disgust. "It's one of the few times I felt ashamed of my town—of the people in it. We're supposed to look after each other, to keep each other safe, but we failed Donald Hickman. My father was the only one who looked after him. Your grandpa kept an eye on him when no one else did."

"Maybe that's why Uncle Donnie became a police officer. To protect others because he hadn't been protected himself," I wondered aloud.

Mom's smile was tinged with regret and more than a little bit of sorrow. "I think you're right, Chey. Sometimes the people who were let down the most in life go on to do amazing things. He turned things around and showed Blue Cliff he was someone worth saving."

*   *   *

Chief Hickman patted my hand. "She needs you, Cheyenne. Don't let her try and tell you otherwise."

Knowing what I did about his childhood made his decency toward my mother, and the rest of the town, even more awe inspiring.

"It means a lot that you look after her the way you do."

Chief Hickman smiled a secret smile and bowed his head slightly. "I've always had a soft spot for your mom. She's special to me. Real special. She was my girl, you know. Back when we were teenagers. I thought we'd grow old together. But things didn't work out the way they should have." His face darkened slightly before he forced a smile back on his face. "But the past is the past, and I'm here now."

"I'm glad she has you, Uncle Donnie."

"She'll always have me. You too, Chey. You're important to me." Chief Hickman's face turned sad. "She's not takin' care of herself. Hasn't really for some time. When the Mason boy went missin', she started actin' real strange. I'd find her out on the road, headin' into town without her shoes. She showed up at the vigil for Dakota, cryin' and wailin' about the Hickory Man. It took myself and two of my deputies to get her home."

The chief's face contorted with worry. "I've done what I can, but I'm not you, Cheyenne. I'm not kin. She needs her flesh and blood. But you're here now. She's always better when you're around. We all are. That's why I called you. I knew you'd come home if you heard how your mom needed you. If you understood how bad off she was. You're a good girl, Chey. In the end, you always do the right thing."

"I'm not sure what I can do. She seems so frantic. It's like last time. Sometimes she's lost in her own world, talking about things that don't make sense. She keeps telling me he's back and that Dakota won't be the last one taken." I closed my eyes briefly, feeling overwhelmed.

Chief Hickman appeared stricken, but not shocked. "She said the same to me. You can't blame her for thinkin' the way she does, though. She was raised to believe she had a special purpose. That your whole family does. Her pa, Charlie, was a hard man. A good man, but tough. He expected her to be dutiful and obedient. You know her pa made her sleep in the forest for days. No food. No water. She was meant to face the Hickory Man and 'introduce herself' to him. She was five years old."

"I didn't know that. Mom talked about Grandpa Charlie, but only the good things, like how he helped deliver the Swanson twins in the middle of winter, saving their lives when they developed jaundice and no one could get through the snow to the hospital. Or how he helped to rebuild the library after part of it burned down," I recounted.

"Your grandpa was a force, that's for sure. And what your mom lived through out here, with her parents, made her think . . . *differently*. And now with Dakota gone, she's gettin' more upset, and her thinkin' is slipping to those old ways. She came into town a few months back covered in blood. She never would say where it came from. I can only assume some sort of animal. But people were talkin.'" He clasped his hands together in front of him.

This wasn't good.

"You need to watch her. Watch her closely, Chey. I'm not sure what she's doin' out there in the woods," Chief Hickman said softly.

His words chilled me.

"What are you two old ladies gossiping about?" Mom reappeared with a tray of cookies and a steaming pot of tea. I could smell the rich sweetness of the berries.

"Chey was just filling me in on things." The chief's eyes crinkled at the edges as he smiled.

My mom sat down, putting the tray on the coffee table. She looked at him, her eyes suddenly hardening. "You shouldn't be sitting in that chair. That's Tom's spot."

My stomach flipped. "Mom, it's okay—"

"Don, you know Tom made that with his own hands. He worked so hard on it. He comes in and takes off his shoes"—her eyes drifted to where the chief's boots rested by the stove—"and I make him some tea. He says it's his favorite place in the world." Her face twisted with sadness. She was doing it again. Talking about my dad as if he were going to walk through the front door and kick Chief Hickman out of his special chair.

I chanced a look at the chief. His face had gone unnaturally blank, a tic noticeable in his jaw, as if he were clenching his teeth. But after a brief, tense moment, he reached out and took my mother's hand. "I don't think he's comin' back to claim his seat, Connie," he said softly.

Mom's lips trembled slightly, and I watched as she struggled not to cry.

"Can I have some tea, Mom?" I asked a little too loudly.

Mom blinked as if waking up. She looked down at the large hand holding hers and patted it absently. "Of course." She started to pour tea in the cups and passed them around. I noticed that her hands trembled slightly.

Chief Hickman lifted my mom's hand to his mouth, kissing it tenderly. "This is the best tea you've ever made, Connie."

"You say that every time, Donald Hickman." Mom laughed. Things went back to some semblance of normality after that.

But I couldn't stop thinking about my mom's strange episode about my dad. And more importantly what Chief Hickman had said about her wandering into town covered in blood. About how quickly she was deteriorating now that Dakota was missing.

I didn't say much during the rest of his visit. He and my mother seemed engrossed in each other. They talked of stories and events that I didn't know about.

An hour later, Chief Hickman cupped her face in a loving gesture. "I've got to get goin', Connie. Thank you so much for the tea and cookies. It's your fault my waistline is growin'."

Mom blushed—yes, she actually blushed—and patted his leg with affection. "You're still as handsome as you were at sixteen, Donnie."

Chief Hickman got to his feet, pulling his keys from his pocket.

I quickly stood up. "Let me walk you out."

"Sure, that would be nice." He put his hand on the small of my back and beckoned me to go ahead of him to the front door. I went outside and waited for him and my mom to say their goodbyes in private. A few minutes later he appeared, zipping up his fleece-lined jacket.

"This is nice of you, Chey, walkin' an old man to his car," he joked.

"Wanted to make sure you don't fall and break a hip," I teased, and we both laughed. "How are things around town?"

"Aside from the Dakota situation, there hasn't been much to write about. Though I've had a few calls about Ed and Linda's son. People findin' him outside their houses. If you see him hangin' around, let me know. Seems jail didn't teach him anything."

I frowned. "Mom says she's seen him out in the woods. I saw him a few days ago. He's always been a creep."

"I hate it for Ed. He tried hard with that boy. Tried to bring him up right. But sometimes an apple is born rotten." The chief sucked on a mint noisily. "But people are more forgivin' when it's one of our own."

Seeing an opening, I took it. "Actually, I did want to ask you something." Chief Hickman raised an eyebrow. "About this stuff with Jasper Clinton." The second his name left my mouth, the chief's entire demeanor changed.

"It's all an absolute load of shit," he barked, startling me with his sudden aggression.

"So you still think he did it? What about the evidence?" I asked.

He clenched his fists like he wanted to punch something— or someone. "It seems I have a snake in my midst. This so-called 'evidence' is a bunch of crap." His jaw was rigid, his eyes stony.

"But the DNA and the old tin and fabric found at the scene—"

"I don't know where that DNA came from. They can't match it to anyone in the system. Seems to me it's been planted. Someone has a lot to answer for. As for the other stuff supposedly found near them kids, it could have been left by anyone. That's why it didn't seem important at the time," he interrupted angrily.

"But could it be possible that someone else did it?" I should have backed off, but I trusted the chief to give it to me straight. At this point I didn't know what to believe.

"And who would have done it?" He peered at me closely. "Who, Cheyenne? Seems mighty strange that the moment he gets out, another of our kids goes missin'. You can't ignore the timing."

I swallowed. "But he never came back to town, right?" I rasped.

"Maybe he didn't. Or—" The chief looked out to the woods, looking thoughtful. "Or maybe he's been here all along. Who can say?"

"That doesn't make sense, though," I argued.

The chief frowned. "Look, Chey, those three kids were loved. Who but an outsider would hurt them?" he reasoned calmly. I wanted to share Chief Hickman's faith in our town. In the people who lived here. But I knew there was darkness at its heart. A blackness that oozed out when you scratched the surface.

Chief Donald Hickman always saw the best in people. It's why everyone loved him. But maybe this time he was being willfully blind. Was it possible he was purposefully looking in the wrong direction?

"What do you think happened to Dakota?"

Chief Hickman looked out to the forest again, his expression unreadable. His eyes fixed on something only he could see.

"Time will tell," was all he said.

"Do you think his disappearance is connected to the other three?"

His focus turned to me, and he placed a heavy hand on my shoulder. I could smell the mint on his breath. "Don't you worry about it. These are questions for the authorities, and I promise you, I'll always take care of you. And this town. I won't make the same mistakes this time." He smiled and I felt a little relief.

He squeezed my shoulder, then got in his truck and drove off into the woods.

CHAPTER

11

—Natalie—

M Y HAND SHOOK as I gripped my full coffee mug. I
stared around the small living room, thinking how
much bigger it seemed this morning. I was used to Hunter
being there. His shoes under the coffee table. His jacket slung
over the kitchen stool. His presence had filled up my home.
But this morning, it was only me and last night's argument.

I was still unsure as to what I was going to do. I understood Hunter's distress, and even his anger. Jasper's getting
out of jail made it feel as if his brother had no justice. But
the things he had said to me—they weren't the flippant
rantings of a hurting man.

I decided the only way I was going to get some answers
was to speak to Hunter directly. I fished my phone from my
purse and called him. After several rings, it went to voicemail. I closed my eyes in frustration.

"Hey, Hunter, it's Natalie. If you can give me a call
when you get this, I'd really like to talk." I went to hang up
but changed my mind at the last second and put the phone
back to my ear. "I know how hard all this must be for you.
But I'm here for you. Whatever you need."

After I hung up, I felt restless. I needed to fix this. As much as his words had stung last night, I was trying to be understanding. I knew I didn't deserve what he had said, but he was in pain. It was easier to forgive when you remembered what his family had been through.

After showering and dressing, I decided to take the bull by the horns and head over to his house. If he wouldn't talk to me on the phone, then he'd have to speak to me face to face. I gave Jamie a quick call to tell her I wasn't coming in today. I felt guilty at how many times I had been leaving Jamie to manage the store recently, but I couldn't worry about that now. I grabbed my purse and left before I changed my mind.

The drive was short, and the nerves had kicked in by the time I arrived at the Caruthers' home. Hunter and I never argued much. I was generally laid back, and he usually got his way because of that. I had been raised on the old adage *Great marriages don't happen by accident, but are small daily acts of intentionality.* I knew I had to put in the work to make Hunter happy, and in the past I had taken that job seriously. Now I was wondering if I had simply been wasting my time.

I knocked on the Caruthers' door and waited. When no one answered the door, I knocked again. I pulled out my phone and dialed Hunter's number in the hopes that he would pick up this time. But then I heard the distinctive ring of his phone coming from inside shortly before it cut to voicemail again. It was official: he was avoiding me. I swallowed my pride and knocked on the door again, more forcefully this time.

"Hello? Hunter?" I called.

Several minutes passed before the door finally swung open and Darla peered out at me, her expression sympathetic. "Good morning, Natalie. Sorry I didn't hear you knockin'. I hope you haven't been waitin' out here long.

Come in." She ushered me inside quickly, her eyes not quite meeting mine.

"Hi, Darla. Can you tell me where he is?" I asked, getting straight to the point.

"He's talkin' to his pa right now. Let me fix you some coffee and warm you up." She started to steer me through to the kitchen. I moved away from her.

"I need to speak to Hunter, Darla. Are they in Chase's office?" I saw her discomfort as she nodded. I headed in that direction, feeling nauseous.

Outside the door I could hear Hunter and his father talking. Their voices were raised, though they didn't sound as if they were arguing. I knew that they weren't going to be happy about me interrupting them. Nevertheless, I raised my hand and knocked on the door, alerting them to my presence, before turning the handle and pushing the door open.

Chase and Hunter sat in leather high-back chairs facing one another, their expressions fraught. They looked up when I entered, Chase's eyes shadowed in annoyance.

"Natalie, what the hell?" Hunter barked with a scowl. "What are you doing here?"

All of my blustered bravado and righteous anger dissipated by the look of displeasure he gave me. My mouth felt dry. I stared blankly at him as I tried to quickly gather my thoughts. He looked like a mess. His eyes were ringed with dark circles. His skin was chalky white. I noticed black smudges across his forehead and cheeks.

Hunter stood up, throwing a look to his father that I couldn't read before approaching me. "You need to leave. Now." He gripped my arm and attempted to yank me through the door. The stench of alcohol and something acrid made my nose burn. He smelled as if he had been standing next to a bonfire all night. I extracted myself from his grip.

"And I think we should talk." I stuck my chin out, affecting a confidence I definitely didn't feel.

"So you said in your voicemail," he mumbled under his breath.

"You *did* listen to my message, then." It wasn't a question. I tried to settle my jangled insides. I attempted to take his hand, but he purposefully avoided my touch. "I know last night got heated, Hunter, but we need to talk about what happened. What I said and what you said."

I was mindful that Chase was within earshot, so I tried to keep my voice low.

"I need some space right now, Natalie. My family has to come first." He stared at a spot over my shoulder, refusing to meet my eyes.

His words were a punch to the gut. "I thought I was your family too," I breathed, trying to keep the tremor from my voice. He knew exactly where to stick the knife for maximum carnage. "Hunter—"

"Oh, for God's sake," Chase snapped. "Hunter, we have more important things to deal with right now than your girlfriend's hurt feelings."

"I'm his fiancée!" I wanted the words to be angry, but they came out shaky and emotional.

"Nat, I'll call you later." Hunter looked tired, and I started to feel sorry for him once more. But then I reminded myself that he was shutting me out—again—and the sympathy turned rancid in my stomach. "Dad's right. We're busy, and I can't deal with your drama now."

"My *drama*?" I blinked up at him, hardly able to believe what I was hearing. I couldn't understand how a drunken disagreement had turned into something potentially relationship ending.

This time I let Hunter lead me out, still too stunned by Hunter's cold dismissal to put up a fight. At the front door, Hunter still wouldn't meet my eyes. I found myself

struggling to hold back angry tears. I was close to breaking my mother's cardinal rule of not letting anyone see me
cry. Hunter may have been a chauvinistic jerk at times,
but he had never treated me like this—with such open
hostility.

"Hunter." I said his name quietly. When he looked
down into my face, he seemed impatient and eager to be
rid of me. But I needed to try one last time to make things
right. "I don't know what I've done to deserve this, but
maybe we can figure things out together—"

Hunter laughed humorlessly, cutting me off.

"What?" My voice was thready, my throat thick with
tears. "We had a fight. A disagreement. Why is this blowing
up into—"

"Because you're part of the problem, Nat! And I don't
want it in my life," he spat out. I took his hand, and I noticed
him wincing when I gripped it. He shook me off, trying to
hide red, angry skin covered in oozing blisters. It looked as
if he had held his hand over an open flame.

"Oh my God, Hunter, what happened? Are you okay?"
I gasped.

"I'm fine, no thanks to you."

I felt like I had been physically slapped.

"What does your hand have to do with me?" I demanded.

"It's you *and* Cheyenne. And the people like you who
think that a child murderer being released from prison is
any kind of *justice*." I recoiled from his fury.

"Hunter, that's not what Chey was saying. That's not
what *any* of us were saying." I reached for him again, but he
stepped away. "If you'd only listen—"

"Jasper killed Mikey and now he's walking free. And
what happens when he kills again, huh? What about
Dakota? What about all the other kids? I had to do something." He looked down at his blistered hand, his mouth
becoming a thin, angry line.

My head started buzzing with misgivings. There was a determination on Hunter's face that I only ever saw when he would psych himself up before a football game. Hunter was a man who would do whatever it took to get the job done. I used to find his "can't fail" attitude charming, but now it scared me.

"What do you mean, Hunter? What did you do?" I asked warily.

"Nothing you need to worry about, Nat. You don't need to worry about anything I do ever again." His words were clipped, cold, and final. He opened the front door and didn't say another word, his intentions clear.

He wanted me to leave because we were over.

I walked out onto the porch. I turned back to say one final thing, but he slammed the door in my face. I stood in shock, both horrified and embarrassed. Had Darla seen? The thought of our breakup being observed mortified me. I stumbled down the steps, barely aware of the cold on my cheeks.

Back in my car, I wiped away the tears that had escaped. Hunter and I had been together since high school. We'd gone through a lot, and I couldn't quite fathom that we were done.

I began to drive, unsure of where I was going. Hunter was all I knew. All I'd ever really known. Yet, as I drove, I recognized a strange sort of relief. We'd put our entire lives on hold since Mikey's murder, and we hadn't moved forward since. I may have a thriving business, but where our relationship was concerned, we were stuck. Hunter still lived at home with his parents. We hadn't gotten married like we'd wanted. We hadn't started a family.

When I thought about it, *really* thought about it, we were practically the same couple we had been in high school.

I wanted to be angry at Cheyenne. I wanted to blame her for everything that had happened. After all, the problems had started when she'd come back to town. It made a sort of convoluted sense to lay the fault at her feet. But I knew this wasn't on her.

This was all Hunter.

And his father.

And his mother.

It was their history and everything in between.

And maybe it was my fault too. For being the type of woman who accepted being a second-class citizen in her own relationship. A woman who swallowed her thoughts and feelings to make others feel better.

Even as I tried to hold it together, I couldn't help letting out a sob. Soon, I could barely see clearly through the blinding tears. I quickly pulled off to the side of the road to get control of myself, pain and resentment flowing through me. I sat there, being assailed by the memory of Chase's dismissiveness. Hunter's angry eyes. Darla's sympathetic smile.

I was embarrassed, angry, and hurt by all of them.

When I finally got a hold of myself again, I realized that I was at the edge of Ashby Woods, as if instinct had brought me there. Sure, I had been in the woods since Chey left, mostly to check on Constance, but I had otherwise kept away. Now having her back in town had made me remember how this was the place I gravitated to when I needed comfort. And somehow I'd driven there without knowing where I was headed.

In my darkest hour, my subconscious had taken me home.

*   *   *

"Kids, you have to be careful out here. Don't go farther than the rocks. That's where the protection ring ends."

Constance Ashby continued down the steps, past where Chey, Jack, and I were sitting. As usual, she carried her hand-woven basket over one arm. It was as much a part of her as her hands and feet. She'd told me once it was made of the same hickory that grew in the forest. That her grandma Lydia had made it, and had passed it down to her daughter, Maud, Constance's mother, who then gave it to Constance. She let me look at it sometimes, pointing out the knots and twists, telling me they were to ward off the evil eye.

"Okay, Mom," Chey had groaned.

"What do we need protecting from?" I'd asked innocently. I'd heard stories of the Hickory Man all my life, and I knew that most people thought Constance was a witch. Or at least, that's what the kids at school said because she was always carrying weird herbs and rocks with her. But Jack and I didn't believe she was a witch—or if she was, she was a good one. She'd only ever been nice to us, and we'd never felt anything but safe at her home.

Chey rolled her eyes and I guessed she was mad at me for asking. Chey loved her ma, but she knew she was weird. I guess there was a difference between weird and cool when it was your ma and not someone else's. Because I definitely thought Constance was cool.

Constance stopped and frowned. Her hair was long and braided down her back. She tucked some stray hair behind her ears as she came closer.

"The woods are always watching. You're protected here, I've made sure of that, but he's always watching and waiting, and you never can be too careful when it comes to him. The three of you tempt him, and it's best to keep away."

"Okay, Mom, we got it," Chey said impatiently. "We won't go past the rocks. We'll stay right here."

Her ma started to turn away, but Jack asked another question.

"Ms. Ashby, ma'am, if you don't mind my asking, but how do you know all this stuff?"

Chey groaned again and elbowed Jack in the side, but he ignored her, as did I. Because I wanted to hear what she had to say, too. My ma only ever talked about keeping clean and not

making a mess. And Jack's ma was nice, but all she did was bake
pies and talk about the farm. They were both ordinary mothers
doing ordinary things. Not like Chey's ma. She was different.

"Well, Jack, my ancestors were some of the first settlers of
Blue Cliff. My family has been on this land for generations, so
we know all about the secrets of the woods."

I stared in awe at this marvelous woman, my jaw slack.

"Natalie Bartlett, you'll go catching flies if you're not careful," she laughed, and I quickly shut my mouth.

"Sorry, ma'am." I blushed.

It was the height of summer, and gnats swarmed in the
shade of the trees. A buzzing and chirping was the backdrop to
everything. The pine and earthy scent of the forest floor filled
the air. I wiped away the sweat from my forehead as Constance
reached into her basket and pulled out a little cloth bag filled
with herbs. She handed one to me and one to Jack, who didn't
seem to know what to do with it. I brought the bundle to my
nose, inhaling deeply.

"What do you know about the Hickory Man?" I asked,
still curious.

Constance froze, her face scrunching up as if she were in
pain. She crouched down in front of me.

"Don't you go sayin' his name like it's nothin' to be scared
of," she scolded, her tone curt. But she didn't shout at me like
my ma would have done.

"I'm sorry," I said quickly.

"Mom . . ." Cheyenne whined.

"I'm not cross with you, but you can't go throwin' around a
name like that. He is not someone you ever want to meet." She
looked thoughtful before sitting down on the step below us. "Do
you know about the first settlers?" We all nodded our heads. Of
course we knew the old stories. You couldn't live in Blue Cliff
and not hear all about how it was settled. Locals took a lot of
pride in being able to trace their families back to the beginning.
But something told us that's not what she was asking.

"But do you know the real story?" Constance asked, peering at us.

"What real story?" Jack frowned.

Constance was quiet for a bit and looked out toward the tree line before continuing. "When the first settlers came here, there were no houses and no streets, and there were no schools . . ."

"Yes!" The three of us cheered, and Constance smiled.

"There wasn't much of anything back then. The old town, the one out at the holler, was built by my ancestors' hands. Your ancestors too." She inclined her head to Jack and me. "They were good people. They looked after one another, but times were tough. Food was scarce and people were dying. Their struggles felt almost like a punishment. As if they had angered something, or someone, by being here. Something had to be done, or they wouldn't survive."

"They must have survived, because here we are," Jack pointed out.

Constance's smile was funny. "Yes, Jackson, here we are." She looked out to the trees again. "That first awful winter, some children went missing. Two little girls, much like yourselves, and then a while later a little boy, like you Jack. No one knew where they had gone, but the forests were vast, and most assumed that they had wandered into them and gotten lost. As winter thawed and spring came, their bodies were finally discovered. They were lined up next to one another, and in their pockets they had coins, and in their shoes there was dirt."

I gasped and looked at my friends, who were both just as interested.

"Like in the nursery rhyme!" I exclaimed, and she nodded. "Keep silver in your pockets, walk with dirt in your shoes, or he'll poke your eyeballs from their sockets, and boil your bones in stew."

Cheyenne, Jack and I laughed because we'd heard the song a thousand times.

"Yes, like in the nursery rhyme," Constance said before continuing. "Well, Brockett Ashby was a long-ago ancestor of mine. And his mama, Eleanor Ashby, had a dream about a being that lived in the woods. An evil being that was as old as the rock and as terrifying as a storm. It was a demon sent straight from the devil. She warned the other settlers that they had to be mindful, that they would never sleep easy as long as this force remained. And everyone listened. Eleanor's dreams were well known because she saw things and predicted things that no one could explain. She said that the monster would destroy all they had built unless he was given the blood of the youngest fruit."

Constance let her words hang in the air for a few seconds before going on. "The people of Blue Cliff were a spiritual group. Godly, yes, but they knew to respect nature. They believed in its power. Back then it was easier to believe in things without logical explanations. But you had to be careful. Brockett's mama knew this. Back then, people hung women who saw things. Remember what happened in Salem," she stated matter-of-factly.

"Can we go play now, Mom?" Cheyenne asked abruptly. As usual, she was embarrassed by all this talk, though I couldn't understand why. I loved hearing the old stories. I loved being surrounded by all the pretend magic. I loved Constance and her free-living ways. My ma was uptight all the time and full of rules. But here, in the woods, anything felt possible.

The spell was broken and Constance smiled. "Yes, of course you can. Just stay on this side of the rocks." She picked up her basket and put it over her arm, pausing briefly before pulling out a handful of silver coins and giving them to each of us.

"Keep these tucked in your pocket at all times, ya hear me?"

"Yes, ma'am," Jack and I said in unison. "What did your ancestor mean when he said he needed the blood of the youngest fruit?" Jack piped up before she could leave.

Constance's expression darkened, and she looked away. "Never you mind that. You three go play. I have things to be doin'."

The coins were cold in my hand, and I quickly tucked them in my pocket.

"You don't have to keep those, ya know," Chey said to Jack and me. "She doesn't know what she's talking about. You guys have heard what everyone says about her."

I looked at Cheyenne, but she was watching her ma disappear into the woods.

"Want to play tag?" I laughed, and she finally grinned. Jack chased us around, making sure to stay close to the house, the silver coins jingling in our pockets.

*   *   *

I reached over and opened my glovebox, feeling around inside until I found the small bag of herbs. I pulled it out and sniffed it. The scent had faded over the years, but I could still get hints of what had been tucked inside. Only now it wasn't just a bag full of plants; it was the scent of cedar chips and rosemary and, very vaguely, cinnamon. I knew these herbs now, what they meant. And unlike when I'd been a child, I realized their importance.

But now I knew the difference between fairy tales and real life. Yet despite this—despite knowing it was ridiculous to still believe in the Hickory Man and the strange goings on in Ashby Woods—I couldn't help but feel safer with the little bag with me at all times.

Feeling I had lingered too long, I started the car back up and put it in gear. From my peripheral vision, something moved and I turned to catch it, but all I saw was the back of someone with light hair disappearing from sight. Even after the person was gone, I still felt as if I were being watched. It was a familiar sensation, but not one I ever grew comfortable with. With the herbs in my fist, I drove home. Far away from the hidden eyes that followed me.

12

—Cheyenne—

"F**ANCY MEETING YOU** here," Jackson greeted me. I had come out of the woods at the edge of the Campbell farm. I hadn't expected to see Jack there, his faded blue pickup parked in the middle of the field. "I needed to stretch my legs," I told him, stopping to watch him nail planks of wood to the fence panel that had obviously come down with the heavy snow.

"Out walking in the woods alone is never a good idea, remember?" He raised an eyebrow, and I rolled my eyes. There was a definite tension between us now. An anticipation that was both exciting and frustrating. The other night, when he had dropped me at home, I had known that he wanted me, and I felt it now as well. We regarded each other with an awareness that only came from knowing and desiring someone in a deep and profound way. He had been my first in all things, and I felt it every time we looked at each other. It was an attraction that seemed to burn brighter than ever before.

"You and Nat sure got yourselves worked up on the drive home." I tucked my hands into my coat pockets.

"We know to take care out in those woods, is all. You've been gone too long, Chey. You seemed to have forgotten how things are around here." I couldn't tell if he was trying to tease me or this was a passive-aggressive attack. Jack stopped briefly and wiped the back of his hand along his brow, leaving a streak of dirt. "I saw your mom walking along the road earlier, heading into town." He inclined his head in the direction he'd said she'd gone.

"Really?" I frowned, wondering what she was up to this time. "I got up this morning to make her breakfast, but she had already left." I let out a frustrated sigh. "I came home to help her out, but she's never home for me to do anything." I didn't like the idea of her wandering off. After my conversation with Chief Hickman, my worries about Mom were stronger than ever.

"I'm not sure, but she looked like she was on a mission. I said hello, but I don't think she heard me. You know how your mom gets when she's focused on something." Jack lifted his hammer and brought it down again, his body vibrating from the impact.

I watched him work for a few more minutes before asking a question that had been eating at me. "Do you remember my dad at all?"

Jack looked surprised by my seemingly random question. I had never really talked about my missing-in-action father. He wasn't a part of my life, and I had never questioned his absence. It wasn't hard to understand that outsiders simply couldn't hack a life in a closed-off community like Blue Cliff.

But my mother's increasingly erratic behavior had me wondering more about the father I had never known. Wondering if he was out there somewhere wondering about me.

"A little bit. Not much. Dad would stop and talk to him when we'd walk through the woods by your house. Always

THE WOODS ARE WAITING 159

said he was a decent man. You know, for an outta-towner," Jack told me.

"All I can see in my mind is this blue shirt he always wore and a ring on his right hand. Mom told me it was his class ring. It had an eagle embossed on a yellow stone. It's weird, I don't know much about him. Only the stuff Mom's accidentally shared over the years. Hell, we don't even share a last name. Mom would only say that we were Ashbys when I asked about it, as if that explained things. I guess he was okay with it, but who knows." I frowned.

"What's with all the questions about your dad?" Jack looked concerned.

"No reason. Just that Mom sometimes acts like he's still around."

"Like a ghost?"

I shrugged. "I don't know. I always thought it was strange how she spoke about him like that. Not like a woman scorned, but a woman still in love."

"Denial is a powerful thing. Maybe she's never gotten over him. When you really love someone, not even time can erase those feelings." Jack's eyes found mine, and I felt my cheeks heat up and my heart pound.

"Jack—"

He dropped the hammer beside the post. "I need to go find more wood to make some stakes for the fence," he said without preamble, his voice rough. He lifted his old Radio Flyer wagon from the bed of his truck and put it on the ground.

"Oh, um, I can come with you if you'd like the company," I offered.

"Sure," he responded, his voice tight. He opened the passenger side door, pulled a small handheld ax from beneath the seat, and laid it in the wagon. He pulled it along behind him as he made his way toward the forest, pausing briefly to allow me to catch up.

"Stick with me, alright?" he remarked gruffly. "We'll stay on the paths."

As we walked side by side, Jack lifted his hand in a wave to someone on the road.

"Is that Otis?" I asked, trying to make out the figure in the distance. He moved quicker than I thought possible for a man his age. He darted off into the woods in the direction of my house. I felt a shiver of apprehension. I still couldn't work out his behavior the other night at Salty's. His comments about Dakota had set off alarm bells inside me, even though Natalie and Jack thought him to be harmless.

"Yeah. I see him comin' and goin' a few times a day. Never seems in a hurry to talk either."

"It's odd he's out here. Most people stay out of the woods if they can help it." I watched to see if he would emerge from the tree line, but he didn't.

"He used to be my scout leader when I was a kid. He probably knows the woods as well as your mom, so he spends a lot of time in them." Jack shrugged.

"But why is he out here *now*?" I went on, not letting it drop.

"I doubt it's anything sinister, Chey," he reasoned.

I hoped he was right. I tried to shake off my misgivings as we made our way into the woods.

"So, the chief told me that the DNA that was turned into the state was bullshit and that they all thought the other evidence found at the crime scene was most likely left by someone else—not the killer ." I watched Jack chop up a thick tree limb into pieces and put them in the wagon.

"Well, whoever turned over the evidence knew it was important. And a big question is who turned it over? Who wanted to get Jasper out of jail?" Jack pondered as we walked farther into the woods. I knew soon we'd be coming to the north fork of old Bobcat Creek. Jack, Nat, and I used to build forts in the dried-out creek bed when we were kids.

"I asked him if he thought the murders and Dakota's disappearance were connected, and he never really answered me. I got the feeling he didn't want to talk about it." I reached down and picked up a twig, snapping it in two.

Jack looked at me over his shoulder, his brow furrowed. "I'm sure he didn't. All of this makes him and the department look really bad. A court decided Jasper was innocent, and now they're looking into whether he purposely withheld evidence. Because if he got it wrong, then he failed to protect his town and let a killer roam free."

"So, who did it then, Jack? Who killed those kids? And who took Dakota?" I asked in a rush. "Everyone is in such a hurry to tar and feather Jasper that they haven't stopped to think about other possibilities."

Jack stopped and turned to face me. "Chey—"

"Because I can't be the only one who thinks it must have been someone from Blue Cliff. That it's someone we know. Someone those kids trusted. I've been wracking my brain, trying to think of who it could be. What about Otis? He works at the elementary school, doesn't he? That would give him access to all the kids. Or what about Ed and Linda's son, Reggie? I know he just got out of jail for peeping in windows. He's always been a creep. I could see him doing something to those kids. He was wandering around by my house the other day, and Mom says she's seen him out there a lot. And Chief Hickman says he's had complaints about him. So that's two guys acting really weird, if you ask me. Or maybe it's—"

"Hey, hey, take a breath." Jack stood close, looking down into my eyes. He cupped my cheek. "Thinkin' like that will drive you crazy."

"But we need to know who did it. We can't live with all these questions. I feel anxious every time I go into town. The kids are all scared to death, thinking they're next. And they should be scared. Because any one of them could be taken. There were three last time. There could be three again." I was having a hard time breathing.

"I get how you're feelin'. I really do." Jack wrapped his arms around me and pulled me toward him. He ran his hands up and down my back. "They'll find who's responsible. I trust the chief to get the right guy. Maybe it's Jasper, maybe not. But you can't spend all your time wondering which of our neighbors might be responsible. That's no way to live."

I pressed my forehead to his chest, breathing in the scent of him. I tucked my hands into his coat pockets to warm them, my fingers brushing against something rough. I pulled out the object, staring at the tiny corn husk doll.

"Let me guess—Mom brought this to you?" I raised an eyebrow.

Jack stepped away from me and took the poppet, quickly putting it back in his pocket. "I trust her when she says it'll keep me safe," he said, his voice hard, our moment officially over.

"But it's all a bunch of stupid superstitions," I challenged.

Jack picked up the wagon handle and started toward the creek bed. "It's not stupid to me. We all believe, and maybe you should too."

"Come on, Jack. We have to focus on what's going on, not some dumb . . ." My voice trailed off as we approached what had at one time been a rushing stream.

Jack's steps slowed, and I could hear his shallow breathing. He dropped the wagon handle, and it landed in the melting snow with a soft thud.

The air was quiet. No birds. No rustling of animals. Just an endless, empty nothingness.

I opened my mouth to say Jack's name, to get his attention, but my tongue felt thick.

A twig snapped somewhere close by, the sound making me jump.

The incline down into the dried creek bed was steep. I remembered Jack, Nat, and I scrambling up and down it when we were young. We'd pile sticks and leaves in haphazard structures, creating forts we'd spend hours in.

Another cracking sound. Then another.

Jack's breathing became raspy, and he blindly reached for my hand, holding on for dear life.

"Chey," Jack whispered, my name sounding like agony.

I took a step toward him, my foot kicking another small bundle just like the one Jack had hidden away in his pocket. I reached down to pick it up, my hand shaking.

"Chey," Jack said again, more urgently this time. "Look."

I didn't want to look. I wanted to shut my eyes.

"Look."

My vision blurred, my pulse pounding in my ears. The rough twine of the poppet dug into my hand, but I only held it tighter.

"Protect me from evil. Protect me from those of evil will."

The words wouldn't protect me from this. Nothing could.

Finally I lifted my eyes.

Jack and I stood side by side on the creek bank, staring down at the tiny figure spread out on the leaves and snow, eyes staring up to the sky above him. His blue plaid shirt buttoned up to the chin. His hands lay neatly beside him, palms upright, silver gleaming in the faded winter sunlight.

"Is that—?"

Jack squeezed my hand hard enough to break the bones. "It's Dakota Mason."

CHAPTER

13

—Cheyenne—

WE RUSHED BACK to the Campbell farm, Jack abandoning the wagon as we ran as fast as we could. We didn't talk about what we had seen. All we could do was *hurry*.

A pang of guilt filled me at leaving Dakota alone once more, but we came to an unspoken agreement that neither of us could bear to remain behind.

Dakota Mason was dead. And he had been for a while by the looks of it. We hadn't ventured close, but I could see the telltale signs of decay. His death hadn't been recent—though he clearly hadn't been left to the elements long; he was untouched by the recent rain and snow.

We ran up to the house, passing the barn where I could see Jack's dad, Paul, as well as Billy Miller and Thad Lewis, who had both worked at the farm since I was a kid. I followed Jack to the backdoor. He called out to his mom as he charged into the Campbells' kitchen.

His mother was sitting at the table, the newspaper spread out in front of her. She looked up in surprise as we entered. "Jack, honey, what's wrong?" Louise Campbell asked, taking in the sight of her son's pale face.

Jack picked his cell phone up from the counter. "I need to call 911. Chey and I found him. Out at the creek bed." He held the phone to his ear.

Louise looked at me, and her hand went to her throat. There was no time for a proper greeting.

Jack's dad rushed into the house, followed by Billy Miller. "What wrong, son?"

Jack was talking to the dispatcher so it was up to me to explain what we had seen.

"We found Dakota out there in the woods. He . . . he's dead." My words tripped over themselves.

"Oh no, please no!" Louise cried out.

"The police are on their way," Jack said a few seconds later, after hanging up. He turned to his parents.

Louise covered her mouth with her hand. "That poor, sweet boy."

This felt the same as five years ago.

We were stuck in an endless cycle of trauma.

Another murdered child.

Another grieving family.

Blue Cliff was cursed.

Paul braced himself on the counter, his complexion ashy. "Out in the woods, you say?"

"At the old creek bed," Jack told him. "He's like the others. Looks like he's been left there to be found. Coins in his hand and everything."

"Funny coincidence that we lose a boy right after that sicko Jasper Clinton gets out of jail," Billy said, his words heavy with accusation.

"Now isn't the time for that, William Miller," Jack's mom chided shakily. "We need to take care of Fred and Lisa. They'll need our support." She reached for a large mixing bowl from the shelf and went about getting together the ingredients for a pie. Our town's way of grieving involved lots and lots of food.

As if potato salad could heal the loss of a child.

As if piles of homemade biscuits could stop a family's pain.

Cooking to deal with an unspeakable tragedy had the feel of putting a Band Aid on a gunshot wound.

Fifteen minutes later five police cars pulled up to the house. Chief Hickman and Deputy Chief Jeff Cross, Jess's uncle, came into the kitchen, faces somber.

"Tell me what you found," the chief instructed Jack and me gently.

We explained what happened. How we found Dakota. The chief listened intently, his eyes never leaving our faces. "What's that there in your hand, Chey?" He indicated the poppet I hadn't realized I was still holding.

I held it out to him, my hand trembling. "I found it out in the woods. Near Dakota."

Chief Hickman turned to his deputy. "Jeff, get an evidence bag will ya? We need to tag this." He carefully wrapped the tiny doll in a tissue and dropped it into the clear plastic bag Deputy Chief Cross brought to him. The chief held it up, peering at it closely. "Looks like the ones your mom makes, doesn't it." I nodded mutely. "And you say you found this near the boy?" He pressed. I nodded again. "Hmm," he murmured before passing it to his colleague.

He put a reassuring hand on my shoulder before standing up. "We need to get out to the woods. It would be best if you folk could stay in the house, or even better, go into town. We'll be cordonin' off part of the farm as a potential crime scene, so it's important you stay out of the way. But first, I need you two to show me where you found him. Can ya do that?" He looked at Jack and me, his expression grim.

"Of course," Jack responded, glancing my way.

"You don't think that boy was killed here do you? On our farm?" Louise exclaimed.

The chief turned his kind eyes to Mrs. Campbell. "It's too soon to know anything, Louise. But I'll get to the bottom of it. I promise."

"He looked like the others, Chief," Jack added, following the men from the kitchen. "He was laid out on his back. Had the coins too."

Chief Hickman paused. "I'm glad it was you two that found him. Seems better that way."

We made our mournful trek back out to Bobcat Creek. No one said a word. The only sound was the crunch of undergrowth as we walked. Ten minutes later we were with Dakota again.

A collective intake of breath could be heard from the police officers. Those wearing hats, took them off and held them over their hearts in a show of respect. The sight of the dead child seemed to bring them all to their knees.

Chief Hickman cleared his throat. "Thank you, kids. We'll need to ask you some more questions later on—for the official record an' all—but for now, we've got it from here." He turned back to Dakota Mason, who wouldn't be going home to his parents.

Jack and I went back to his house and found his mother pouring sugar and flour into a bowl, her cheeks streaked with tears.

"Where's Dad?" Jack asked.

"He's gone back out to the barn, though I don't expect he'll be doing much work now. We're going to head over to Fred and Lisa's later tonight."

Louise turned to Jack, pulling him into her arms. "Are you okay?" She reached to embrace me as well. "And you, Chey, are you alright? I can't imagine what it must have been like."

She didn't have to say out loud what she was thinking.

That I had been through this before.

With another dead child out in the woods.

"I'm okay, Louise," I said, trying to speak around the lump in my throat.

"You two should go into town like the chief said. Get away from here while this business is being taken care of."

Jack picked up his truck keys. "She's right. Let's get out of here."

"Okay," I agreed, "I think we should go and tell Natalie."

"Yeah, that's a good idea," Jack agreed. We headed out to his truck, our hearts heavy.

We slowly made our way to the main road. It took some time to get through the police cars barricading the driveway.

We drove in silence, both of us too shell-shocked to speak. The image of the tiny boy played on a loop in my mind. But his face kept getting mixed up with that of the other dead boy I'd found in the woods. What were the chances of me finding two dead children?

On our arrival into town, I wasn't surprised to see it was again heaving with people. News crews still wandered about, but it was too soon for them to have heard about Dakota. When word got out, the streets would be full of strangers picking apart our town once more.

"What's going on at the square?" Jack slowed down to a crawl, unable to get past the massive crowd congregating around the small communal park in the center of town.

"There's Natalie." I indicated where she stood on the sidewalk, arms crossed, staring at the people clumped together.

Jack pulled over on the side of the street and parked the truck. We got out and rushed over to Natalie. "Hey," Jack called out.

Natalie looked at us, her eyes wide, her expression bleak. "Did you see it?" she asked, her voice trembling.

Jack and I both frowned. "See what?"

"Someone put it on the square. I don't know what it means, but it can't be good." Natalie looked terrified.

Jack, Nat, and I made our way to the crowd that had gathered. Voices were loud with suspicion and fear.

"What is it?" Jack asked, trying to peer over the heads of everyone.

"The fire department just left. Someone reported a fire on the square about an hour ago. I was in my shop and saw it. It looks like a scarecrow. I don't know why anyone would build that and then torch it. It's really strange," Nat explained, shuddering.

An hour ago.

Around the time Jack and I were stumbling across Dakota's body.

"I need to see it." I started pushing my way through the crowd. Jack followed in my wake, coming up short once we reached the square.

"What the hell is that?" Jack breathed, his front pressed against my back.

I was thankful for his solid presence, otherwise I might have fallen to the ground. Because in the middle of the square, tied to a large hickory tree, were the burnt remains of a life-size effigy. The same kind I remembered making as a child.

An image of the Hickory Man.

"I feel like I've seen one of these before." Natalie had come up beside me, her eyes on the effigy.

"It's the Hickory Man," Ed Grady said. I hadn't seen him in the crowd, but now he stepped forward, his voice rising. "These are meant to be out there—in the woods. Not here. This only invites him closer. Who would have done this?" He glared at the people standing around. "If you did this, say so!"

"It was probably looney Constance Ashby. I saw her hanging around here earlier," Hunter called out, his eyes hard. I noticed how Natalie stiffened at the sound of his voice.

"Yeah, I saw her too!" Jess Cross piped up.

"Maybe you need to keep better track of your crazy mom, Cheyenne," Hunter shouted at me as everyone started talking at the same time. Speculation went hand in hand with accusation in Blue Cliff.

"I think you should focus on your own house before worrying about anyone else's," Natalie shot back, surprising me, and probably everyone else. She turned away from her fiancé, not giving him a second glance. After a few awkward minutes, Hunter said something to Jess, and the two of them left.

"I take it things still aren't good between you two?" I surmised.

Natalie gave me a bland look. "He's going through a lot, but that doesn't give him a right to be a dick."

"Never thought I'd hear you say something like that." I gave her a grim smile.

"Well, things change . . . people change." She took a long, ragged breath. "I think it's over between us. Actually, I know it is."

I wasn't sure how to respond to that. In my opinion, she'd always been too good for him, and I had made my thoughts on the subject clear. But regardless, she had cared for him deeply. It had been a sticking point of our friendship. Until now it seemed.

"I think I'm sort of glad," she added, glancing up at me.

"I think I'm sort of glad too," I replied, fighting to hide my grin.

Natalie rolled her eyes. "Oh, you can cheer if you want to."

"I've never really liked him. He was always an ass. I was civil for your sake, Nat." Jack shrugged.

"Well, you won't need to be anymore." She sighed.

The crowd had started to disperse, with no clear proof of who had built the effigy or set it on fire.

But my suspicions circled dangerously around my mom, whom Jack had seen headed toward town earlier, and Hunter had seen as well.

As we too turned away, Natalie eyed Jack and me curiously. "What are you two doing here together?"

I wished I could tell her something good, but there would be no good news today, it seemed.

"We found Dakota," I told her.

Natalie looked between Jackson and me in obvious shock. "What do you mean you *found* Dakota? Is he okay?"

"We found him out in the woods. In the old creek bed where we used to build forts," Jack explained. We didn't have to say he was dead. Saying we found him in the woods was enough.

The three of us were quiet, staring at the smoldering figure of the Hickory Man. Otis Wheeler, back from his woodland trek, was dismantling it piece by piece, muttering to himself.

The smell of the burning wood lingered in the air. Otis hefted chunks of charred stump, dropping them into the garbage can. Charcoal blackened his hands, and he wiped them on his jeans.

"He got back here pretty damn quick," I observed.

"What are you talking about?" Natalie questioned, watching as Otis pulled an old Altoid tin that he used to store loose tobacco from his coat pocket. He rolled a cigarette and put it between his lips, lighting it. He looked long and hard at the pile of sticks and leaves, a strange expression on his craggy face.

"Jack and I saw him heading into the woods a little over an hour ago. Not long before . . ." Jack and I shared a look.

"Just spit it out, Chey," Natalie urged impatiently.

"It was right before we found Dakota," I told her.

"These people never learn unless you show 'em," we heard Otis say as he continued to take apart the effigy.

The Hickory Man loomed large over the town. The burnt remnants of his effigy felt like a threat. A warning.

"It's probably only a coincidence—" Jack began.

"There's no such thing as a coincidence in Blue Cliff," I interjected, and neither Natalie nor Jack argued.

"It's happening again," Natalie remarked as journalists started circling, taking pictures, making notes. "And it'll keep happening."

*   *   *

Jack, Natalie, and I remained in our morbid vigil. The three of us, like the innocent faces hammered to the telephone poles, were our own tangled chapters in this town's painful story.

We stood silently, all thinking the same thing: Blue Cliff had opened its jaws and gobbled up another child.

The Hickory Man was meant to remain in the trees. The town worked hard to keep him there. People tried to protect the streets, their homes, *their children*, from his ever-present evil.

Only now, someone had burned his likeness in the square. The scorched earth served as a beacon, welcoming him in.

My skin erupted in goose bumps. I ran my hands up and down my arms, trying to get warm. But this was a chill that went deep into my bones.

He had been allowed to burrow into the heart of Blue Cliff, and the people had a right to be afraid.

In the back of my mind, I heard menacing laughter.

Quiet. Almost a whisper.

The sound of malignant satisfaction deep within the forest.

CHAPTER

14

–Natalie–

T HE HALL WAS packed to the gills. As soon as news had spread about Dakota, people demanded a meeting to discuss what was happening. Only days had passed since the boy had been found, and people were scared sick. Children weren't playing outside, and parents were in a constant state of panic, terrified their kid would be next. Not enough time had passed for us to forget what this felt like. Something had to be done. The culprit had to be found. Blue Cliff townsfolk demanded justice, and they'd get it one way or another.

As the mayor, Chase Caruthers had hastily called everyone together. Time and place was communicated by word of mouth rather than an official notice. Meetings were a normal part of life in Blue Cliff. However tonight, the mood was far darker than it had been in a long time.

I was seated near the back, trying to disappear into the crowd. I noticed Hunter at the front with Jess. My ma was seated with Nancy and Jackie. I had purposefully avoided her when I arrived, not wanting to get corralled into sitting with her. I also saw my dad, who, like me, had taken a seat at the back of the hall, hoping to go unnoticed. He had quickly become public enemy number one. Most believed it was due to his negligence that a murderer was free. And now, with Dakota an obvious victim, no one would be happy to see him there.

"These seats taken?" I looked up to see Jack and Chey standing in the aisle.

Cheyenne seemed incredibly uncomfortable to be in a room crowded with people I knew she'd prefer to avoid. "Surprised you came," I said to her.

"I found him, so I thought I should." She gave a small shrug, but her jaw was clenched. "Are Dakota's parents here?" she asked, looking around.

I shook my head. "I don't think this is a place they want to be when they're grieving."

"Can't say I blame 'em. People are angry. And an angry crowd is a scary crowd," Jack stated, his eyes on Hunter and Jess, who were talking to a group of people at the front.

"I don't trust those two," Chey remarked softly, saying out loud what Jack and I were thinking.

"That's because you're smart," I replied, still feeling a twinge of conditioned guilt at not automatically defending my ex-fiancé. I looked down at my bare left hand. It felt ten pounds lighter without the weight of his ring. I had put it in a box and dropped it off at his house yesterday. I hadn't heard from him, not that I expected to.

Someone coughed behind me, and I turned, making eye contact with a man a few years older than me, with unkempt blond hair and shifty eyes.

"Good to see you here, Natalie," Linda Grady said from beside the man I knew to be her son.

"Hi, Linda. Where's Ed?" I asked, looking away from the blond man's eager expression.

"He's closing up the store. He should be along any minute now. You remember my boy, Reggie?" She patted his leg.

I didn't want to look at Reggie Grady again, but felt compelled to out of politeness. I gave him a half-hearted smile. "Yes, of course. Hi."

Reggie didn't smile, but I noticed him lick his lips, his nostrils flaring. I quickly looked away.

"It's horrible about Dakota," Linda exclaimed, wringing her hands together. "I heard you two found 'im," she said to Jack and Chey, who had finally turned around.

"Yes, ma'am, we did," Jack said with a grimace.

"What was it like?" Reggie asked, his eyes now unnaturally steady.

"What was *what* like?" Jack frowned at him.

Reggie leaned forward slightly, and I instinctively backed away.

"Finding the body."

Jack, Chey, and I shared a look, and Linda seemed uncomfortable by her son's inappropriate question.

"I don't think we should talk about that," Linda cut in.

Reggie sat back in his seat, a surly expression on his face. "I was just curious is all," he muttered, deflating slightly.

The three of us quickly turned back around.

"Well, that was bizarre," I said, low enough so that only Jack and Chey could hear me.

"Reggie has always been a weird guy," Jack remarked.

"Alright, alright," Chase called out loudly, getting everyone's attention. "Let's get started. I know people want to get home for supper. I'm going to turn it over to Chief Hickman. He can fill everyone in and hopefully put some minds at ease."

The chief stepped forward, his face bleak. "Thanks, everyone, for showin' up last minute like this. I know it's not easy to do durin' the week." He cleared his throat and took a mint from the tin in his pocket before continuing.

"By now, I'm sure everyone has heard about Dakota Mason. Our hearts are with Fred and Lisa durin' this awful

time. Jackie Lytton and Cynthia McIlwee are organizin'
a prayer vigil for Saturday night at the church. They'll be
stickin' around afterward to give you all the details." Chief
Hickman inclined his head in the two women's direction.

"What's prayer gonna do? We need to find Jasper
Clinton!" someone called out angrily. There was an instant
cacophony of voices as everyone agreed.

"We know he's the one responsible. People have seen
him around," Darla piped up from where she sat with her
son Craig.

"Dakota was scared before he was taken. He said he saw
him out in the woods," Otis shouted, and everyone looked
at him.

"What are you talking about, Otis? What do you know
about any of this?" my aunt Margaret challenged, her mouth
pursed in disapproval.

Otis got to his feet, his hands balled into fists. "I talk to
the kids. They tell me things. Dakota said he saw a man out
in those damn woods. That the man spoke to him. Everyone knows it was Jasper Clinton!"

Gasps echoed through the hall as everyone started talking at once.

"Okay, everyone calm down," Chief Hickman bellowed, to be heard over the din. "Thank you, Otis, for
sharin', although, if you have any information, it would
be good if you came down to the station to make a
statement."

Otis, having been politely chastised, sat back down, his
face dark and dangerous.

"I understand things are tense right now. We all want
the person responsible to be caught," Chase placated.

"I'd think you'd want that psycho caught more than
anyone," Abel Fry said, Jamie beside him. "That monster
killed your boy, and now he's gone and killed Dakota.
Enough is enough. If he hadn't been allowed to get out on a

technicality, none of this would have happened, and Dakota would be home with his parents."

All eyes turned to my father, who hadn't escaped the notice of his neighbors.

"What are you even doing here, Stew? Shouldn't you be tryin' to fix this mess you caused?" Billy Miller spat out, and I felt the swell of rage directed at my dad. He visibly shrank in his seat, as if wishing the floor would open up and swallow him. I saw my ma purposely look away from her husband, as if distancing herself from him.

"Everyone, please. Throwin' accusations around won't solve anything." Chief Hickman motioned with his hands for everyone to settle down. Cheyenne reached across Jack and took my hand. Jack put his arm around my shoulders.

"While we're talking about all this, we should find out who burned the man out there on the square. That's dangerous. Whoever did it should know better," Ed said from behind me. I hadn't seen him come in; I had been too fixated on the train wreck in front of me.

"Maybe it was Connie. She's always lurking around, looking sneaky. I heard she was in town that day too," Nancy stated from her seat near the front. My ma nodded beside her, and others murmured in agreement.

"Who cares about a pile of sticks? I want you to find the person who killed my Livvie. Who killed Dakota!" Tammy Bradshaw wailed, her husband, Earl, holding her. Her face was full of so much anguish it was painful to look at.

"We need to find Jasper Clinton!" Hunter shouted, jumping to his feet. "We can't let him get away with this!"

"Let's get 'im!" Cherry Rhinehart screeched.

"This is two seconds away from turning into a modern-day witch hunt," I said to Jack and Chey.

"Grab your pitchforks, ladies and gents," Cheyenne murmured. "I'm just glad my mom didn't come to this."

I squeezed her hand. "Me too."

"Find the person who put the man in the square, and you'll find Dakota's killer! Only a maniac would invite *him* into our town!" Ed insisted.

"Maybe the effigy was to remind us to be careful. It's a warning," Otis argued.

Things were quickly spiraling out of control, and it felt a little like the chief and Chase were allowing it to happen. Both of them sat up front, watching the chaos unfold.

"Someone needs to calm this situation down before it's too late," Jack urged anxiously.

"That's the chief's job," Chey retorted, letting out a frustrated breath.

Jack looked around at the crowd that was getting more and more riled up. Their voices rising, their expressions becoming more menacing. Nothing brought a town together quite like shared righteous anger.

Finally, not able to stand it any longer, he stood up and cleared his throat, though no one seemed to notice right away.

"What are you doing?" Cheyenne hissed under her breath. "Sit down."

He ignored her, and all Chey and I could do was watch our best friend throw himself into the lion's den.

"Excuse me . . . can everyone listen up for a minute?" He sounded unsure, but his back was straight.

Slowly, voices quieted as people turned to look at him. Chief Hickman inclined his head in Jack's direction, encouraging him to speak.

"The thing is, we all need to be pulling together as a community right now, and pointing fingers like this isn't going to help."

"So what do you think we should do then, Jack? You and Chey found Dakota—you know what that evil son of a bitch has done to our town," Ed yelled, clearly not ready to calm down.

Jack seemed to consider the question for a minute. Finally, with a sense of resolve, he addressed our frightened town. "No one feels safe, so that's where we start. Maybe we should have volunteer patrols around town. There's safety in numbers, right? Groups can walk kids to and from school, make sure they get home to their parents. The kids would feel better, and we'd be able to keep an eye on them." There was some head nodding, accepting the good sense of his suggestion.

Feeling emboldened, he went on. "What about holding a fundraiser to help out Dakota's parents? We need to do something more than offering thoughts and prayers. This is Blue Cliff." Jack looked around at the angry faces of his neighbors and friends. "We pull together and help each other out. We don't go accusing people and threatening them. Because then that makes us no better than the monster that hurt those kids."

"What a crock of shit!" Hunter hollered from his seat. He stood up, his face filled with rage. "We need more than patrols and fundraisers," he snapped, "Stewart Bartlett screwed up, and now that sicko is back on our streets, killing our kids. Dakota's blood is on his hands!"

The room erupted into angry shouting again, This wasn't a group wanting to come together. This was a town ready to rip itself apart in its grief and fury.

My dad quickly left as people hurled abuse at his retreating back. Any sense and reason Jack had tried to impart was lost in people's drive for vengeance.

"We need to find that murderer and give 'im a taste of his own medicine!"

"Make him pay for what he's done!"

"It's time we showed people that the children of Blue Cliff will be protected no matter what!"

Hysteria ensued as more and more voices sounded out, each angrier than the last.

"I think we need to get out of here," Jack said under his breath.

The three of us got up and snuck out the back. No one noticed.

"I need to find my dad," I told them once we were outside.

"Yeah, okay." Jack sounded distracted.

"Call me later and let me know how it goes," Chey said, giving me a quick hug.

I ran off in the direction I knew my dad would have gone. I caught up with him quickly, finding him sitting on one of the memorial benches in the center of town. He looked up as I approached. I hated the pain I saw in his eyes. As mad as I was at him, he was still my dad, and I loved him.

I sat down beside him. We were both silent for a while before he spoke.

"I'm sorry for all this, Natalie." His tone was defeated, his misery obvious.

"It was pretty bad back there," I said.

"I know they need someone to blame. I guess it makes sense that it's me; it doesn't matter if they're wrong." His words were tinged with a furious bitterness.

"But they're *not* wrong are they, Dad?" It wasn't a question—it was confirmation. And when he wouldn't meet my eyes, I forged ahead with all the truths I had come to realize. "I don't get it. You always seemed certain that it was Jasper. How could they have evidence that proves otherwise?" We both knew the answer, but I needed to hear him say it. To admit it.

"You're a smart girl, Natalie. I know you've figured it out." His words were full of shame. He finally lifted his eyes to meet mine. "I withheld evidence so Jasper would be sent to jail. I knew that DNA would prove he didn't do it, so I made sure no one saw it. But nothing stays hidden, does it?"

I was horrified. Even though I had suspected it, it was still a shock to hear.

"He was innocent, Dad." It was a statement. A harsh reality. There was no avoiding this now. We couldn't bottle it back up and pretend it didn't exist.

His face darkened with irritation. His sad eyes sparked with annoyance.

"He was far from innocent, Natalie." My dad stared off into the cold night as he chose his next words carefully. "That boy and his family were trouble from the day they moved in. A blight on this town. Drinking all day, partying all night. They weren't good people. The parents were as bad as the son. Do you know, Donald had more complaints from Clinton's neighbors in one month than he'd had from the entire town in a year? They weren't a good fit for Blue Cliff. This isn't a place for outta-towners."

"Not growing up in Blue Cliff doesn't make him a murderer," I reminded him fiercely. "He didn't kill those children, Dad. How could you have done that?"

Dad sat up a little straighter, steel in his spine. "I had a duty to this town—to preserve their *idea* of safety. Our lives are saturated in a fear that goes back hundreds of years. You can't grow up in this town and not feel it. When those kids were killed, it was time to give them a new kind of monster. One they could put a face to. Blue Cliff *needed* Jasper to be guilty. People can stomach murder a lot easier when it's committed by someone that isn't one of them. People had been through enough!" He clenched his fists. "Natalie, you have no idea the sacrifices I have made to keep you safe. To keep you happy. I chased away your nightmares. That's what I've done!" he shouted. "Everything I have done has been to protect *you*."

I stared at him in disbelief. "How dare you put this on me! I didn't ask you to make awful choices for me. I didn't ask for you to lie and break the law. All of this is on you and no one else."

He flinched but then stiffened. "Blue Cliff would have fallen apart. I saved these people more misery than they could have survived."

"You didn't protect us, Dad—you sentenced us all!" I yelled, the explosion coming from deep within me. I stood up, not able to sit next to him any longer. "The killer was out there this whole time. And now Dakota is dead. How is that protecting any of us? You're as responsible for that boy's death as the person that killed him! And everyone knows that. They see you for what you are."

"You don't understand!" he roared, "All I had was three dead kids and a terrified town. I had to do something. I made a choice. One I could live with. It was better than the alternative. *That* I couldn't live with." He stared up at me in exasperation. Dad got to his feet and began pacing back and forth. "This will all go away soon," he said quietly, but it was obvious he didn't believe that. "I'll fix it for you, Natalie. I'll do whatever it takes."

"This isn't going away. Dakota is dead. Whoever did it the first time is killing again, and they won't stop until more children die."

"I can't do this again. I thought it was over. I thought you were safe," he moaned more to himself than to me.

Suddenly it all made sense. The case had made his career, but in the process I'd lost part of my dad, and now I finally knew why.

Guilt.

He'd sent an innocent man to prison, and he hated himself for it.

His body seemed to deflate, and he collapsed back onto the bench, putting his head in his hands. I watched him, appalled by the person he had become, or maybe it was the person he had been all along. Part of me still wanted to comfort him; he was my dad, my one time hero. We'd always been close. He was the parent I counted on. The one who loved me without condition.

But I couldn't.

He'd allowed a killer to live among us.

Suddenly, breathing the same air as him was too much. I walked away, leaving the broken man my father had become all alone.

CHAPTER

15

—Cheyenne—

THE WOODS WERE quiet. They were often silent, but this heavy lack of sound felt like a terrifying beginning. Pregnant and waiting. I couldn't remember the last time I had heard the crows and the magpies in the trees.

Three days ago, Jack and I had found nine-year-old Dakota Mason's body. The feeling of familiarity was unavoidable.

Things had gotten ugly at the town hall meeting last night. I hadn't expected it to be pretty, but I hadn't been fully prepared for the borderline violence. People were terrified. And frightened people did stupid things.

The town of Blue Cliff wasn't open to peace.

It was ready for war.

Everyone was turning on each other. Neighbors were now suspects. Friends were now mistrustful. I wasn't immune to the instinct to look at everyone with suspicion. I'd found myself scouring the crowd last night, wondering if the killer could have been there.

The investigation into the murder had begun. But we all knew how it would turn out.

Dakota had drowned. Like all the others.

With dirt in his shoes and old-timey silver coins in his palms. I had seen the glint of silver in the sun.

Keep silver in your pockets,
Walk with dirt in your shoes,
Or he'll poke your eyeballs from their sockets,
And boil your bones in stew.

Once again the silver and the dirt hadn't done their job.

Dakota had been dead for some time. The county medical examiner reported he had probably been killed not long after he was taken. So where had he been kept all that time?

The town was in turmoil, and there was an anger that was visible. Someone would have to burn for this. And who better than the man who had so recently been released from prison?

On top of all that, the dream was getting worse too. I was only sleeping a handful of hours a night now. Every time I closed my eyes I was back out there. In the woods.

But the dream kept changing. Altering in ways it never had before.

Last night the images had been startlingly clear. I felt strangely lucid as I waited among the trees.

This time I looked down at my left hand, noting a deep cut in my palm. Warm blood flowed sluggishly from the long incision. I felt it dripping between my fingers. Warm. Sticky.

*   *   *

"Wait for him. The blood will call him to you. Be brave, Chey. Be brave and you'll be safe."

Was that my mother's voice? I turned and looked around me, but she was nowhere to be seen. She had walked me deep into the forest and left me all alone.

"Just as my pa had done," she had told me. "And his pa before him."

I was too young to know what that meant. I didn't understand what I was supposed to do. All I knew was I couldn't move. I couldn't leave. I had to wait for him. And I knew he'd come. He couldn't stay away from the blood.

Day turned into night and still I remained. Alone and terrified. I was far from home. I had no idea how to get back. I worried what would happen to me out here, all alone in the woods. Would I be forgotten? My hand throbbed; the cut was no longer bleeding, but it was painful every time I moved my fingers. I wanted to cry but I didn't.

"Cheyenne."

I heard him before I saw him. My name on the wind. The crunch of dead leaves under heavy feet.

"Cheyenne."

I could feel his excitement. The air practically vibrated with it.

He was there. I could see him now. He was big. I'd expected a monster. Something like a ghoul or a vampire. My child's imagination had created something fantastical in my mind. But that wasn't what he was. This was no mythical nightmare. This was real. He was real.

I began to shake so hard that my legs couldn't hold me upright anymore.

He moved closer, his white teeth gleaming in the moonlight.

I trembled, frozen to the spot, unable to cry out.

He was going to take me away. I knew that with total and absolute certainty.

"Cheyenne."

* * *

I stood on the porch, staring out into the quiet woods. The door opened behind me, and I turned to see my mother shuffling out, her long hair looking grayer than it had before. Her face was drawn, and she wouldn't quite meet my eyes.

"Morning," I greeted as she moved past me and down the stairs.

"Stay inside," she said, her voice oddly monotone. "Don't disturb the salt." Without another word, she headed across the gravel driveway and disappeared into the trees.

I stood there watching until she was gone, and even then I waited. Wondering. She was worse than before. She had taken the news of Dakota's body being found particularly hard.

And last night, when I came home from the town meeting, I walked inside and knew instantly that something was wrong. A sharp, coppery scent hung in the air. I made my way into the living room, almost screaming when I saw what waited there. There was blood and what looked like entrails coagulating on my mom's ceremonial table. I started to gag, feeling vomit rise in my throat.

I had gone to the kitchen and gathered cleaning supplies. Breathing through my mouth, I quickly scooped my grisly find into a bucket. With shaking hands, I began to mop up the blood. It was then that I saw the small corn husk poppet wrapped in a scrap of blue plaid cloth. I picked up the handmade doll and looked at it closely. Mom had rubbed it in the blood. I stared at the fabric, my heart beating wildly. I recognized the material. It was the same color and pattern as the shirt Dakota had been wearing when we found him in the woods. The shirt he had been killed in.

I abruptly dropped the poppet in the bucket and rushed outside, burying the contents deep in the ground, where no one would ever find them.

Was it Dakota's shirt?

No. That was ridiculous. It made no sense. But I had buried it anyway.

*   *   *

I stood a few minutes longer on the porch, willing the morning air to clear the cobwebs from my mind. The sun was out, and the snow was finally melting. We were predicted to have a spell of unseasonably warm weather over the next week, but I couldn't summon any excitement for the reprieve from winter.

With my mother gone, I figured now was a good time to have a look in her bedroom. Something was wrong, and I needed to know what it was if I was going to help her. What better place to look than the room she sequestered herself in for hours at a time?

The door was locked.

I jiggled the knob, pushing it with my shoulder, but it wouldn't budge. Since when did my mother lock her bedroom door? I was debating what to do when a knock startled me.

"I come bearing food," Natalie said by way of greeting, standing on the porch and holding a covered dish. "When I'm stressed, I cook. I've already taken fried chicken and two cobblers to the Masons, so I thought I'd bring you and your ma my sausage and grits casserole. Constance loves it. I'll put it in the fridge, and you can eat it when you want." Natalie was rambling. Her cheeks were flushed, and she had a wild look in her eye that she only ever got when she was overwhelmed.

"Thanks," I replied.

I stepped aside to allow Natalie to head to the kitchen.

"Or I can heat some up now if you want. Where's your ma? She should eat," Natalie suggested, already getting some plates from the cabinet.

"She left."

Natalie frowned. "The woods?"

"Yep," I answered. "But I could eat."

Natalie scooped some casserole onto a plate and put it in the microwave.

"How's she been?" Natalie asked.

"Weirder than usual. I want you to check something out." I motioned for her to follow me out to the backyard.

I walked straight to the mound where I had buried the poppet. Using the trowel I had dropped on the ground, I quickly dug it up again and handed the doll to Natalie.

"Who is this meant to be?" Nat asked, looking at it closely. She recognized what it was, especially having seen them all over town. She handed it back to me. "And what's with the blue fabric?"

"I don't know. But I'm telling you, it looks like the same material as the shirt Dakota was wearing when Jack and I found him."

Natalie blanched. "Come on, Chey. I've seen most of the men around here wearing a blue plaid shirt at one time or another. It could belong to anyone." She pursed her lips.

"It's not only this. When I came home last night, there were blood and guts all over the table inside with this poppet lying in the middle of it."

Natalie looked at me incredulously. "What are you saying?"

"What if she did something? What if she . . . what if she hurt Dakota?" I couldn't quite meet her eyes as I confessed the grisly suspicions in my heart.

Natalie gaped at me. "Come on, Chey! Even you can't believe that. Constance is a lot of things, but she's no killer." Natalie said it with such confidence. Her belief was unwavering. I had always thought Natalie was better suited to be Constance Ashby's child than I was.

I curled my fingers around the small doll. "Then what about this?"

"Whoever killed Dakota probably killed Mikey, Livvie, and Danielle too. And they've been living here this whole time. But that poppet can't be connected to all that. It's just not possible. These are meant for protection. Not destruction." She watched me bury the doll back in the ground, her face troubled. "But why was a child killed now and not years ago?" she wondered aloud. "There's such a huge gap between murders that it can almost feel like some awful coincidence."

"But it's not a coincidence, Natalie. You know that as well as I do. It's all connected. Livvie, Danielle, and Michael. Dakota. Whatever's going on with my mom. I just can't figure out how."

She let out a sigh. "What are we going to do?"

"What can *we* do? We're not police officers. We're not investigators. It seems that's who needs to figure this out—"

"Because they did such a great job before," Natalie cut me off angrily. "They railroaded Jasper, and they'll try to railroad someone else this time."

I knew Natalie was struggling with the things her father had done.

I put an arm around her shoulders. "Come on." I turned us back toward the house. "Let's go eat some of that casserole."

*   *   *

"Yep, it's definitely locked," Natalie announced, rattling the doorknob to my mother's room. Now that we were both fed, I wanted her help in figuring out what was going on with my mom.

"Unless we want to break down the door, which I don't advise, I say we start by looking somewhere else. Maybe there are other places that could provide clues. " she suggested.

"Like where?" I frowned. "Trust me, I've searched through this house. If there's something here, I haven't seen it."

"Have you looked in the old root cellar? I know Constance keeps her jars of herbs and random family stuff down there."

I had almost forgotten the root cellar existed. When I was younger I had never been permitted down there. Mom had said it wasn't a place for kids, and I'd never argued, mostly because the dark, dank space freaked me out.

"I doubt there's anything of significance—"

"I don't know—there's a lot of stuff from your grandpa and great-grandpa. It might be worth a look," Natalie interjected.

"You've been down there?" I asked in surprise.

Natalie shrugged. "Only a few times, but not for a long time. Your ma would ask me to go fetch some old jars from time to time. She doesn't go down there anymore now that her knees are giving her trouble."

"Well, let's go check it out." I led the way around the side of the house, stopping in front of a nondescript wooden door that looked as if it led straight into the ground. It was hidden behind overgrown shrubs, and if you didn't know it was there, you'd never notice it.

I pulled the handle of the ancient-looking door, and a waft of mildew and decay drifted out. The opening was dark and cavernous, a narrow set of stairs descending into total blackness. I leaned inside but couldn't see anything.

Natalie reached around me and pulled a string hanging from the ceiling. A yellowed bulb flickered to life. She started to head down the stairs but realized I wasn't following. "You comin'?"

"Do I have to?" I grimaced.

"Since when am I the brave one in this partnership?" Natalie teased, taking my hand and giving it a tug. "Come on. There's nothing down here that will bite you. Or at least I hope not."

"That's not very comforting," I deadpanned, carefully walking down the steps.

Natalie turned on another light when we reached the cellar floor. I blinked my eyes as they adjusted. The cellar was much bigger than I'd imagined. The dirt-packed walls were lined with wooden shelving in various states of decay. Some of the wood was rotted through, and other shelves were sagging from years of disrepair. Cobwebs hung from the ceiling, brushing my face. Something scurried in the shadows, making my skin crawl.

Jars were lined, some four deep, on every available surface. There was a huge metal table in the middle of the room, like the kind you'd find in a military tent on a battlefield. It was covered with old notebooks and piles of newspapers that looked older than the hills.

Natalie started sifting through the items on the table, and I began to circle the room. The jars were all filled to the brim. Some of it appeared to be normal preserves, though half of them could have been easily a century old. The fruit that may have once been cherries and peaches had turned brown and was clearly spoiled.

I pulled the string on another light; a dusty bare bulb came to life, illuminating the back wall, which was bare of any shelving. I noticed that, unlike the others, this wall was made of stone, and it was covered with drawings that looked etched into the rock.

"Nat, check this out."

"What is it?" she asked, coming to my side.

I pointed to the wall. "Have you seen it before?"

Natalie moved closer and squinted, trying to see in the gloomy lighting. "No, I only ever got stuff off the shelves for her, and I never ventured far from the steps." She reached out and lightly touched the wall with her fingertips. "Are these names?"

I stared at the wall, trying to make sense of what I was seeing. There were drawings of trees and paths. Faded writing and arrows pointing in various directions. Symbols had been etched in places, and I tried to work out what they all meant.

I traced my fingers over the scrawling. It was a hand-drawn map of Hickory Woods. And below it was a long list of names scratched into the stone. One after the other.

HENRY BAKEMAN. ALICE LEE. BETSY HUNT.

HARPER   MARSHALL.   JOSEPH   SCOTT.
DUNCAN WILLIAMS.

The names went on and on, in groups of three, my stomach turning as I read them. My fingers moved over the letters, needing to touch them to know that they were real and that I wasn't imagining them. Most I didn't recognize, so they meant nothing to me.

But it was the handful of names at the bottom that had me struggling to breathe. That made my blood run cold and my heart race.

BRADLEY MOSES. LYDIA STRUTHERS. SALLY BURBANK.

CLARA   WHITMER.   BILLY   WALKER.   JANICE BROWN.

I heard Natalie gasp.

"Olivia Bradshaw. Michael Caruthers. Danielle Torrents," she read out loud in a strangled whisper. "Cheyenne? Why are their names here?"

The room suddenly felt too small. "I don't know."

"Jesus, look." Natalie had started to shake beside me.

There, at the very bottom of the list was one final name. Freshly etched into the stone, chips of rock littering the floor.

DAKOTA MASON.

Natalie's eyes were saucers as she turned to me. "These are all the dead kids."

"There's at least thirty names on this list. I recognize some of them, but the others—" I pointed to the ones at the top that had been written in an almost aggressive, spiky script. "I think these must be older. From a long time ago. Clara, Billy, and Janice disappeared back in the fifties; their missing posters are still up on the board outside Grady's. And I know Bradley, at least, was from the twenties. I'm guessing Lydia and Sally must be from that time as well since they're grouped together."

I was trying to think logically, not to jump to the most horrific conclusion, but Natalie got straight to the point.

"Did your ma write all this?"

"I don't know," I said again. It seemed to be my de facto response. I looked closely at the names of Livvie, Danielle, and Michael, wondering if the letters were written in my mother's handwriting. "I can't be sure, though I'm certain she didn't write those." I indicated the names above Livvie's. "And actually, if you look at all of them, they seem to be written by different people. Some are thick and deep cuts, while others are nothing more than scratches on the rock. Clara, Bradley, Lydia, were clearly written by one person; and Billy, Janice, and Sally's names by someone else. And these too." I ran my finger over the names of Henry, Alice, and Betsy. "And these are different still," Natalie pointed to the faded names of an Edith and Clementine Baker next to a Hugh Fuller. They were the oldest, the cuts almost entirely smoothed out from age.

"Why would there be a list of dead children on the wall of your family's root cellar?" Natalie asked.

I didn't have an answer. And the ones floating around in my head were too horrible to say out loud. I turned my attention to the map. "This is Hickory Woods."

"It sure is. I recognize some of the landmarks." Natalie stood back to get a better look. The map, like the names, seemed to have been added to and drawn by different hands. It was massive, taking up a good portion of the wall. "There's your house." Natalie circled the drawing of my home with her finger.

"And there's Bobcat Creek. That's the dried-up bed at the north fork, where we found Dakota." I indicated the curving line that cut through the woods.

"There are a lot of spots I don't recognize," Natalie observed. "Like this over here. What was it meant to be? It looks like a clearing of some kind." I recognized it, even crudely drawn. It was the spot where Mom and the others erected the effigies.

"That's the old Ashby hunting cabin," I said, pointing to a square in the middle of the trees far to the west. "I remember Mom taking me out there one time, and it was basically falling down by that point."

"The map stops here. And is this black paint?" Natalie leaned closer to the wall, scraping at it with her fingernail.

She was right: it did look as if the map ended abruptly, and the rest of the space had been covered in a thick coating of black. "What's this round thing?" I frowned.

"It's a well," Natalie said with authority. As though she knew exactly what it was.

Why would there be a well in the middle of the woods? It was drawn as being nestled in between the trees, and beyond it was where the blackness began. As if it was an endpoint of some kind.

We were interrupted by the sound of gravel crunching beneath tires.

"Someone's here," I said. "We should go."

We hurried up the steps, both of us eager to get out of the cellar, away from the list of dead children on the wall. Once outside, we saw Jackson's truck parked in the driveway.

He was knocking on the door when he saw us. "Hey, there you are."

"What's up?" I asked as he walked toward us.

"I came to make sure you and your mom were alright. Shit's gettin' rough out there. Everyone's all riled up." Jack jingled his keys in agitation. "Did you hear that someone set fire to the Clinton place? It happened the night we went to the bar. I drove over there earlier, and it's practically burned to the ground. Police aren't in a rush to find out who did it either. Everyone's angry and lookin' to make someone pay for Dakota. There's talk of forming a group to track Jasper down."

Natalie covered her mouth with her hand. "That's horrible!"

"This all feels like it's building toward something," I murmured.

"We need to show Jack what we found," Natalie said to me. "I don't think this is going to stop with Dakota."

"What did you find?" Jack asked, looking between us.

"Come on," I said with resignation, gesturing for him to follow as the three of us made our way back down into the cellar.

CHAPTER

16

—Cheyenne—

"I HAVE NO IDEA what this is," Jack said after we showed him the back wall of the root cellar. "But whatever it is, it doesn't look good."

I grabbed a couple of old journals and sat on the bottom step. There was no way I was going to sit on the dank, dirty floor. "I can't help but worry that Mom's done something really bad. Or at least, she knows a lot more than she's ever let on. There's no way this has existed here for god knows how many years and she didn't know about it."

Jack settled on a step above me, with his own pile of papers. "Okay, but that doesn't mean she did whatever awful thing you think she did."

Jack might be right, but do we ever really know people? Even those closest to us?

"Listen to this. This journal is dated 1703," Natalie called out from where she was perched on a rickety stool at the table, an electric camping lamp providing some light. Her eyes ran over the pages in front of her as she started to read.

"*The winter is long, and the people are afraid. The animals are dying, and we don't know if we'll make it to spring.*

Isaac says he saw the man in the trees again. His teeth blood red and eyes like hell. I know what he wants. Moder says he comes to her in her dreams. Tells her the truths of the woods. We're dying. All of us. The land is making it clear we don't belong. Our crops won't grow. Our houses burn down. Babies are stillborn. He demands the blood of the youngest fruit. But how can I give it to him?"

"Sounds like the start of every summer camp ghost story I've ever heard," Jack quipped, but his joke fell flat. Sitting in the root cellar with the names of dead children on the wall, it was hard to find the humor.

"'Blood of the youngest fruit'? What the hell does that mean?" I asked.

"I'm not sure but it gets more interesting." Natalie turned the page and kept reading.

"There's power in numbers. There's protection in threes. The number of the Holy Trinity. Moder and I sent three of our beautiful children into the woods. One by one I led them there. The dying wouldn't stop unless we gave him what he wanted. Give him the three, and he is satisfied."

"Something tells me he wasn't taking them to the woods for a picnic," I muttered.

Natalie shushed me before reading some more.

"I give him thrice, hoping it binds him to his promise and protects us from his evil. Moder assures me that the threes are our salvation. Their blood saves us all. I tell them not to be afraid, that this is their duty. But I'm deceiving them. Because I am afraid. We all are. I avoid their eyes as their blood flows."

"Jesus . . ." Jack gasped.

I wanted to tell Natalie to stop reading, but she was relentless.

"He has been here since the beginning. The man in the shadows is as old as the mountains. We made the mistake of living on his land. But if we want to stay, we have to do what he

wants. We have learned not to go beyond the water. We built the well to remind us. We take silver when we venture close to the rocks. Moder tells us to put soil in our shoes to bind us to the earth. So far it has worked. Except when the babies die and the houses burn—then we know what we have to do."

"It's just a bunch of old stories. We shouldn't take this stuff seriously," Jack protested weakly, but we all knew they were more than that.

Natalie flipped through the pages. "This one is from May sixteenth, 1785."

"The time has come for spring cleansing. I know my part. The three were chosen with great care. The best of us. The brightest stars. Harper, Joseph, and Duncan. Even though I knew what I had to do, I couldn't take the blade to their throats. Instead, I led them to the well. I put them in. Enough to submerge their faces. The smell was horrid. There's something wrong with the water there, but he approves. The old stories say he comes by stream or river or brook. It flows from one plane to the next. It cleanses them, and their suffering will be less. When they were still, I laid them out on the forest floor as an offering. It is done. Our town is safe for now."

I hadn't realized that I was trembling until I felt my teeth chatter. I opened one of the journals beside me, my stomach lurching. This one was dated July 21, 1923, and I read it aloud for Natalie and Jack to hear.

"Bradley, Lydia, and Sally. I knew them. I looked after their families and sat beside them in church. Bradley was friends with my boy, Charlie. So young. Younger than the others have been. I did it because I didn't have a choice. I knew it when the Bartlett baby died in his sleep and when Bobcat Creek dried up. I offered them in the way my father has taught me. Drowning is a kinder way to go, and he doesn't seem to mind. All he wants is the death. I only hope these are the last in my lifetime. I can't do this again. I give him the three, and I hope he is satisfied."

I lifted my head, my mouth dry. "Seems Great-Grandad Jonah was more squeamish than his ancestors. I'd almost feel sorry for the guy if he wasn't a cold-blooded murderer."

My ancestors were killers. This was the blood-soaked past our town was founded on. All the superstitions, all the illogical beliefs, were rooted in my family's murdering ways. Had my mom followed in their footsteps? Is that why she was the way she was?

"This doesn't mean anything, Chey," Jack pressed. "Your mom's a good woman." It seemed I wasn't the only one who had made the connection to my mother.

I got up and handed Natalie the papers. She frowned as she skimmed them.

"What is it?" I asked, looking over her shoulder.

She went and stood in front of the wall of names. "Bradley Moses. Lydia Struthers. Sally Burbank. I remember these names now. We were always told they were accidents. But they weren't." She held up the journal, my great-grandfather's words stark on the pages. "They were murdered. Just like all the others."

Jack stood up, his face pale. "Shit. Shit. Shit." He swallowed thickly. "Chey's family have been killing kids. Shit."

"It's these damn woods. It does strange things to your head," Nat stated matter-of-factly.

"I think it's more than the woods," I challenged. "It's this whole damn town. It's the way we live. We can't blame the trees. This is about the people who live here." My voice shook with the force of my anger. All of my bitterness toward Blue Cliff bubbled over.

Jack and Natalie wore twin expressions of sympathy that I really didn't want. I had to look away from both of them.

Jack shuffled through papers. "There are some old newspaper articles mixed in with the journals. This one is from 1951. "*Local Children Still Missing: Two Days Since the*

Disappearance of Clara Struthers, Billy Walker, and Janice Brown, With No Leads."

"Give him the three," I murmured.

"We have to find your mom," Nat said, her voice hard. "Maybe she'll tell us what all this means."

"We don't really think Constance killed those four kids, do we?" Jack asked with worried incredulity.

"I think she knows more than she has been saying, and I think we need to find her. Now," I told him.

Natalie got to her feet. "So where do we start?

Jack looked back at the map on the wall. "We go to the woods."

Natalie ran her hand over the black paint coating the stone. "I'd like to check out this old cabin you say belongs to your family, Chey. It's isolated, out of the way, and close to whatever all this dark stuff is."

"Seems as good a place as any to start." Jack checked the time on his phone. "We need to get going while we still have daylight. The last thing any of us want is to get stuck in those woods at night."

Natalie looked down at her shoes. "If we're going to go wandering around the woods, I need better footwear." She pulled her car keys out of her pocket. "I'm gonna head back to my house and change. Let's meet at the old holler in an hour."

"It's a plan." I gave her a grim smile that didn't reach my eyes.

With a final look at the map on the wall, Natalie hurried up the steps.

I watched Jack clean up the papers into piles. Neither one of us said anything. The reality of what was happening settled uncomfortably between us. There was a connection between the murdered kids and my mom. While Jack and Natalie were hesitant to accuse her outright, I had no such qualms. I was her daughter; I should be defending her.

But I couldn't.

Because I came back to Blue Cliff expecting the worst. It seemed I had gotten it.

"Want to help me break into my mother's room?" I asked, only half joking.

Jack gave me a piercing look. "You really believe she had something to do with this?"

"I don't know, Jack. I really don't. But not knowing is driving me nuts."

Jack stared at the names on the wall, his expression bleak. "Okay, then, let's go." We went back to the house, feeling a sad sort of resignation.

I jiggled at the locked doorknob. "You don't lock a door unless you're hiding something."

Jack gently pushed me aside. "I'm not a fan of breaking and entering, just so you know. But I get what you're saying. We have to know what's going on with your mom." He took out his wallet and retrieved his county library card. "Lucky for us these doors are dirt cheap and not even remotely secure." He carefully slid the card down the crack, wiggling it between the lock and the jamb. A few seconds later the door popped open. "Voilà."

"Thanks, Campbell." My smile was half-hearted as Jack pushed the door open.

The room was much the same as I remembered from my first night. Thankfully, Jack didn't mention the chalk symbols and burnt candles on the floor.

I started opening drawers and rifling through my mom's things. Jack stood awkwardly by the door. I looked over my shoulder at him, raising an eyebrow. "Not gonna help?"

"I'm not going to rummage around your mother's underwear. There are lines I won't cross, Chey."

A few minutes later I came across an old pile of photographs. "Check these out." I motioned Jack over.

The one on top was of my mother at least thirty years younger, her arms around a good-looking man with my same crooked smile and cleft chin. He was both familiar and a stranger.

"I think that's your pa." Jack was right. I recognized the class ring on the man's hand.

I had to force myself to put the picture aside, even if I wanted to memorize the face I had never really known.

"Hmm, this is interesting." I held up a folded newspaper clipping dated 1968.

Jack pointed at the small script beneath the photo. "That's your grandpa, Charlie Ashby."

The photograph was blurry due to its age. Charles Ashby, my grandfather, stood in front of the town square in what looked like some kind of ribbon-cutting ceremony. Young children flanked him on either side, all smiling broadly. But Charles wasn't smiling. He looked severe and forbidding, like a chiseled piece of granite.

"He died before I was born, and all the stories I've heard involve him doing some great deed for the community. The Ashbys worked hard at hiding the evil parts of themselves." There was something soulless about Charlie Ashby's eyes and the set of his mouth. He was tall, towering over the kids surrounding him.

"Is that my mom?" I scanned the list of names below the photograph.

"Yep. See? Constance Ashby," Jack answered, his finger hovering over her name. "There's Natalie's dad. And those are my parents at the back."

"But who's that?" I indicated the boy huddled against my grandfather's side. The child acted as if he wanted to hide behind the large man's legs. Charlie's hand appeared heavy on the shoulder of the boy, who appeared small for his age and uncomfortable with being in front of a camera. He was cute, but with hesitant eyes. He didn't smile, and his clothes were torn and dirty. Charlie seemed protective of him.

"Huh. It says here that's Donald Hickman," Jack mused. "I've never seen pictures of Chief Hickman as a kid."

There was something about the chief as a child that made me sad. Maybe it was the worn clothes or his tentative posture. All the kids in the photo were young, probably no more than eight or nine, but there was a maturity to young Donald Hickman's expression that shouldn't have been there. I knew he'd lived a life that had caused him to grow up faster than he should.

I put the pictures back where I'd found them. "I was really hoping I'd find something that would prove my mom isn't who I suspect she is." I looked around the room again, frustrated when it revealed nothing of use. A sob erupted out of me before I could hold it back. The realization of what I suspected about my mom hit me hard. I covered my face with my hands, feeling myself start to fall apart. Jack came closer, but I waved him off.

"I just need a minute. I need—" I couldn't finish my sentence. Suddenly, being in the same space that Mom slept in was too much. Her things, these pictures, her scent . . .

I ran from the room and escaped across the hall. I sat down on my tiny twin bed and sucked the tears back where they belonged. Now wasn't the time to feel sorry for myself.

The mattress sagged as Jackson sat down beside me. I rubbed my temples. "I'm sorry. I can't seem to get it together."

Jack looked at me, his brown eyes warm. "You don't have to apologize. Not to me."

We stared at each other. "You deserve more than any apology I could ever give you."

We both knew that I was referring to my running out on him all those years ago.

"I really am sorry, Jack." I pleaded with my eyes, because for some reason, right now, with my entire world being torn apart, it felt important to have his forgiveness. "I just couldn't stay and deal with it anymore."

Something on Jack's face seemed to crumble. He touched my face, his fingers lingering on my skin. "I know, Chey, but I didn't care about your family or your baggage. I only ever wanted to be with you." He met my eyes. "And God help me, I still do."

"Jack," I said, his name leaving me like a sigh. We reached for each other and kissed like we were never coming up for air. Seconds turned to minutes as the heat built between us. Clothing was thrown to the floor. Naked skin pressed together. We moved in perfect unison as we had always done.

This was what coming home felt like.

When we were finished, we curled up together beneath the blanket, trying not to fall off the narrow bed.

"We definitely had more room in this thing five years ago." Jack gave me a knowing grin.

I laughed as I sat up, propping myself up on my elbow. I looked down at his much-loved face. "I missed you."

His expression became tender as he tucked my hair behind my ears. "I missed you too. You have no idea how much."

My chest suddenly felt constricted. Images flashed in front of my eyes, and then I wasn't here.

I was *there*.

* * *

I was crying. It was cold and I was alone. I knew I had to wait. It wouldn't be long.

Day turned to night, and then I saw him. Big and covered in shadow as he called my name.

But the sound of his voice was familiar.

"Mom?" I called out, terrified.

It wasn't my mom. It was the Hickory Man. There was the sound of crunching, like bones being ground between teeth, accompanied by a smell I should know . . .

* * *

I recoiled at the memory of my dream. I felt unsettled and off-kilter. Why was I thinking about it now?

"What is it?" Jack asked, noticing the look on my face.

I shook my head and kissed him again. "It's nothing." I sat up, grabbing my shirt and putting it on. "As much as I hate it, we should go. Natalie'll be waiting for us."

"Yeah, we can't put this off," Jack started to get dressed but then stopped and leaned back down to kiss me again. He cupped my face in his hands. "We'll get to the bottom of all this, Chey. You're not alone anymore—you have me. And Nat. Always."

I wanted to cry at the heartbreak of it all.

To have found the love of my life again when everything was falling apart felt like the worst kind of irony.

17

–Natalie–

THE DRIVE TO Ashby Holler was quicker than I'd thought it would be. I almost longed for a deep snow to make the road impassable. I couldn't summon the usual excitement for the warmer than normal weather. Because with each passing mile, I came that much closer to a truth I wasn't sure I was ready for.

The road was desolate. I didn't pass another car. This isolated stretch of highway edged close to the mountain, heading north. Not many people drove out this way, and those who did had no idea that a long abandoned town lay just beyond the tree line.

I noticed the dilapidated bridge to my left that disappeared into the overgrowth of Hickory Woods. I knew it stretched over the empty gorge of Bobcat Creek.

I took a sudden right, my car bumping along the old path heading to the holler. I briefly worried about my tires. My car wasn't meant for off-roading, which I very much was doing. The dirt road that had once lead to the holler now blended in with the rest of the forest. It was nearly impossible to discern the road from the trees, but I knew my way, even though it had been years since I had been there. I recognized the fence we used to climb over and the rotted bench we'd carved our names into. When Chey, Jack, and I were kids, we used to play hide-and-seek in the deserted buildings. It was our make-believe world, and we had spent hours out in the middle of nowhere, with hollow houses as our castles.

This was the Blue Cliff that everyone had tried to forget about, and after reading the Ashby journal entries, I now knew why.

Jack's truck was already at the edge of Hickory Woods. Chey and Jack jumped out as I parked.

I reached into my glove box and pulled out the small bag of herbs. Fingering the soft material, I fleetingly wished I'd replaced it at some point. It felt like a bad omen, to go into the woods without a fresh bag, and this one was long overdue a replacement. I'd always relied on Constance for that. Though knowing what I knew about her now, I felt silly for believing in it.

In her.

I shoved it back, jumping as Chey tapped her knuckles against the window. She stepped away as I opened the door and climbed out.

"Well here goes nothin'. Time to track down my potentially murderous mother." She gave me a wry smile, her attempt at humor failing.

"Whatever we find out there, we'll deal with it together. The three of us have always been stronger as a unit." Jack's voice was firm.

I reached for Chey's hand, and we clung to one another. It would be so easy to fall apart. To curl into a ball and wait for all this to be over. But deep down I knew it would never be over. Not unless *we* stopped it. We couldn't count on the police. We only had each other, and that had to be enough. I was filled with a strength I didn't know I possessed.

We stood side by side.

The three of us.

"I think the cabin is a few miles west," Jack said, indicating the thicket of trees to our left. "It was past the well and near what looked to be the old Hickory Hill cemetery. I'm pretty sure we need to cut close to the slate cliffs and curve around to Black Cedar Falls. It seems to be a straight shot."

We began to walk, the trees enveloping us and pulling us in. The air was cooler here. The soft squelch of thick mud underfoot and the crunch of leaves were all we could hear as we moved in silence.

I wasn't sure what exactly we would find when we reached the cabin, but I only hoped that at least some of the answers we were looking for would be there. No matter what, nothing would be the same after today. For better or for worse.

We'd been walking for around thirty minutes when I asked to stop to catch my breath. The mild weather paired with the physical exertion was making me sweat. It had been a long time since I went on a hike. I may have grown up in the country, but I wasn't exactly an outdoors kind of gal.

My muscles were aching from trudging through mud and rock. I leaned my back against a knotty tree, resting briefly. Chey came to stand next to me, our breaths beginning to even out.

"How does your ma do this all the time?" I asked Chey, genuinely curious. "She's not exactly a spring chicken anymore. This is exhausting."

"She probably knows a hundred different ways through these trees." Her tone was bitter, her anger and hurt evident.

"Have you thought about what you're going to say if she's there?" I asked.

Chey's jaw twitched. "Maybe: 'I know you've been killing kids, and now you're going to prison'?" She zipped up her jacket, her eyes hard. "I have to face the fact that my mom, *my family*, is responsible for a lot of death."

We lapsed back into silence after that. We knew we needed to keep going, but we seemed reluctant to.

The sound of a branch cracking somewhere in the distance had us scrambling. We looked in the direction that we'd come, half expecting to see someone behind us.

"Are we being followed?" I whispered.

"I'm not sure," Chey whispered back as we hurried faster. "These godforsaken woods—they play tricks on your mind."

Less than twenty minutes later, we came to a small brick well, the stones slimy and covered in moss. A metallic scent filled the air. As we approached the cavernous opening, the smell became stronger. It burned my nose.

"This must be the well mentioned in the journals," Jack observed quietly.

I swallowed, recognizing the spot instantly. "I've been here. With Constance."

Cheyenne frowned. "What? When?"

"Sometimes she would take me into the woods. You'd be off with Jack and Hunter was busy, so I spent time with your ma. And one time we came here. I remember it taking forever to walk through the woods. And then Constance had me drop something into the well. She said—"

"Let me guess: it was for the Hickory Man? That he'd what? Reach up from the water and take whatever gross thing you offered?" Cheyenne cut in, sounding irritated.

I cast a scared glance around me. I didn't like her saying his name. Not out here. All of my old childhood fears had resurfaced with a vengeance as soon as we stepped foot into the woods. "Shh, Chey, not so loud," I begged.

"Christ, Nat, there's no goddamn Hickory Man!" She stomped over, gripping the edge and peered down inside. "It's a disused well, not some portal to hell." Moss and algae crept up the side of the crumbling bricks, and when I leaned over, rocks fell as the weakened sides gave way.

It was hard to tell how deep it went because it was full of water. It came almost to the top. There were strange-looking mushroom-like growths all along the inside. They were covered by a greenish fuzz and oozed a slimy substance.

I covered my nose. "It smells awful."

"Yeah, like something metallic but rotten." Chey coughed. "I hope we don't get some kind of lung disease breathing all that in. God knows what's growing in there."

I remembered the smell of dead and dying things that had emitted from its depths. I recalled the feeling of abject terror as I stood over the opening, fully expecting the Hickory Man to grab me and pull me in.

"Whisper a prayer, you'll need them there, as he pulls you into the mud," I said softly, trying not to hyperventilate.

"You okay, Nat?" Jackson looked at me with concern.

"What did the journal say? *'He comes by stream or river or brook. It flows from one plane to the next.'*" I stared into the brackish water. "Makes you wonder what purpose this served so far out in the middle of nowhere."

"This place feels strange," Jack said in a hush, his shoulders hunched up as if trying to protect himself.

He was right. The air felt different by the well. As if the trees themselves were holding their breath. And it was quiet. Too quiet.

"We built the well to remind us."

"On the map, everything beyond this point is blacked out. What if the well is where the old settlers thought he came into this world. What did you call it, Chey? Like a portal from hell or something? That means everything out there"—Jackson pointed off into the forest—"belongs to *him*."

The three of us looked at each other.

"'I submerged their faces,'" I whispered, the words choking me. I felt vomit rise in the back of my throat. The truth

pummeled me. "The Ashbys took the children to the well. They drowned them. They left them in the woods for *him*."

I couldn't get enough air into my lungs.

"It wouldn't be hard for a much larger man to overpower a little kid," Jack pointed out. "The water is high enough that it makes sense why their clothes were not submerged. They weren't held under running water. The Ashbys would simply lean them over the side and push their faces in."

The three of us wore the same expression: absolute and complete horror.

"This is where they were killed." Cheyenne looked around at the thick trees that stood in silent witness to generations of atrocity.

"And this is where it's *still* happening," I added, my voice broken and bleeding. "Olivia, Michael, Danielle, and Dakota were all found with water in their lungs. Tainted water."

We stared down into the old well. Smelling the stench of metal and fungus. The scent of contamination.

The memories of childish screams echoed around us. It hung in the air. It soaked into the ground.

This was an evil place. And I didn't want to stand there a second longer.

"Let's go," I pleaded. "Now."

Cheyenne and Jack nodded, both as eager as me to get away.

We carried on walking, each of us lost in their own thoughts, the specters of murdered kids following us the whole way.

Minutes began to feel like hours. We walked farther and farther into the woods. We went through what seemed to be miles of wilderness. With every step it felt like we were getting closer to some indescribable horror. As if we were walking toward a collective doom that we had no power— or will—to stay away from.

Finally, late in the day, we came upon a small wooden building. The doors and windows were still intact, and despite it being the middle of the woods, the path to the front door was clear.

A large tree had fallen over at some point. Part of it had been hacked up and disposed of, but the massive trunk still stood, split at the base.

"It's not what I expected it to look like," Chey eventually said. "I remember it being a lot more *Texas Chainsaw Massacre* than this. And someone's definitely been out here—and often by the looks of it."

Jack continued toward the door, his footsteps crunching along the jagged path. He reached for the handle, and we all expected it to be locked, so when the handle turned, we shared a look of surprise. The air whispered out, stale and warm. The door complained against the rusty hinges as Jack pulled it wide and went inside.

The cabin was bigger than it seemed from the outside. Four walls, two windows, and a large hearth along the far side. It stank of death and decay. There was no denying the smell. Living in a rural community taught you early to recognize the scent of dying things. Despite the smell, the place was surprisingly neat and tidy. A little dusty, but otherwise clean.

Jack wrinkled his nose. "It smells like someone's gutted a deer in here."

Some places held onto death. You could feel it. Taste it. Smell it. This shack, in the middle of nowhere, had felt violence, and the stench of it was everywhere.

The connection to Chey's family was evident by the pictures of Ashby kin on the wall, next to a framed hand-drawn map of the Hickory Woods that was a near replica of the one in the root cellar—down to the black smudge past the old well.

I turned my attention to the rest of the room. A blackened fireplace took up most of the far wall, complete with an old poker and an ancient set of billows. Shelving ran along the left-hand side of the entrance, but I automatically looked at the wooden table opposite the hearth. We all gathered around to have a better look.

"Is that . . .?" Jack began.

Chey's eyes were sad, as if the truth was killing her. "Silver coins. Old ones too. If I were a betting woman, I'd say they're the exact same kind found on those kids." Chey moved on to the object beside it. She picked up her mother's basket and the corn husk poppet and showed it to us. "We know who makes these. I even found one in the woods near Dakota's body," she exclaimed with finality, the sight of the coins and the dolls explaining everything. "Goddamn silver coins in my mother's herb basket. She said she lost it, but that was obviously a lie. And there's only one person that makes these poppets. She's been handing them out like candy all over town for years." Her words sounded forceful and angry. She lifted her hands in frustrated defeat. "Well that's that. The basket. The coins. The corn husk dolls. All here in my family's serial killer hunting cabin."

"This doesn't mean—" Jack began, but Chey silenced him with a furious glare.

"It was her . . . all these years . . . it was her." She looked between Jack and me. "We knew it before we came out here. And this . . . this is proof." She gestured to the room around us. At the undeniable link between the murders and Constance Ashby.

I didn't know what to say to make her feel better. There really wasn't anything to say. The basket was Constance's; we'd both know it anywhere. I began to scan the room for anything else. Anything that would prove or deny what we were seeing. I headed to the shelves, picking up dusty glass jars and wooden boxes. It was the same stuff we'd seen in the cellar. Everything about this place reminded me of Constance.

My foot kicked something as I reached up on tiptoes to a top shelf. A large wooden box with iron fastenings lay by my feet. I crouched down to look at it. The lock slipped free from the clasp with little effort, and I pushed open the lid.

I made a strangled noise and stood up, still looking at the box.

"What? What is it?" Chey asked, coming over with Jack right behind her. "Christ," she hissed.

Jack reached inside to pluck out a handful of photographs. There seemed to be hundreds of them. Black and white, sepia, color. Some were sketches, hastily drawn. But all of them were of children.

Dead children.

CHAPTER

18

–Natalie–

"WHAT DO WE do now?" I asked.

Chey hadn't spoken since we'd found the pictures. She stood by one of the windows, staring out at the forest, her expression blank. She looked broken. I had never seen her like this.

Jack was still sifting through the photographs. He'd found pictures of Danielle, Olivia, and Michael, and even Dakota. His, the most recent, was placed right on top. Like the cherry on top of a gruesome sundae.

There were so many children. Some of their faces were recognizable from the posters in town. Some were much, much older.

In the photos they were clearly dead. Their little bodies laid out in offering. Pale skin, eyes closed, hands positioned beside their bodies, prostrate on the ground in almost peaceful repose. All of them were exactly the same. The differences in hair color and clothing was eclipsed by the same careful precision in which their deceased bodies had been placed. The newer ones—the pictures of Michael, Olivia, Danielle, and Dakota—were obviously taken here, at the cabin. Now we knew where the bodies were kept for weeks until they were displayed in the woods. And why the room reeked of death and decay. Dakota's body had rested here until recently.

The thin paper of the photos was well worn, as if they'd been handled many times.

"Stop looking at them," I begged Jack.

I reached for the box, taking it from him, closing the lid on the photographs. "No good can come from seeing those." I put it back where I had found it. But I could feel them there, pleading with me to give them justice.

"We need to get help. We need to go to the chief and let him deal with all this." I gestured around me. "He'll know what to do."

Chey turned to us suddenly. "I need some air." She headed to the door, flinging it open with force and darting outside.

A few minutes later we heard shouting.

"How could you?" Chey's voice called out.

Jackson and I shared a startled look before rushing to the door.

Outside, Constance was frozen in her tracks, her eyes wide with horror at finding her daughter there, more so when she saw Jackson and I come out of the cabin.

"No, no, no, you shouldn't be here!" she shrieked. "Not all three of you! It's not safe. You need to go!"

"We're not going anywhere. Not until you admit what you've done!" Chey cried.

"He'll come for you kids. He's wanted you from the beginning. It's you he's after. You have to go, please," she pleaded. Her whole body was trembling. Her eyes were wild, and I barely recognized the woman I had always loved. She looked like someone lost to the woods. Lost to the demons in her own mind. The person in front of me wasn't familiar. She was a killer.

I was terrified of her.

"Stop it, Mom! Just stop it!"

Constance hurried forward, reaching for Cheyenne's arm. "You need to go—"

"Don't touch me!" Chey snatched her arm away, "I know what you did. You, Mom—not the Hickory Man. We all do. And I won't let you get away with it anymore." Her voice broke, and I felt my throat squeeze tight.

"I wanted to protect you, Cheyenne," Constance whimpered, her eyes beseeching. "Everything I've ever done was to protect you. All of you." She looked over at Jack and me. "But I failed." Her face scrunched up as if in pain. "My God, how I've failed."

She was deceptively nonthreatening. But she'd hurt so many children. Ruined so many families. Destroyed so many lives. How could anyone say they did such awfulness out of love? The recent memory of my father saying something similar rose to the surface.

The crack of a stick snapping echoed through the trees, and we all looked out to the clearing. We could hear someone moving out there. Getting closer.

My mind jumped to the Hickory Man, the dark, menacing presence of my childhood.

But now I knew better.

The Hickory Man didn't exist.

Evil was a person.

Of blood and bone and with a wicked heart.

Jack came to my side. I gripped his arm, my fingers digging into his flesh. I broke out into a cold sweat as leaves rustled and branches moved. I couldn't breathe. My heart hammered in my chest.

"It's too late. He's here," Constance rasped.

Despite now knowing how psychotic Constance Ashby was, a chill still slithered down my spine, and the hair on my arms stood up as I watched a large shape emerge from between the trees.

I was so focused on the figure that I didn't notice Constance running toward us. She stood as a barrier, her body guarding ours.

"Chief Hickman?" Jackson called out as the man became clear. The chief came trudging out of the brush, his hat pulled down low over his eyes.

He stopped when he saw us, though he didn't appear surprised, as if he had known he'd find us out here in the middle of nowhere. His expression turned resigned when he saw Constance. He reached up and pulled off his hat, running a hand through his thin hair.

"Good God, Connie," he said softly. He turned to Chey, who had grabbed a hold of her ma's arm and held her in place. "I'm so sorry, Cheyenne." he said, his voice filled with agony. "I'm so sorry, you had to find out about your mom like this."

"You knew?" Chey demanded, her voice like steel. "All this time, you knew what she was doing?" She didn't bother to hide her disgust. I was pretty sure Jack and I wore similar expressions.

The chief looked at the three of us, giving us all his attention in that way of his that made you feel comforted and special at the same time.

"Not at first, no," he began, "I always wanted to believe we'd gotten the right man. It wasn't until Jasper was released that I figured it out. I knew the stories, of course. There's been talk in this town for years about the Ashbys. And your mom has told me stories, plus there was all that business with your grandpa after the kids went missing back in the fifties. It made people start to question things and what went on out here in these woods. People started lookin' closer at all those kids dyin'. Like maybe they weren't all accidents."

"You're lying!" Constance yelled.

Chief Hickman ignored Constance. His face was haggard, but kind. "Your family's special, Cheyenne. But they've got darkness in them. You can't be raised in Blue Cliff and not know that your ancestors did some horrible things thinkin' they were keepin' this town safe." He looked at Constance, his affection obvious. "I didn't want to believe that that same darkness dwelled in your mother. I love her. I've always loved her. Even when she chose someone else. I would do just about anything in the world for her—and for you, Cheyenne. I didn't want to believe she could hurt those kids. But when the truth is obvious, you can't ignore it. You have to make sure that darkness doesn't burrow into your own heart too."

"Don't listen to him!" Constance bellowed before reaching into her pocket and pulling out a handful of herbs, flinging them at the chief as if warding off evil. "Your words are an abomination, Donald. I see that now! You thought you could fool me. And you did. For years you blinded me. You rendered me deaf. But I see now. I hear now. Tom saw it too! He told me there was darkness in your heart, and I wouldn't listen." She let out a sob. "I wouldn't listen! But my Tom knew!" She turned to us, her previously wild eyes now steady. "He speaks poison with his viper's tongue." She turned to Chey, reaching out to put her hands on her face, but Chey leaned away from her touch.

"Mom, you're sick. You're really, really sick, but it's over now."

"I did what I could to protect them. To protect *you*, my sweet girl." Constance reached for Chey again, and Chey turned from her. "I didn't realize that all this time I had to protect you from someone much more insidious. Someone I trusted. Someone full of more evil than the thing that dwelled among the trees. It didn't make sense with Dakota. He was the only one . . ." She seemed to be struggling to understand something.

"Stay away from me," Chey begged and began walking back toward the cabin. "I don't believe a thing you're saying." She held out her hands as if to fend off her mother. She turned and ran into the cabin.

I went after Cheyenne, ignoring Constance's shouts of protest. The chief was here. This was over. Inside the cabin I found Cheyenne sitting on the floor, her forehead pressed to her knees, her arms wrapped around them. I sat by her side and let her cry.

The door swung open and the chief came in, the heavy stomp of his boots sounding too loud in the small cabin. He glanced down at us, his mouth pinched with worry.

He pulled a chair out from under the table and sat down. The wood groaned beneath the weight of his body. He sighed wearily. "There's only one thing to do now, girls. I have to take her in. As much as it hurts me to do so. She has to pay for this."

Sympathy for him bloomed in my chest. Everyone knew Chief Hickman had been in love with Constance for years.

"I'm so sorry," I said to him. Because Constance's victims were many. We had all been damaged by her actions.

He offered me a morose smile before reaching into his pocket and pulling out a small tin of mints. Cracking the lid open, he pulled several out and popped them in his mouth. As he put them away, he crunched noisily, the sound loud. I was grateful for the strong smell of mint. It made the scent of death and rot less nauseating.

But that smell . . .

There was something about the fear fermenting in my stomach that caused a memory to slam into my consciousness. It came unbidden with the force of something I couldn't ignore . . .

*   *   *

It was hot in my room. Too hot. But Dad told me not to open the window.

"Leave it closed, Nat. Don't open it. Not ever."

But I was sweating. The fan was only moving around warm air.

Careful not to make a noise, I got up and, with all my might, lifted the heavy wooden sash, grateful for the immediate rush of the cool night breeze. The screen had a hole in it, and I watched as a firefly made its way through the opening. I caught it between my hands, laughing as its tiny legs tickled my palm.

There was a sound from outside. My bedroom was on the bottom floor. My window faced the backyard. I squinted at the dark shape of my swing set as it moved slowly in the wind.

Then he was there.

The giant shadow.

He moved slowly, melting out of the trees.

He came close to my window but stopped beneath the large elm. I knew he saw me. Fear made it hard to breathe. I had seen him before. Out there. In the forest.

I knew who he was. He was the Hickory Man, and he'd come for me.

"Natalie." He said my name softly. "Natalie, come with me. Come to the woods."

I started to shiver as he moved closer, fear threading through my tiny body. The smell hit me as he reached the window. The strong smell of mint. My stomach churned.

"Natalie . . ." He whispered my name again, and I whimpered as he reached a hand up for me. "Come and play in the woods with me."

"No!" I turned around to see my dad rushing into my room. He stopped, looking outside at the man moving away from my window. "Go away! I told you, you can't have her!" he shouted, slamming the window closed and pulling the curtains back across the glass.

He turned to me. I expected him to be angry because I hadn't listened. But he didn't look angry; he looked afraid. "I told you never to open your window, Natalie. It's not safe—do *you hear me?" He gripped my arms so tightly I cried out, but he didn't let go. "Do you promise, Natalie?"*

"I promise, Daddy," I whimpered.

He let me go and ushered me back to my bed, tucking me in. I thought he would stay with me, but he didn't. Daddy rushed out of the room as quickly as he'd come in.

Heat burned through my body, but this time I didn't complain. Because I was really terror-stricken. Afraid of my daddy's face when he saw me by the window. And more than that, I was frightened of the man outside.

I knew who he was.

He was the Hickory Man.

I pulled the covers over my head as if they could shield me from the boogie man.

But I could still hear him crunching the bones of little children, and I could still smell mint—the surprising scent of the Hickory Man.

*   *   *

The memory went as fast as it came. I had experienced snippets of this recollection over the years, but I had been so young I couldn't be sure what was real and what my child brain had made up. But I clearly remembered the terror. The image of the shadow in my yard coming for me. I was pretty sure it hadn't been the first time I had seen *him*. I vaguely recalled telling my dad about *him* weeks before. And I definitely remembered bringing it up again years later, only to be told by my seemingly trustworthy father that I had imagined the whole thing. I could add that to the list of things he had lied to me about.

I started to tremble, unable to calm myself.

The chief continued to crunch on the candy, and I felt as if I were in quicksand, clawing desperately to hold on. To not be swallowed whole.

Something wasn't adding up.

Memories were fuzzy. Coming and going.

But the danger felt real. It was here and waiting for us.

Cheyenne looked up, her eyes fixing on the chief. "Where is she? Where's my mom?"

"She won't be hurtin' anyone now—don't worry. Jack's out there with her. Such a decent boy. I always had a soft spot for him. For all of you. My three perfect kids," he said with an indulgent smile.

"The evidence against Constance all seems a little circumstantial, don't you think, Chief?" I found myself piping up. My unease was growing.

The chief's eyes fell to me. He regarded me as if trying to figure me out. Then his mouth broke into a large, delighted smile. "You've got a sharp mind, just like your pa. Always thinkin' of the details. He did the same thing with Jasper."

I frowned, feeling more and more uncomfortable.

His expression was contrite. "I feel horrible about my role in all that nastiness. I knew there was a chance Jasper was innocent, but I let Stew talk me into it. Said we needed to get someone behind bars and fast. I had more than a dozen complaints about Jasper already. No one liked him. Then there was Connie, spoutin' off to anyone who would listen about seein' him in the woods. So, I trusted your pa to put together a good case. I believed the evidence would show we had the right man." He shook his head. "I was caught up in the rush of findin' the bad guy, I guess. I let your pa talk me into something I would never have normally agreed to. We were comin' from a good place—or at least I was. I can't speak for Stewart and his motivations."

So this was how he was going to play it. He was throwing my dad under the bus. Not that my dad didn't deserve it, but I knew they were equal parties in what had happened. But it seemed the good ol' chief was already polishing his image as the local hero who had been bamboozled by the wily assistant commonwealth attorney looking to build his career. And he knew that everyone would believe it. People loved the chief. My dad, not so much. At one time my dad had been well thought of, but with his extravagant house and too expensive suits, the kind regard of his neighbors had disappeared. The citizens of Blue Cliff didn't like a show-off, and my parents' airs and graces were not appreciated.

Even though the chief was saying all the things I myself had already thought, somehow hearing them from him made it ring false. As if he was trying *too* hard.

"Seems to me after the Jasper stuff, you'd be more careful about who you put in jail. You'll need a better case than last time. Public goodwill only gets you so far," I went on. Why was I arguing? Up until ten minutes ago, I had been convinced Constance was the killer. All signs pointed to her.

So why was I second-guessing things now?

Because of how Constance stood between us and the man coming out of the woods, convinced we were in danger. Because of the love I saw on her face when she looked at Chey and me.

Because for all of her sometimes terrifying eccentricities, when face-to-face with Constance Ashby, in my soul I couldn't believe that she would *ever* hurt a child.

Sometimes, the so-called truth was an illusion force-fed to you by a guilty conscience.

"We have to let Chief Hickman do his job," Cheyenne argued quietly, her face stricken. "Stop fighting it."

The chief was looking out the window, presumably at Constance and Jack, and I realized how awfully silent things were out there. Constance had been yelling only minutes ago. Why had she suddenly gone quiet? Was Jack restraining her?

"You saw the coins in Mom's basket. We read the journals. This place belongs to my family. Hell, you even said Mom brought you out to the well. One plus one equals two," Cheyenne exclaimed, pitching her voice low. It was obvious that she'd already given up. That she'd accepted who she thought her ma was.

"Constance will pay for her crimes. Then we can start puttin' all this behind us." Chief Hickman stood up and put another mint in his mouth, the smell now making me want to retch.

The smell.

That goddamn smell!

Familiarity and fear clawed their way up from my subconscious as the room spun.

"The mints . . ." I started to say, but the words died in my mouth as the door flew open and Constance appeared in the entryway. She looked like a vengeful goddess. A blade gleamed in her hand, and a thin trail of blood dripped down the left side of her face.

"Mom!" Cheyenne yelled.

I could see Jack on the ground behind her, apparently unconscious. Or dead. I felt light-headed with panic.

"Oh my God," I gasped.

Constance lifted her hand. "I won't let you hurt them, Donald. I know what you did. I've been wondering about things for a while. But I told myself those thoughts were wrong. When you showed up at my door five years ago, your brown uniform torn and scratches on your arms, I didn't ask questions because I trusted you." She drew herself upright, her face furious.

"And when I saw you only a few weeks ago with that boy in the woods, I should have said something. I shouldn't have believed you when you said you were only showing him the old trails. I didn't want to listen to what my heart was telling me. I didn't want to think the worst of you." She looked over at Chey and me, her eyes bleak.

"But I knew. Deep down, I think I always knew—I just didn't want to believe it. I had seen that look before. On my pa's face. I saw it and I looked the other way because I couldn't bear the truth then, and I can't bear the truth now. This is as much my fault as anyone's. But I won't look away this time. Your evil ends here."

Chief Hickman snorted as if she were telling a funny joke. "I have no idea what you're talkin' about, Connie—"

"I know about Tom," she interrupted him. The chief's mouth shut, the denials silent. "It was staring me in the face the whole time. It looked at me through the eyes of my oldest and closest friend." She wasn't screaming or yelling. She was deadly calm.

The chief's eyes hardened. "Jesus, Connie, you're always yammerin' on and on about that do-nothin' husband of yours. If you had any self-respect, you'd shut the hell up about that no-good outsider." He sounded like a man with wounded pride. It was obvious he was pissed Constance had taken up with someone else. It was a grudge he'd held onto. But why were they talking about Chey's dad when it seemed there were more pressing issues?

"I knew something was wrong when he didn't come home. He said he was going to see you. That he needed to talk to you about Chey. Said he saw you out there in the woods with her. He knew you watched her. But then Stew said he saw Tom leavin' town, and stupid me didn't question it, as much as it hurt. Because I believed you with my whole heart. I listened when you told me my Tom wasn't happy. That a man from out there could never be content with a Blue Cliff life."

It was obvious that Constance was angry, but there was now a deep sadness as well. Neither Chey nor I moved, afraid of breaking whatever this was. We were terrified as it built toward a horrible climax.

Chief Hickman spat on the floor at Constance's feet, startling me. "Don't go talkin' about your whole heart, Connie. I loved you and you shit on me. Gettin' with some lowlife outta-towner. Everyone expected us to be together. Your pa expected it too. It's how it was meant to be. You humiliated me." His features turned harsh, his face warping into something dangerous.

Constance shook her head. "It was never about love with you, Donnie. It was about getting what you thought was owed to you. Your *entitlement*." Her eyes flashed in our direction, and I saw the very real fear there, and it froze me from the inside out. "You wanted me, so you killed him, didn't you. You killed my Tom!"

The chief laughed. A rich, awful sound that filled the room. "Sure, I killed Tom. He was like a fly in the ointment, always buzzin' around, pokin' his nose where it didn't belong. But it wasn't about you, Connie. It never has been." Then he turned and looked at Chey and me huddled together, and his smile was full of nightmares. "That stupid man of yours thought he knew. Came at me with all his empty threats." His lip curled. "As if I'd ever be scared by a weak man like Tom Jenkins. A man that didn't even give his family his name."

"I'll stop you! I swear I will!" Constance shouted, taking his attention from us, which I could tell was her intention.

There was a brief moment of tension. as if everything was poised, waiting. Then the chief started to laugh again. When I was younger his laugh had been a comfort. It was the laugh of a costumed Santa Claus at Christmas. It was the laugh of a man beloved by everyone.

That laugh, I now realized, was a total lie.

He stopped abruptly and took a step toward Constance. "I'll do whatever the fuck I want, Connie, and there's not a damn thing you can do to stop me." These weren't the words of a man in love. This was a man ready to stop whoever got in his way.

With a quickness I didn't know Constance possessed, she thrust the knife toward him, but he grabbed her arm, wrenching the weapon free from her grip. With a sudden, violent movement, he twisted her body and embedded the knife in her stomach.

Cheyenne screamed and tried to get to her ma, but I held her back, instinctively pulling us as far away from the scene as possible.

Constance's face crumpled, tears wet on her cheeks. She reached out toward us. "Chey. Natalie." Her voice was broken. "My babies. I'm so sorry." And then she fell to the floor, blood pooling around her unmoving body.

Cheyenne had stopped screaming, but the echo of it still reverberated around us. We were both quiet as we watched Chief Hickman slowly wipe the knife on his pants leg. He stared down at Constance. "Why do you always have to ruin everything?" He kicked her still form with the tip of his boot, as if she were roadkill.

He turned to us, his face eerily blank. His eyes were flat, like a snake's. He gripped the knife at his side, and his eyes bore into mine. Then Cheyenne's. He turned to look at Jack, who still hadn't moved from the ground outside.

He walked back to the table and sat down again, resting the knife on his thigh. His gaze held us prisoner. We were trapped.

"Well, girls," he said, his voice low and unemotional. "I think the cat's out of the bag now, don't you agree?"

19

—Cheyenne—

REALITY WARPED AROUND me. Things went hazy, as if I were dreaming the events that began to unfold. Nothing felt real.

But it was. All of it.

I screamed, my throat raw and bleeding. My mom's expression shattered like glass as she fell. The look of total betrayal and fear in her eyes would haunt me forever.

Chief Hickman towered over my mother's seemingly lifeless body. She had to be dead. She was losing too much blood. It seeped between the wooden slats beneath her. And she hadn't made a sound when the chief kicked her. Not a peep.

I had believed my mother had killed four children.

I had been convinced of it.

Yet if my mother was a killer, why was Chief Donald Hickman wiping my mother's blood on his pants and watching Natalie and me with a look of calculated cruelty? A look I had never seen on his face before?

And why had he admitted to killing my father?

The truth of that slammed into me.

Chief Hickman had murdered my father.

Tom Jenkins hadn't walked out on his family. He hadn't abandoned my mom and me. He had been taken from us. A part of me felt an intense relief, but that part was quickly drowned out by the voice inside my head, yelling at me to *get out.*

"Mom?" I croaked, watching for any sign of life. There was none. I let out a guttural cry, unable to contain it any longer. Natalie held me together. In the history of our friendship, I had always been the strong one.

Not this time. This time I needed *her* strength.

"Shh, Chey, shh," she hushed me. Her calm steadiness did the trick, and I swallowed the sobs.

My mother was probably dead. And I no longer believed she had killed those kids. The moment the chief sank the knife into her, I knew she was innocent. It was because of the total devastation on her face at the realization of what was happening. It was how her eyes clung to mine in desperation. How she said my name with a love I didn't deserve.

No matter what her family had done before her, that wasn't my mom. In my heart, I knew my earlier suspicions had been wrong. I felt ashamed at having believed the worst about her for most of my life. I hardly remembered a time when I hadn't been embarrassed or annoyed by her. And these last few days, since I'd found Dakota in the woods, I had even believed her capable of the worst kind of atrocities.

What sort of daughter does something like that?

A shitty one, that's who.

I was spiraling downward in a wave of self-recrimination. I had failed my mother. I had failed Natalie and Jack.

"So what are you gonna do, girls? You gonna play nice?" Chief Hickman licked his lips and watched us with emotionless eyes. He may have had the face of the man I had known all my life, but he was a total stranger.

Where was my protective "Uncle Donnie"? The man who loved my mother and watched out for us? Where was the kind Blue Cliff chief everyone could count on? Where was the man who had looked so upset when we led him to Dakota's body? I was having a difficult time meshing these two diametrically opposed individuals together. It seemed my mother's first love was not only evil, but he was also one hell of an actor.

It was as if he had finally taken off the mask he always wore, in order to reveal the monster beneath.

"You killed Chey's dad," Natalie said, her voice rough. It wasn't a question, it was a statement.

Chief Hickman tapped the knife blade against the table top. *Tap. Tap. Tap.* "Blue Cliff isn't a place for outsiders. Just ask Jasper." He chuckled as if telling a funny joke.

"But why?" I croaked out.

A sadistic smile spread across his aged face. "You weren't mine, Cheyenne, but you should have been." His eyes pinned me in place. "I waited a long time for you."

I felt Natalie squeeze closer to me, her hand clutching mine, and I held on, afraid to let go. "I don't understand . . . I thought . . ." I shook my head. "I thought you loved my mom."

The chief got to his feet and walked to the door, looking out at Jack's still body. He braced himself against the jamb. "This was never about Tom, or even Connie. This has nothing to do with any of that."

The chief turned back to us, his face now tender. That gentleness after the violence was obscene.

"You were always meant to end up here. This would have concluded a long time ago if I hadn't been so sloppy. I've been payin' for my mistakes ever since. I tried again, you see. I had to." He put his hand in his pocket, jingling something that sounded like change. "But they weren't right. They weren't special like you, Natalie, and Jack. I tried to make it work. Michael, Livvie, and Danielle should have made me feel . . . something. But I was tryin' to fit a square peg into a circle hole. I should have known better. When you build somethin' up in your head and the parts change halfway, it's never going to work out the way you want it to." He snorted in apparent disgust. "It didn't feel the way I expected. Not with them. It will never feel right because it *always* should have been you three. And I almost screwed up everything with my own carelessness."

"The Altoid tin. That was yours. My god, and the fabric was from your police uniform. How did no one see it?" Natalie sounded numb.

"The DNA too. Good thing I had a man on the inside to make all that go away. I worried a little when someone found it and handed it over to the state. Should have known Stew would mess that up too. He swore he got rid of all that. I shouldn't have trusted him. That man's a snake through and through. That was my stupidity. I thought the jig was up. Luckily, I'm smarter than Stew Bartlett. Because you have to be in the system to be a match. And no one will ever look my way. I've made sure of that." He gave her a wink, and I felt sick with revulsion.

"But what about Dakota? Why did you kill him?" Natalie demanded, her entire body shaking either in rage or fear. Maybe both.

Chief Hickman ran his tongue over his teeth. "Ah yes, poor, trustin' Dakota Mason. He really sent Connie over the edge, didn't he?" His grin was horrible. "She was doin' okay, you know, but it wouldn't take much to make her lose it again. She did it before, remember? I knew she wouldn't be able to handle another missin' young'un. In fact, I banked on it."

"You murdered him to get me back here," I deduced. "Because you knew how my mom would react. Everyone saw how she was five years ago. You knew another child going missing would trigger her in the worst possible way. And you also knew I could never say no if I thought she was getting bad again. Even though that was the reason I left, if my mom needed me, I'd come back. Like you said when you called me, 'You're an Ashby.' You gambled on my sense of duty, and you were right."

"I've always been good at readin' people. I know what they want. I know what makes 'em tick. And I know that, deep down, you want nothin' more than for your mom to love and need you. So I gave you your heart's desire, Cheyenne. You should be thankin' me." He smiled, as if had given me a Christmas gift I had been asking for.

"That boy lost his life because you wanted to get Cheyenne back to Blue Cliff?" Natalie was aghast.

He stared at us for a long, uncomfortable moment. "You're here, aren't you? All three of you. My plan worked." He seemed barely able to contain his excitement. "You three were mine. Do you realize how hard it was for me to live here, watchin' you and Jack live your lives, knowin' Chey was out *there*? I was damn near out of my mind. So I waited. I'm a patient man. I knew I had to make up for my mistakes. This is my chance to get it right. I looked for the signs." His words were quiet and deadly, and his features were scarily calm.

Natalie squeezed my fingers hard enough for them to lose circulation.

"You killed those poor kids," I accused, sounding out of breath. "They trusted you! We all did!" I felt myself getting worked up. Anger overtook fear.

Chief Hickman gave me a fond smile. "The Ashbys are special. I've felt a closeness . . . an *affinity* to your family my whole life. Did you know your grandpa Charlie would come visit me when I was a young boy? My own pa was an alcoholic. A mean one too." He ran his hand along his arm absently, stroking the scars that were there. "Used my skin as an ashtray when I didn't listen. It hurt, but it only made me tougher. That son of a bitch didn't live long enough to try somethin' worse. No one mourned him. Especially not me."

He hadn't bothered to acknowledge my accusation. That's not how he wanted to tell his story.

"But Charlie saw something in me. He said I was an Ashby in soul if not in blood. Connie and I were friends of sorts. But she was soft. Always wantin' to help people. I hated her pity, but I allowed it. If only because it gave me access to somethin' better." He pressed the tip of his thumb into the sharp blade, a bead of blood rising to the surface. "The first time she brought me out to the woods, it felt like comin' home. Your grandpa had strung up a deer he had killed. He saw me watchin', so he handed me a knife and told me to help him gut it. That was the beginnin'."

I didn't want to listen to him. I wished I could block him out. But I couldn't. He wouldn't let me.

"He saw I had a taste for the darker things, like he did," he continued.

The chief ran his hand along the shelves, stopping periodically to open a box. "Charlie was a cold man. A tough man. He wasn't all about makin' friends. Yet everyone respected him. They knew he kept them safe. Or at least that's what he made them believe. He told me once that trust concealed everything. People would look the other way as long as they trusted you. As long as they believed. And Charlie fed their trust and their belief by elaborating on the local legends and by remindin' them of our shared history. All the Ashbys did the same. They built a legacy for their family that got rid of all doubt. They knew how to keep this town docile while they lived—and killed—as they wanted."

Chief Hickman spoke about my family with complete reverence. He actually thought the fact that these men killed children was something wonderful.

"I wanted that. I wanted their trust for my own reasons. Charlie recognized the thirst in me because it mirrored the one in him. So he'd take me into the woods. He'd show me things. I knew the secrets before Connie ever told me. Because they were mine first." There was that word again.

Mine.

Donald Hickman was a man who needed to be in charge. He needed to *own*. And he needed *power*.

It all made sense now.

The pitiful runt of a child cowering against my grandfather's side. Mistreated and abused. A town that looked the other way. He had grown up with nothing. Even his name hadn't mattered.

That sad boy had been molded in the image of an Ashby. My grandfather's twisted and disturbed guidance had fueled the fire that burned in his belly. He grew up entitled. Bloodthirsty.

And cruel.

The chief became the demon in the woods. The evil we should have been fearing all along.

The chief looked down at my mother, his expression icy. He had done a good job of making everyone think he actually loved her, because it was clear now that this man had no idea what love really was.

"You're deranged!" Natalie yelled, her body still clinging to mine.

Chief laughed. "I knew about the other children. Everyone suspected, but only I *knew*. People accepted them as "accidents," even if in their hearts they wondered. It had never been spelled out for what it was. Not until Charlie told me. Because he knew I could handle it. Your mom never had the stomach for the tough stuff. She was weak." He curled his lip in obvious disgust.

"My mother was not weak," I spat out. "She was stronger than you'll ever be."

The chief's smile grew. "You goin' all high and mighty on me, Cheyenne? After the way you left her here to rot?"

His words were like a slap in the face. I had left her alone with a killer.

"So you believe in all that bullshit about the Hickory Man? That he needs the blood of the youngest fruit? That's why you did all this? You know it's crap, right?" I taunted, my words sounding braver than I felt.

Chief Hickman's smile twisted into a sneer. "Of course not. I'm not a fuckin' idiot, Cheyenne. Though you have to admit there's somethin' about these woods that doesn't sit right." He looked out the window, suddenly thoughtful. "I can see how easy it was for our ancestors to believe a demon lived out here. Sometimes you see things or hear things, and you wonder." He turned back to us. "But there is no Hickory Man. Those kids are dead because of a tale perpetuated to hide the bloodthirsty urges of men like me. Your grandpa knew there was no evil bein' needin' appeasement. That's not why he took them. And that's not why I followed in his footsteps when your mother refused to." He bared his teeth. "You see, it's easy to blame murder on a ghost when an entire town is raised to believe in monsters."

"Jasper wasn't a ghost. He was a man, and you sent him to prison," Natalie shot back.

"Jasper had it comin'. I couldn't have him hangin' around after everything he saw. Always snoopin' where he shouldn't. Eyes on everything. He saw me with Olivia that day she went missin'. And Danielle too. He was gonna be a problem, so I made sure he went away." The chief seemed pretty damn proud of himself.

I remembered that conversation with Jasper all those years ago. His sad eyes and his insistence that he was innocent.

"I see stuff. Things they don't realize I see."

"You're a psycho, and from the sounds of it, Chey's grandpa was too," Natalie snarled. "And you got my dad to somehow go along with your crimes."

Chief Hickman gave her a shrewd look. "Your father had his own reasons for doin' what he did. Who's to say his motivations were any better than mine?" He lifted his shoulders in a nonchalant shrug.

"If my dad had known what you really were, he would have stopped you," Natalie said through gritted teeth.

"You don't know your pa at all, Natalie. Stew and I had an understandin'. He kept his mouth shut so I'd try to forget all about his beautiful baby girl." His look was indulgent. "But you're impossible to forget Natalie. You, Chey, and Jack are mine. It was only a matter of time before I claimed you."

His words sunk in, their meaning clear. Stewart Bartlett knew what Chief Hickman was and had said nothing.

"No, he wouldn't do that. He wouldn't stay silent if he knew you had murdered those kids." Natalie's face paled.

The chief cocked his head to one side. "Men will do just about anything to protect their own. It's instinct. Your fool of a pa couldn't accept that you belonged to me. He kept me from what was mine for long enough."

I could feel Natalie start to tremble. Her palm, pressed against mine, was slick with sweat. "It was you outside my window," she whispered. This didn't sound like a revelation—more of a confirmation.

The chief pulled out another mint and popped it in his mouth. "I'm surprised you remember that. You were so young—only four years old—and perfect. Just like Cheyenne. And just like Jack." In any other situation, his words would have sounded like those of a caring uncle. Now they dripped with sinister meaning. His intentions toward us were all too obvious. "It was always you three for me."

My stomach fell.

He gnashed his mints, the sound loud, like crunching bones.

"You were there and my dad *knew* it was you." Natalie was practically vibrating with anger.

The smell of mint was strong. It mixed with the aroma of damp earth and wood rot. It was a combination of scents that was both unique and familiar.

I had smelled them before.

I let out a gasp, and both Natalie and the chief looked at me.

"I remember too," I breathed, my mind opening up and swallowing me whole.

* * *

"You have to wait for him. Just as I did when I was your age. You have to present yourself to him. To offer him your service. If your intentions are pure, he won't hurt you, Chey." My mom gripped my small shoulders hard enough to bruise. We were standing deep in the woods. Mom had led me past the old well, which she explained was how he came into our world.

"You have to stand here until he comes, do you understand? You can't run. You have to wait. Don't run, Chey. It will be worse for you if you do."

I was young. I had just turned five. But I wasn't too young to know my way around the woods. I knew that beyond the stones was the old cabin. It wouldn't take me long to get there. I wished I was there now. I didn't want to stand out in the woods all by myself. Even though Mom had been preparing me for this, I still didn't understand.

"Don't leave me, Mom," I begged, trying not to cry.

My mom pulled me into a hug. "We're doing things our own way now. You'll see that one day. But this has to happen if it's to be different. We can alter the path, but not the first step."

I didn't understand, and I knew she wouldn't explain. So I swallowed my cries as she took out a knife and cut the palm of my hand. Blood dripped onto the ground. I heard her say that the blood would call him to me. I was scared, so scared as I watched my mother leave in the direction we had come from.

I stood there for a long time, waiting. It was fall and got cold in the woods at night. My mom had made me dress in an old-timey nightgown. I hated it. It made me all itchy.

It was getting dark when I heard the trees move. I was so scared. I could scream, but I didn't dare. Mom had told me to keep quiet. To stay still. And to wait.

I heard the crunch of what sounded like bones grinding together before I saw him.

He pushed through the branches, his breathing heavy. My knees were shaking. I started to cry, even though I knew I shouldn't.

I wanted my mom.

He smelled of earth and dead things, of blood and leaves and something familiar. He breathed again, and the scent of mint washed over me. It reminded me of the mint that grew in my mom's garden.

"It's okay, Cheyenne. I'll take care of you," he promised, his voice low and deep. I didn't believe him. It was almost nightfall, and his face was in shadow, but I knew him. I knew who he was.

"Are you the Hickory Man?" I whispered.

"I'm here to protect you from him, Cheyenne." He took my hand and tugged me forward. I stumbled over a rock and fell to the ground.

"I want to go home," I wailed.

I felt myself being lifted to my feet, a hand heavy on my shoulder. "You're so important, Cheyenne. You mean more to me than you will ever know." I looked up into Uncle Donnie's eyes. He pushed a piece of hair back from my face. I listened to him because Uncle Donnie never lied to me. He liked me. He told me so all the time.

The crunching came again. Not bones at all, I realized, but mints.

"Mom says I have to stay here and wait for him," I argued.

"Your mom will never know. Once she realizes you're not here, everything will be over. You'll have saved the town!" He said it like I was going to be a superhero. He took my hand. "Come on, before it's too late."

I followed him into the woods, toward the old hunting cabin.

I trusted him.

I had no reason not to.

CHAPTER

20

—Cheyenne—

I CLUTCHED A HAND to my chest. Every new truth fell with the impact of a nuclear bomb.

"It wasn't a dream. My God, it wasn't a dream." I covered my face with my hands. I felt Natalie's arm go around my shoulders, and I began to cry. I wasn't even sure why I was crying now. The loss, the devastation, the fear . . . the pointlessness of it all.

"Stop crying. Now," he demanded loudly.

I dropped my hands and met his gaze head on. I wouldn't look away. I wouldn't give him the satisfaction.

"You were going to kill me all those years ago. Nat and Jack too. They used to see you outside their houses. You were planning to take us to the woods just like you did the others," I growled.

Chief Hickman tapped the flat of the blade against his leg. Minutes ticked by, and I was starting to think he wasn't going to respond. The metallic tang of Mom's blood made me want to gag.

"I always liked this place, tucked away in the woods. Far from everything," he mused, changing the subject drastically enough to give me whiplash. "Connie used to bring me out here when we were younger. Back then it wasn't much more than a pile of timber with holes in the roof. But over time I fixed it up. Sometimes with Connie, sometimes by myself. She didn't care that I came here. She didn't know her father used to come here as well. And her grandfather too. And every Ashby before her. And then it became mine."

He turned his attention to the framed map—the replica of the one in the cellar. "It's the perfect spot. The well is close, only a short walk. It made it all so easy. Dunk 'em in, drag 'em out, bring 'em here. Then wait. Until the time was right for them to be found." He grinned at me. "And who better to find 'em than you, Cheyenne. My perfect girl."

He lifted one of the coins from the basket and jingled it in his hand. "The coins are a nice touch, don't ya think? You have to appreciate the irony of all those dead kids who couldn't be protected by their silly superstition." Then he picked up a poppet and looked at me, a pleased expression on his horrible face. "And this was just for you, Chey. I knew you'd make the connection when you found it by Dakota. Because you're a smart girl. I raised you to be that way."

"So those kids died not because the Hickory Man would destroy the town if he didn't get his sacrifice, but because you and the Ashbys liked killing little kids," Natalie spat out.

The chief appeared frustrated with Natalie's assertion. "This goes back hundreds of years. This is all wrapped up in this town's history." He held his arms out in dramatic flair. "Charlie explained the importance of storytellin'. How there comes a point when people's fantasies become their reality. That's what's happened in Blue Cliff. There's no movin' on. There's no forgettin'. It's always there. Brockett and his mom killed those three kids for reasons that most people today would never understand. But Blue Cliff understands,

4

and it always will. Places like this breed men like me. We're a natural consequence to all that darkness."

"Are you seriously blaming the town for your actions? You're even more deluded than I thought," Natalie said incredulously.

The chief lifted the knife and pointed it at her menacingly. "This town made me who I am. Who Charlie was. Who the Ashbys became. And those kids died because *we* wanted them dead. It was the town's belief that made it possible. So you tell me who's really to blame here."

Natalie looked like she wanted to argue more, but the sight of the knife waving dangerously in our direction had me changing the course of the conversation.

"So you're saying that I come from a long line of psychopaths? That what? Murder is my birthright?" My fight-or-flight response was making me restless. I needed a plan and I needed it fast.

"Not all of them were like Charlie. I think Brockett and his mom truly thought that some wicked thing lived out here, and the only way to keep it happy was to give 'em the kids. Who knows how they came to that idea. But they were livin' in a time when you shit in a hole in the ground, so there wasn't a lot of rational thinkin' going on." Chief Hickman tapped the side of his head for emphasis. "Some thought they were protectin' the town, like your great-grandpa Jonas. Apparently he cried and cried over those kids. Was sick for weeks afterward. Charlie hated him. Said he was too soft. He hated that Connie seemed to take after him. He showed me the old journals that he kept down in the root cellar, where his pa whined about it. But he still took those kids and drowned them, right out there in that well. So he wasn't completely yellow-bellied."

The chief walked toward Nat and me. He towered over us, his presence tall and overpowering. I felt like a child again. Terrified of the boogeyman. Except the boogeyman stood right in front of me, and he was someone I had loved and trusted.

"Charlie showed me how to use the story. Back in the old days, the Ashby men simply waited for somethin' bad to happen. A house to burn down. A baby to die. Then they knew the time was right. It was the perfect cover. But Charlie didn't bother with that. He killed when he felt like it. And that's what I did. I planned it out for years. Waitin' for the perfect three."

"But you're the chief of police!" Natalie exclaimed, her firm voice breaking. She turned and looked at me, still struggling to make the connection.

Chief Hickman looked thoughtful. "You know, girls, it's awful hidin' who you really are. To put on a badge and a smile and pretend I don't have these thoughts. These urges. Even if bein' the police chief was the perfect mask for me to wear, I've hated every moment of it. Except for those moments out here in the woods with those kids. Then I could be who I wanted to be. But it wasn't enough. Not until I had my three. Who knows? Maybe if things had gone right all those years ago, Mikey, Livvie, Danielle, and Dakota might still be kickin.'" He smirked and I could only stare at him in horror.

"Oh my God," Natalie groaned beside me.

Chief Hickman seemed unaffected by our revulsion. He lifted his shoulders in a careless shrug. "I knew I was different, and I knew I had to be smart. Every decision I've ever made has been about layin' the groundwork and coverin' my tracks. I needed to take lessons from the men who came before me. Men who wanted the same things I did." I forced myself not to flinch as his fingers worked through my hair. "I crave things, Cheyenne," he said quietly, making my skin crawl.

"Why us?" I whispered, not wanting to know, but needing to.

He gripped my chin, forcing me to look him in the eyes. "I don't know why you called to me. Maybe because you're an Ashby. Or maybe because of somethin' inside you. I felt it when I looked at you. Natalie and Jack too. It was powerful. I thought of nothin' else but you and all the things I wanted to do to you. It became an obsession." He closed his eyes, his fingers still holding me captive. "You, Natalie, and Jack were wanted. Your families adored you. All three of your families were trusted and loved by everyone, and I needed to shatter this town. I needed to remind them of what it meant to truly fear. To truly grieve." He opened his eyes, and I had never seen such desire on someone's face. "I wanted to break them like I had been broken."

Then I saw it: the hate.

Donald Hickman *hated* Blue Cliff. He hated it more than perhaps even I had. The town had failed him as a child. People had turned the other way when he was abused and mistreated. The only person to show him what he perceived as kindness was the worst possible man to look up to. A man who twisted a child's innocence. A man who turned trust into terror.

Donald Hickman blamed Blue Cliff for what had happened to him. For not getting what he wanted, what he felt he deserved. For having to deny that part of himself that clawed at his insides.

Chief Hickman hated Blue Cliff, and he had wanted to make it pay. He wanted to break it apart and then be the one to pick up the bloody pieces.

Another terrible thought settled over me. "My mom took me to the woods. Did she hand me over to you?" I asked, my heart splintering.

His hand dropped and he thankfully backed away. "No, she left you out there because she's a fool. Because she thought it was some kind of rite of passage. Do you remember me tellin' you about her being left by herself for days when she was a child?"

I nodded. I had never heard that story before Chief Hickman told me.

"Apparently there was a tradition in your family where the firstborn would be left to the elements. I suppose in the olden days it was to see whether a kid was tough enough to survive out here. But given our town's fixation on the Hickory Man, it became some bizarre introduction to a forest demon. All seems a bit overdramatic to me. So, of course I knew the day would come when Connie would do the same with you, and then I would take you. I watched you three. I bided my time. Chey, you would be the first, and then I'd come for my other two. One by one." He came alive as he spoke about what he had planned for me—for us. He was disgustingly proud of himself.

I realized with dread that this was the happiest I had ever seen him. All those other times I now knew to be fake. Those smiles, those laughs, they had all been lies. But this, right now . . . here in these woods, with the memories of dead children all around him, he had found bliss.

"But it didn't work. Your plan failed, because here we are," Natalie interjected with obvious loathing.

The chief's expression became thunderous. "I know these woods. These trees. I had planned for so long. I don't know how it happened. The sky was clear. No storms that night . . ." He frowned, as if struggling with his recollection. "But the wind picked up. It was like a damn hurricane. We had just gotten here. Everything was fallin' into place, and I was so close. You were almost mine. Then a tree fell. It startled me is all. And you got away." He glared at me, as if it were my fault he hadn't gotten to murder me.

"After that, Stew became a bit more . . . stubborn. Decided to put his pathetic foot down for once. After losin' you, Chey, I let him. And Louise, the superstitious bitch, didn't leave Jack alone for a moment. Slept in his goddamn room for almost a year," he growled in frustration. "I had to force myself to give up on you three, as much as I didn't want to. I had to move on. I had to wait for others." He let out a slow breath. "I was on pins and needles for months after that, though. I didn't know what you would remember. Would you tell someone? But if you mentioned it to your mom, she must not have believed you, because she never said a word to me about it. You were young after all. Who takes a child's crazy stories seriously?"

I couldn't remember if I'd ever said anything to my mom. But I suspected I hadn't. Because even back then, a part of me was terrified of her. Of her making me go back out to the woods by myself. And like most early childhood memories, they eventually became hazy with time until they were forgotten altogether.

Except I hadn't really forgotten them. They became the fabric of my nightmares.

I could hardly believe my life had been saved by a freak accident. If not for a sudden storm, I would have become another name on the cellar wall.

He turned to stare out the window again. "The tree shouldn't have fallen. It had survived a hundred hard winters. It was strong." He wore a look of confused anger. "It had to have been a fluke. I'm not a believer and I never will be. It's *my* fault things got messed up. No one else's," he muttered to himself. "Mistakes happen. That's all it was. Mistakes and chance. This time will be different."

At that moment, outside, Jack let out a moan, and Chief Hickman's head swiveled in his direction. Jack had started to sit up, his hand going to the back of his head. His fingers came away wet.

"What the—?" He looked in our direction, his eyes meeting mine. They clouded with worry and fear. "Chey . . ."

"Seems you've woken up just in time, Jack, my boy," the chief said jovially, his demeanor changing completely as he walked outside and hoisted Jack up on unsteady feet. Jack wobbled and swayed, his eyes looking glassy. Blood had trailed from the head wound, but it didn't appear to still be bleeding. Jack had a good four inches on Donald Hickman and normally would have easily been able to overpower the older man, but not in his condition.

The chief shoved him into the cabin with us and closed the door behind him. Jack stumbled, almost pitching forward, but regained his balance. Chief Hickman took his gun from its holster and pointed it at Jack's chest. Still holding the knife in his other hand, the chief pressed the blade against the side of Jack's neck. "Go sit with the girls. Don't want you missin' out on story hour. It was startin' to get good."

Jack immediately held up his hands, his eyes going wide with shock. "What are you doing, Chief?"

Chief Hickman waved the gun in our direction. "I said, have a seat. You've always been a nice, obedient boy—don't go gettin' a backbone now."

Jackson had to step over my mom to get to us. His breathing became ragged as he took in the sight of her still form, but he wisely kept his mouth shut. He sat on the floor beside me. "What's going on, Chey?"

Chief Hickman dropped the knife onto the table and looked at us indulgently. "Look at you guys. All together, the way it used to be. My three perfect children."

"I don't understand. What happened to Constance?" Jack's face brightened. "Did you stop her, Chief?" He looked so hopeful. I hated to be the one to tell him that his childhood hero was actually the villain.

"Mom wasn't the one who needed to be stopped," I told him.

"What do you mean? Your mom hit me over the head with a goddamn rock, Chey. She knocked me out cold. She was saying some crazy stuff about the chief, and I was trying to hold her back . . ." His words trailed off. I saw the moment he caught on to the situation we were in. "Shit," he breathed.

"We were all wrong. It wasn't Jasper and it wasn't Mom," I whispered. All of us kept our eyes on the chief, who had started pacing again. "The chief planned to kill us when we were kids, Jack. He killed Michael, Olivia, Danielle, and Dakota."

"I can't believe this." Jack ran a hand down his face. "Why?" He sounded agonized.

Chief Hickman focused on us again, and I could sense a change in him. A note of finality. "We've talked enough. This has to end now. I've waited too long."

Natalie whimpered beside me, and I took her hand. Then I took Jack's.

It had always been the three of us.

In life, and now it seemed in death.

"Are we all ready?" he asked with an eager smile. "This moment is as much about you as it is about me."

I was so lost in my own fear that I didn't realize Jack had let go of my hand until he was on his feet.

He charged forward, slamming into Chief Hickman. Their bodies collided and fell sideways onto the hard floor.

The sound of the gun going off, not once, but twice in quick succession, was almost loud enough to pierce my eardrums. I couldn't tell if anyone had been shot. It was all a tangle of limbs, their bodies making it hard for me to see. I started to scramble toward them when another shot went off.

This time I could see everything.

"Jack!" I screamed, as he rolled sideways with a groan, his shirt now red with blood.

I began to rush toward him, but Chief Hickman was getting back onto his knees, still clutching the gun, his finger on the trigger.

"Sit back down, Cheyenne." He waved the gun in my direction. He looked down at his brown button-down shirt, which was also soaked in red. He, too, had been shot in the scuffle.

"Damn, that hurts," he panted, pressing a hand against the wound. I expected him to be furious, but instead he began to chuckle. "That wasn't part of the plan, but it'll do, don'tcha think? I put up a good fight."

He stumbled to his feet, looking a little unsteady.

"So, this is how the story's gonna go. I tracked your mom out here. I figured out she was the one who had murdered Dakota. I knew about this place because Connie and I are close, so it makes sense that she would have shown it to me at some point." He lifted the gun and pointed it in our direction again. "I found her here with the three of you. You two were dead already, but Jack here . . . he was her accomplice all along."

"Who the hell would believe that?" Natalie scoffed, a tremor in her voice. "People know Jack. They know his family. They're good people. He's not an outsider like Jasper." She glanced at Jack's still body on the floor. "They know he'd never help anyone hurt a bunch of kids. That's ridiculous!"

Chief Hickman seemed to consider her words. "The funny thing is, people will believe it because they will have a face to a crime. That's something they can wrap their heads around. There's no way anyone would think frail ol' Connie could do all this by herself. She'd need some help, and who better than the local farm boy who still visits her every week?" He tapped his chin as if putting a lot of thought into it. "Yeah, that seems about right. Jack has always been a malleable boy. Not a lot of grit. We all saw the way he trailed after Chey like a brainless puppy. You could've told him to jump off a bridge, and he would've done it."

"That's not true," I protested.

"Doesn't really matter if it's true or not. It won't take much for people to believe he'd had his mind twisted by all that Ashby nonsense over the years. You Ashby women are awfully compelling." He wiggled his eyebrows suggestively. "And I'll be *so* upset to learn the truth about a boy I cared so much about. Everyone will take their cues from me."

"Why my mom? Why pin it on her? Why not find someone else?" I asked, my voice sounding small.

"I had planned to pin it on Jasper when he got released. It felt like a nice piece of irony. Wrongfully jailed man let out of prison to go on and commit a crime just like the ones he was accused of five years ago. Sounds almost poetic, doesn't it? His release felt like a sign. That it was time for me to get what I wanted." His eyes lit up like a child's on their birthday, only for that light to be replaced by smoldering anger.

"Thought he'd come back here. Where else would that piece of shit go? But he never came back to town, and then his parents up and moved. It destroyed my carefully laid plans." His face split into a disturbing grin. "But necessity is the mother of invention, so they say."

He walked over to my mom's body and stared down at her, his expression almost tender. "No matter—it all worked out in the end. Everyone will believe she did it. Most already think she's guilty. She doesn't have the fear or respect of the people that her pa did." He glanced at Jack. "Sure, the boy might be difficult to believe, but people will buy anything if you sell it hard enough." He straightened up and had a look of resolve. "So, I'll say I figured it out. I pieced it together from conversations I had with Connie. She let things slip from time to time that made me wonder. And bein' the smart man that I am, I put two and two together. Of course, I had to stop 'em. I couldn't let 'em get away with everything they'd done. Jack and I fight, and he shoots me." He looked down at the blood seeping through his shirt before turning back to us. "But I'm the better shot."

He aimed his gun at Jack and mimicked shooting it. "I am the chief after all." He was enjoying himself. He liked creating this story that painted him as the town savior once again. Jasper had been his villain five years ago, and my Mom and Jack would be the villains this time.

"My dad will tell everyone what you are. What's to stop him if I'm dead?" Natalie challenged, and I felt a flash of hope. Mr. Bartlett loved his daughter more than anything.

The chief braced himself against the table. His face had gone white from blood loss. He held his hand to his side and grimaced. "Stew can say what he wants. Who will listen to him now? He's a disgrace. His mishandlin' of the Jasper situation makes him less than trustworthy." He looked like he was having a hard time standing. Blood seeped through his fingers and dripped onto the floor.

"People aren't stupid," Natalie shouted. "They'll see—"

"People will see what I want them to see," he barked. "I'm the goddamn chief!" Natalie fell silent, because he was right. No one would question him because no one ever had.

Chief Hickman started to cough, a deep phlegmy sound. It winded him, and he started to wobble on his feet. His pants were now coated in blood. He was bleeding too much. "Looks like the bullet went deeper than I thought." His voice was thick and wet. He unbuttoned his shirt to get a better look at the hole in his gut.

"What is *that*?" Natalie gasped, her eyes wide and horrified. I followed her gaze and couldn't quite believe what I was seeing.

On Donald Hickman's chest, tattooed in dark, black ink, the letters no more than an inch high, were three names. Etched into his skin like those on the root cellar wall.

While my ancestors had carved names into rock, the chief had carved them into flesh. The letters were wavy and uneven; the chief had obviously done it himself.

CHEYENNE ASHBY

NATALIE BARTLETT

JACKSON CAMPBELL

These were "his" names. The most important ones.

He had claimed us.

His "perfect" three.

Natalie dug her nails into my arm as we huddled together, too terrified to move.

Chief Hickman poked around the wound before carefully buttoning up his shirt again. Covering the evidence of his deranged obsession once more.

"You need a hospital. Let us help you," I offered carefully. "You won't make it—you're losing a lot of blood. I doubt you can walk back all those miles on your own."

The chief's face morphed into something ugly and filled with fury. "I've always made it on my own!" he bellowed, causing Nat and me to flinch. "That's what this is all about. This fuckin' town. These goddamn people. Always turnin' a blind eye. They're like a bunch of sheep, one followin' the other, no mind of their own. They carry the silver because that's what they're told to do. They believe Jasper's a murderer because that's what everyone says. They let a kid get the shit beat out of him by his own pa, and they do nothin' because everyone says it's not their place. " He ground his teeth, and his nostrils flared. "But now, *I* tell them what to believe. *I* call the shots. It's *my* word they listen to. I will dig the heart out of this town and crush it in my hand."

He staggered over to Natalie and pressed the barrel of the gun to her forehead. I noticed his entire body was shaking; he could barely hold his arm straight.

He looked at me with a horrible mixture of hunger and desperation. "I want to save you for last, Cheyenne."

Natalie and I were both sobbing. We couldn't stop. This was it. It was all over. And I hated that people would think my mother and Jack were responsible. That they would be remembered as murderers while the chief would be venerated.

I cried harder as Natalie straightened her shoulders and looked the chief straight in the eye. Finding courage at the very end.

"No, please, no . . ." I begged with everything I had. "Please!" I was entreating a madman. I knew my tears—my pleas—wouldn't matter, but I used them anyway. He cocked the gun, and I had to look away. I couldn't bear to witness my best friend's murder.

"Arghhh!" the chief suddenly yelled. I looked up to find him hunching over, and then he collapsed onto the floor. He rolled onto his side, his hands flailing frantically for the fire poker that was now sticking out from the middle of his back.

And there, standing over him, was my mother, covered in blood and looking every bit as terrifying as the Hickory Man.

"Mom!" I cried with fresh tears. She didn't look at me—her entire focus was on Chief Hickman, who was trying to stand up. She reached down and snatched the gun now held loosely in his hand. Without a moment's hesitation, she shot him in the head. He crumpled to the floor and was still.

Natalie and I were both shaking violently, unable to move. We watched as Mom, who was still bleeding from the wound in her gut, pushed Donald Hickman onto his back. She reached into the pocket of her long skirt and took out a handful of herbs and sprinkled them over his body. She began to mutter something under her breath, closing her eyes, rocking back and forth.

When she was finished, she went to Jack and knelt beside him, putting her fingers to the side of his neck. "He's alive, but we need to get him to the hospital," she said. Then she ripped a length of cloth from the bottom of her long skirt, wadding it up, and pressed it to his side.

"Mom," I whispered, hardly able to believe what I had witnessed.

My mother finally looked at us, and it was then that her calm broke. She crawled across the floor and took us in her arms. "My girls. My poor, poor girls," she soothed, kissing the top of my head and then Natalie's. "I'm so sorry."

The three of us cried for only a moment. It's all we could allow ourselves.

"We need to get help," my mom said, breaking away. "I'll go, I'll be the quickest—I know these woods." She stood up, placing the gun on the table.

I looked at the red patch on her stomach with uncertainty but she waved a hand in the air. "*Trust me.* You stay here—you'll only slow me down." She didn't sound like the disturbed woman I'd found when I came back to Blue Cliff. She sounded strong. Like the Mom I remembered.

"Be careful," was all I could say, wanting to go with her, but not wanting to leave Jack.

Natalie was still sobbing uncontrollably, and I turned to her. "Go with her, Nat. She'll need you. She's hurt."

My mom stood in the doorway, a determined look on her pale face. She tore some more material from her skirt off and pressed it to the wound in her belly.

"I can't leave you here . . . with *him*!" Natalie whispered, her voice quivering. She glanced at the chief's body and then away again.

"You have to. The town won't listen to her; he made sure of that. But they'll listen to you," I urged. "You don't need to worry about him." I looked at the dead chief. "He won't be hurting anyone ever again."

I crawled across the floor to where Jack was lying. I crossed my legs and pulled his head into my lap. "You're gonna be okay, Campbell. You're not going anywhere without me," I murmured, my eyes never leaving his face.

Moments later, I heard Natalie and my mom leave, and I squeezed my eyes shut, cradling Jack. I pressed my other hand firmly to his side in an attempt to stop the blood flow.

"We're safe, Jack. Finally, we're safe." I repeated it over and over, needing the reassurance.

The monster had finally been slain, and we were once again safe in the woods.

I had to believe the worst was over.

EPILOGUE

–Cheyenne–

Three weeks later

F IVE YEARS AGO, I had been eager to leave Blue Cliff. I had left without saying a word to anyone. I had slunk out in the dead of night, disappearing, like all those lost children, into the forest.

Now I was cleaning out my childhood bedroom, stripping the walls of old posters and cleaning the surfaces of long-outgrown knickknacks. I was preparing to start again in this place I had been determined to leave behind.

Tragedy and trauma had me reevaluating all the things I'd thought I wanted.

"Wow, it looks like a totally different room." Jackson crossed his arms over his chest and leaned against the doorjamb, looking every bit like the boy I had fallen in love with all those years ago. He still made my heart flutter and my stomach flip-flop. I had been a fool to think I could outrun those feelings.

I wiped my forehead with the back of my hand. "Yeah, well I figured if I was going to stay, I needed a room that didn't look like a sixteen-year-old still lived here." I stared admiringly at my handiwork. I had painted the walls a soft yellow. New, patterned curtains hung from the window. The wooden floors had been mopped and polished so that now they shone with a brilliance they hadn't seen in decades. But we had done more than a bedroom makeover. I needed to eradicate the darkness that had permeated the house for far too long.

*   *   *

Jack had been with me that day, not long after everything had happened, when I made the decision to go back down to the root cellar. Armed with an electric sander and a can of white paint, we erased the names and got rid of the map.

"Your mom didn't put those there," Jack stated as he sanded over Michael, Olivia, Danielle, and Dakota's names.

I shook my head. "The chief did. He must have done it once Mom was no longer able to get up and down the steps on her own. She wouldn't have seen the additional names." I realized now that they were in Donald Hickman's handwriting, the letters were the same as those on his chest. Further testament to his obsession with the Ashby birthright.

Though the names of the children he actually killed hadn't been tattooed on his skin as ours had been.

His fixation was reserved for the three of us alone.

Our names were his.

We wouldn't have been added to the wall because our deaths would have belonged to him and not the Ashby legacy. It made the murders of those four kids all the more senseless.

*   *   *

"I've put together your mom's new bed. We should finish getting things together if we're going to pick her up by four," Jack told me.

Mom's injuries had been significant, requiring several surgeries. Her recovery period was longer than for the rest of us. Jack had been lucky that the bullet hadn't gone deep, though he needed several pints of blood. It was the blood loss that could have killed him.

Jack tucked his thumbs in his jean pockets and cocked his head, watching me as I finished making my bed—a double now that I had a frequent visitor sharing the space with me. "You're sure about this? Staying here I mean?"

He sounded so hesitant and unsure, and I knew his question was merited. He was trying to trust my renewed presence in his life, but we had a history of me abandoning him that would take longer than a few weeks to get over.

I walked over to him and wrapped my arms around his waist. I leaned up on my tiptoes and kissed him. Jack held me close, and we breathed each other in. Tied together tighter now after everything. Ours was a bond forged by childhood and first love. And from devastation and terror. It was the kind of chain that could never be broken.

"I'm not goin' anywhere. You're stuck with me," I threatened teasingly.

"What would I do without you, Chey?"

I burrowed into his embrace. "Lucky for you, you'll never have to find out." And I meant it. I couldn't imagine being with anyone else. I couldn't imagine being *anywhere* else.

After a few minutes, Jack released me, and took my hand. "Come on—let's finish up here so we can get goin'." He looked out the window and beyond to the trees. "I hope one day I can be here without feeling like I'm crawling out of my skin."

Of the three of us, Jack seemed to be struggling the worst. His confidence in people had been shattered that day out at the Ashby cabin. Chief Hickman had destroyed Jackson Campbell's trust. I hated Donald Hickman more than I thought it possible to hate anyone. Not just for what he had done to those children, or for killing my dad and nearly killing my mother, but for what he had taken from Jack. And from Natalie. He had destroyed their faith in this town. In the people they had known their whole lives. I had always held myself apart as much as possible from the roots that had been dug for me. I was suffering, but not in the same way. Their whole world had been decimated.

I leaned into Jack's side. "These trees are ours. He has no right to them—remember that," I said with a vehemence that shocked me.

I had spent most of my life hating the forest and its trees. I resented and loathed them equally. But now I was determined to reclaim them. They were only branches and leaves. Nothing sinister rested among the hickories. I had to learn to love them because they were my home and always would be.

Jack let out a long, painful sigh. "Yeah, you're right. My mom says time heals all wounds. Though I'm not sure how time can help us get over all this." He put a hand on his side, over where the chief had shot him. One thing was for sure: it would take more than three weeks to move past what we had been through.

*   *   *

After Mom killed the chief, she and Natalie had made their way back to town in the pitch-black darkness, injured and in shock.

If it hadn't been for Natalie, Mom and Jack would have died. She half carried, half dragged my mom back to her car, with my mom giving her directions on how to make it out of the woods. She took her straight to the hospital.

At some point, hours later, the police had turned up. Natalie had sent them to come and get Jack and me. She had told them everything, including about her dad's involvement. She hadn't left out a single detail—from the past or the present.

We were no longer the town that gobbled up children, yet nothing came without a cost. Our town had lost its belief in the people we trusted. Donald Hickman had betrayed everyone, and we were all broken because of it.

We fell into a new kind of normal after that as people adjusted their lives in the wake of the horrific truth.

Otis admitted to being the one to build and burn the Hickory Man effigy in the square. He drunkenly confessed one night at Salty's to anyone that would listen. He claimed he only wanted to remind everyone to be safe. That there were evil things lurking in our town, and we needed to be on guard. It appeared his bizarre behavior came from a good place. He cared about the town, and while the adults didn't understand his peculiar relationship with their children, it didn't seem to be anything other than benevolent. Otis might be strange, but he wasn't a predator or a killer.

Neither was Reggie Grady, though he was currently behind bars for looking in windows again. It turned out that's what he'd been up to when Mom saw him out near the house. All those times I felt someone watching me from the woods, it could have been the local neighborhood Peeping Tom. He had been skulking around the town and in the woods, watching everyone for a long time. All those years ago when my mom thought she had seen Jasper in the forest, it had probably been Reggie. After all, they looked startlingly similar. Reggie admitted to watching Mom and me since he was a kid. He had a history of wandering where he shouldn't. It would have been easy to mistake one man for the other.

I felt better knowing he'd be gone—for a while at least. Because this time he would probably spend considerably more time in jail. Hopefully, Blue Cliff had learned its lesson. We couldn't look the other way when we knew something was wrong. We had to face the ugliness in the people we had known our whole lives.

And as for Jasper Clinton, his name had finally been cleared in the eyes of the town that had vilified him. Not that it mattered to him, but it was something.

* * *

Jack drove me to the hospital to pick up Mom around four. Her discharge was straightforward, and twenty minutes later we were walking her up the path to the front door.

I put my hand to the doorknob, ready to turn it, when Mom stopped me. "Not yet," she said quietly.

She turned and walked back down the steps and around the side of the house. Jack and I shared a glance. "You go after her. I'll get a fire going," he said, leaning down to kiss me.

I found her at the edge of the woods, head bowed. With the snow finally melted, I noticed for the first time a mound of rocks fanning out in a spiral pattern. "What's this?" I asked.

The wind picked up slightly, and there was the sound of crunching leaves somewhere in the distance. I didn't wonder about the source now that the demon had been confirmed to be men.

"I made this years ago as a memorial to your pa," Mom finally said, her voice rough. "The spiral represents the eternal cycle of life and death." Tears began to drip down her cheeks. "I knew, deep down, that he wasn't alive out there somewhere. In my heart I knew he was gone."

I put my arm around her shoulders and held her close. "I'm sorry I didn't have the same faith in him you did."

"Why would you have? You didn't really know him. He was only a story to you. The barest hint of a memory. You have nothing to be sorry for, Cheyenne." She reached into her pocket and pulled out a small bag of herbs. With shaking hands she untied it and sprinkled the contents over the rocks. "I only wish I knew where he was. Where he rested." She looked up at me, her expression one of total heartbreak. "He never said where Tom was?"

"No, Mom. I'm sorry."

Mom took a deep breath and let it out slowly, closing her eyes. "I'll have to trust the woods will protect his spirit then."

We stood quietly for a while, staring down at the rocks she had fashioned to memorialize her lost love.

"I've decided to stay, Mom. I'm not going back to Roanoke," I told her after a few minutes. "I thought maybe . . . maybe it's time I learn the old ways."

I expected her to be happy at my news. She had been forcing duty down my throat my entire life. Her reaction, however, was unexpected.

"I'm glad you're staying, Chey. I want you here. But I think . . ." She paused. "I think it's time for you to create your own future—your own life. The old ways are done. There's no need for them anymore."

"But Mom, what about . . ."

Mom took my hand and gripped it in hers. "I have to face the truth about what my family has done to this town. The evil they have wrought had nothing to do with the Hickory Man." I startled at her saying his name. She had always been so careful not to before. "I refused to follow the path the way it was set by my pa and by those who came before me," she revealed. "Pa told me what I had to do, what was expected of me." She was crying again, harder and quieter. "It broke something inside me, Chey. I knew I couldn't do it. So I tried to do things differently. I left animals—" Her voice broke and she struggled to clear her throat.

I stayed quiet, letting her continue when she was ready.

"I left the animals. I left the blood. I would never feed the darkness Pa seemed to crave. That Donald craved.

And when those kids were found five years ago, I truly believed that it was the Hickory Man come to claim what belonged to him. I felt so much shame. I thought it was all my fault for not givin' him what he wanted. When Dakota went missing I thought I'd lose my mind with guilt. I was raised to believe I had to keep everyone safe. And I had failed." Her face filled with agony. "I was so blind, so stupid. And I'm sorry I tried to drag you into all this. That I was going to force you into the same horrible life I had suffered through because of misguided family loyalty." Her entire body seemed to deflate. "They never deserved my loyalty or my love." Her lips trembled.

"Mom, what was that doll I found on your table? The one with the blue cloth?" I had to ask, I needed to know.

Mom took my hand. "Dakota's dad, Fred, came to see me. It was the day after you found the boy. He wanted to make sure his son's soul was at rest. He gave me Dakota's shirt, the one he'd been found in, to bind the spell. I did what I could. I only hope it did something. I'm not sure anything I ever did helped anyone." She sounded ashamed and defeated. Her entire life had been built around her beliefs. All of that had been shaken, possibly ruined forever.

I hugged her. "That's not true, Mom. You helped people so much. You helped them believe. You gave them hope. That's more powerful than anything." I meant every word I said. Because the magic might not be real, but she was important to our community. She gave them comfort.

She didn't respond, but she heard me. Her smile was confirmation. Finally, we walked back to the house. I followed her to her bedroom and watched as she took in the newly clean space and brand-new bed. Jack had sanded and polished the floors. The scorch marks from the candles and the strange symbols were gone.

"I like it," she said, giving Jack and me a smile. Then she crawled under the covers, and Jack and I left her to rest.

* * *

"What did she say?" Jack asked when we were settled on the couch in front of the fire, his arm around me.

"She's hurting. She seems so lost. So broken," I murmured, staring at the flames.

"I wouldn't underestimate your ma. She's made of stern stuff. Something tells me she'll get through it and be just fine."

I believed him. Because Mom was right, it was time to forge my own path, to make my own future. To walk away from the past.

And I would do that in Blue Cliff.

Where I belonged.

–Natalie–

M Y PHONE BEGAN to ring, and I saw Hunter's name
lighting up my screen. He had been calling on and
off for the past few weeks, ever since he'd learned what had
really happened to his brother.

He'd apologized. He'd begged. He'd raged. He'd gone
through the full cycle of emotions one would expect when
someone's whole world had turned upside down. Eventually it escalated to a drunken late night phone call where
he confessed that he and Jess had been the ones to burn
down Jasper's family home. The next day, I heard that he'd
turned himself in. He and Jess were charged with arson,
which carried with it a five-year prison sentence. No one
actually believed they'd be convicted. Chase Caruthers's
son wouldn't spend a second inside a jail cell.

Despite all this, it didn't change anything. Not for me
at least.

I wasn't the same person I'd been before. My experience
inside the cabin in Ashby Woods had taken a part of me.
Chief Hickman, a man I had loved and trusted, had wanted

to kill me for most of my life, and that was a revelation that I still hadn't come to terms with. Maybe I never would.

The phone went silent. I wouldn't listen to the voice-mail I knew Hunter had left me. I was done listening to his apologies and his excuses. Even still, grief filled me. I had lost the man I loved and the life I was supposed to have. I had accepted it, but I could still mourn the loss. No matter what had happened, I did love him. I probably always would. But that didn't mean we should be together. I couldn't be the woman he wanted me to be. My days of unquestioning obedience were over.

As for the rest of the Carruthers family, I hoped now that they knew what had actually happened to Mikey, maybe they could find some peace.

Then there was my dad. He *had* gotten away with his crimes. Of course he'd lied when he'd been questioned by police about his prior knowledge of the murders. With no proof, he could only be sanctioned by the state bar association for withholding evidence and perverting the course of justice. He would likely be disbarred, but there would be no criminal proceedings against him. I had sincerely hoped that almost losing me would force him to reevaluate his choices. To see what he had put into action because of his selfish cowardice. But like with the Caruthers family, I knew better than to hold my breath.

I pulled my car up outside Cheyenne's house, parking next to Jackson's truck. The cardinals were singing extra loud, their sweet voices trilling high in the treetops. I stood and listened for several moments, thinking how so often Ashby Woods had been quiet. But now, since everything that had happened, it was like the woods had been set free.

"You comin' in or what?" Jack called from the porch. "Got a pot of coffee going." He jerked his head inward and I smiled, trailing after him.

Inside, the house was clean and tidy. Much tidier than I had seen it in years. Books were stacked on shelves, photos hung on the walls, and dried flowers sat in vases on the windowsills. The house, just like the woods, had been given a new lease on life.

"Go on over—I'll bring you a cup," Jack said with a smile, nudging me toward the two women sitting by the fire.

Constance glanced up, her eyes meeting mine. Her smile grew at the sight of me, and she patted the spot beside her on the couch. "Natalie." She said my name—no more, no less.

Jackson came in, carrying a small round tray with four mugs of coffee on it. Constance closed her eyes and smiled, inhaling deeply.

"Reminds me of my Tom," she said fondly. "He sure did love a strong cup of joe."

Constance had been talking about Cheyenne's dad a lot recently, and Chey enjoyed it, eager to learn more about the man she'd barely gotten to know. And after I shared with her what I'd discovered, he would always be her hero.

*　*　*

My dad revealed the truth about what happened to Tom Jenkins not long after the events at Ashby cabin. He had shown up at my house, wanting to talk. I hadn't let him inside, but I let him explain some things.

"What happened to Cheyenne's dad?" I had asked him. "Connie said it was you who told her he had left town."

Dad hung his head. "I never had a problem with Tom Jenkins. He was a nice enough man. Sure, he wasn't one of us, but that was a good thing. Made it easier for him to see things that everyone else overlooked." The same had been said about Jasper Clinton, and they had both paid the price for it.

"Don came to me and told me to tell Connie that her man had left town. That I saw him leaving. When I asked him where Tom really was, all he said was that he'd taken care of

him. Seems Tom went to see Don, to tell him to stay away from his daughter. He had noticed Donald's particular . . . interest in her. Tom threatened to tell everyone that the local chief was a little too nice to the kids."

"And again you said nothing." My lip curled in disgust.

"From the way Don shared it, Tom attacked first. It was self-defense. Don was furious, saying he'd be damned if was going to get in trouble because of some nosy outta-towner. So, I told Connie that Tom had left. I didn't want to risk Don's anger directed at me. I didn't want to think about what he'd do if I didn't help him." Dad's shoulders sagged in that defeated way that was becoming familiar.

I held up my hands, stopping him. "Enough. I don't want to hear anymore."

"I wanted to make it right. I didn't want to see the revulsion in your eyes, Natalie. I knew I was the only one that could do anything. I tried. I really did. I had to do something to make up for all the wrong I had done."

I stared at him in dawning understanding. "It was you. You were the one who leaked the evidence to the attorney general's office."

My dad wouldn't quite meet my eyes, He let out a long, tortured breath. "It was the least I could do after everything. They had to know. Everyone needed to know."

So my dad had done a good thing in the end. But it wasn't enough. He had still kept his mouth shut, and he had still been lying for years. Kids had died because of his inaction.

"Natalie . . ." my dad started to say, but I could only shake my head, tears in my eyes, as I closed the door in his face. That was the last time I had spoken to my dad, and I wasn't sure when, or if, I would again.

* * *

Constance patted her daughter's cheek lovingly before turning to Jack and me. "Now I know the three of you have things you'd rather be doing than hangin' around an old lady."

"Are you trying to get rid of us, Connie?" Jack teased.

"Never. You three are my heart. It makes me so happy to have you all here, together again." Constance smiled, and she seemed truly at peace for the first time. I had never seen such contentment on her face before.

A few minutes later, Constance started to nod off, so we left her to sleep and headed to the kitchen. "She seems happy. I wasn't sure it would be possible after everything that happened," Jack commented.

"She's given up on all that Ashby family stuff. It's like a weight has lifted from her shoulders," Cheyenne said. "I think that she's finally found some semblance of calm."

"I think we all have," Jack responded, and I couldn't agree more.

Blue Cliff felt different now. Still small. Still familiar. But the heaviness that had blanketed the streets was gone. Hundreds of years of secrets had disappeared in light of the truth.

A little while later, Jack headed back to the farm, promising to come back later that evening. Once he had left, Chey and I put on our jackets and headed into the woods. Constance's basket hung from her arm.

Newly appointed Chief of Police Jeff Cross, had brought it to Cheyenne after the cabin had been processed for evidence. It turned out Donald Hickman had taken it during one of his many visits. He must have enjoyed using an item belonging to the Ashbys to store the coins he placed with his victims.

"Your mom has been through enough. The least I can do is return her things," Chief Cross said to Chey. He handed over the basket and pulled a ring from his pocket. "Someone told me this belonged to your pa. Found it in the chief's things."

Cheyenne took the ring, a gaudy thing with a bird on a yellow stone. Cheyenne's eyes lit up. "This is my dad's class ring. It was in Donald Hickman's house?" She slid it on her thumb, where it fit snugly.

Chief Cross cleared his throat. "Yes, in a box with some . . . other things. We found Olivia's bracelet and a Matchbox car that Dakota's parents said he took everywhere. Seems he liked to keep trophies. There were pictures too. A lot of 'em. Some were over a hundred years old. We've been able to put names to the children in them. Guess he liked to look at photographs of those dead kids. Seemed to have taken some himself too."

He wouldn't quite look at us. I knew how he must have felt making that discovery. It was the same way Jack, Chey, and I had felt when we found the photos in the cabin. It was a sight you would never forget, no matter how much you wanted to. It made a sick sense that Donald Hickman had kept some pictures close at hand. I had no doubt he spent a lot of time looking through them, imagining Chey, Jack, and me among them.

"I'm sorry about not seein' things clearly before. I think everyone in Blue Cliff has some soul searchin' to do about why that is," Chief Cross remarked gruffly. Neither Chey nor I said anything as he turned and left. It seemed people in town felt guilty about thinking the worst of Constance. They would make amends in their own way.

"We actually stay up and talk now. We've never done that before. She makes breakfast in the morning and has taken up knitting. She's like a new person," Chey said in disbelief.

"After everything the chief put Constance through, she deserves nothing but happiness. You both do," I said, leaning down to pull up some sassafras root to make tea with later.

"She's had so many visitors since she's been home. I can't get Ed and Linda to stop bringing food to the house. Neither will say it outright, but both feel horrible about their creepy son peeping in our windows. To think he's probably the one Mom saw all those years ago, believing it was Jasper," she exclaimed, adding some Joe Pye weed to the basket.

I expected it to be difficult for the people of Blue Cliff to adjust to life after learning the truth about Donald Hickman. We had lived a certain way for generations; a change of thinking wasn't going to happen overnight. But it *was* changing—slowly. For a long time, the town had felt like a place one step out of time with the rest of the world. Now it seemed people realized we needed to wake up and take control of our story. The Ashbys' family secret and Donald Hickman had dictated things for long enough.

Blue Cliff was a place that looked after its own, and that was one thing that would always stay the same. Now that everyone knew what had really been going on in the woods, people were more forgiving and understanding of Constance.

"You have a lot of people that love you and your ma, Chey. And you've got Jack and me. Nothing will take that away from you. Not my lying father, not Hunter, and not . . ." I hesitated, still feeling the deeply entrenched superstition to not say the name. Not out here.

"The Hickory Man?" Chey laughed, and I laughed right along with her, shaking off my misgivings.

"You're the strongest person I know, Chey. Whatever happens in life, we'll get through it together. You, Jack, and me. Because that's how it should be." I reached for her hand again.

The trees seemed to embrace us. Comforting us in the way only the forest could. The woods weren't something to fear. They never should have been.

I was full of hope for the future. I was buzzing on it. Which is why it took several minutes to realize something was different. I frowned and looked up.

"What is it?" Chey asked, stopping and following my gaze up into the canopy above us.

My frown deepened. "Where did all the birds go?"

The air had become oppressive, the forest silent. I hadn't realized how dark it had gotten, and quickly too.

A familiar fear began to crawl up my spine.

"Let's get back, okay?" I said and Chey nodded in agreement, not questioning me. I knew she felt it too.

We made our way back to the house a little quicker than when we had left it.

And from somewhere deep within Hickory Woods, a twig snapped as a dark shape moved among the trees.

ACKNOWLEDGMENTS

Abbi's Acknowledgments:

This book is all about Claire. We've been on a crazy, topsy-turvy journey to get this book out there into the world. I am forever thankful for your drive and passion for writing and pushing me when I needed it. I never could have gotten here without you.

To my family, who have always had my back, no matter what. Ian and Gwyn, you are my world.

To my dear friend, Kristy. Thank you for all your feedback on the early iterations of this book. You've known me since we were two kids growing up in a place very much like Blue Cliff, so you got this book on a level few will.

To the amazing beta readers who helped craft this story into what it is today. It was a painful process, but an important one. Thank you!

To our editor, Tara Gavin, and everyone at Crooked Lane—thank you for taking a chance on this story and on us. Your support means so much.

And finally, to all those with a story to tell—just go tell it, even when people tell you it won't sell or there isn't an audience for it. Because seriously, what do they know?

Claire's Acknowledgments:

As always, there's so many people to thank in these things, but I guess the first person I should thank is Abbi. Thank you so much for being my friend and for always having my back. In this crazy world of publishing, I'm glad I have you by my side.

Thank you so much to our editor, Tara Gavin, for loving our creepy little story and believing in its—and our—potential. You'll never understand how grateful we both are for everything.

Thank you also to Rebecca Nelson and the entire team at Crooked Lane Books. We are so proud to have our book represented by such a great publishing house, and we're so grateful that you took on us and our story.

To my favorite people on the planet—my daughters, Becca, Abbie, and Lilah. You never let me give up and always have so much enthusiasm for my stories (no matter how weird they might get!). I am grateful every day that I get to be your mum.

And to my husband and best friend, John, who always pushes me to chase my dreams. I love you—sorry for weirding you out with creepy stories!

And finally, with huge thanks to readers everywhere. I hope that you enjoy this story.